CLOSING IN

E. D. THOMPSON

HACHETTE
BOOKS
IRELAND

First published in Ireland in 2022 by HACHETTE BOOKS IRELAND

1

Cataloguing in Publication Data is available from the British Library.

Paperback ISBN 978 1 52937 043 0

Typeset in Cambria by Bookends Publishing Services, Dublin
Printed and bound in Great Britain by Clays Ltd, Elcograf S.p.A.

Hachette Books Ireland policy is to use papers that are natural, renewable and recyclable products and made from wood grown in sustainable forests. The logging and manufacturing processes are expected to conform to the environmental regulations of the country of origin.

Hachette Books Ireland
8 Castlecourt Centre
Castleknock
Dublin 15, Ireland

A division of Hachette UK Ltd
Carmelite House, 50 Victoria Embankment, EC4Y 0DZ
www.hachettebooksireland.ie

To Nikki,
with much love and admiration

1

I only saw him from the back, and in a long black overcoat that gave no more than an approximation of his shape and size. My hands, holding the new pyjamas I'd chosen for Ray's boys for Christmas Eve, seemed to lose their grip and I hung the garments shakily back on the rack. Part of me wanted to pursue him through the throng of shoppers, spin him round, find out if it was really him. The other part wanted to bolt.

Because if Mark was here, in the town where I lived now, where I had worked and built a life for the past thirty years, then he had come for me – hadn't he?

Or could it be coincidence, him turning up?

All around me, Christmas shoppers were lifting down

merchandise and examining it. 'Do you not want those?' a woman asked, looking at the pyjamas.

I was, as they say, lost for words and could only shake my head.

The festive party music suddenly seemed oppressive. Had it always been this loud? And I was too hot. I should have left my coat in the car. Someone said, 'Are you all right?' but the voice floated away before I could catch it.

A huge yawn reared up in me so that I couldn't hold it in. Now the shop was starting to swim and I felt unsteady. I thought there was something I was meant to do, something important, but I couldn't remember what.

I kept picturing Mark – if it was Mark – striding away from me through the people and clothes and tinsel. He'd got that limp from jumping into a haystack when he was fifteen, not knowing there was a pitchfork in it. I had given up wondering if I would ever see him again. To be perfectly honest, I had thought he might very well be dead.

Someone knocked over a display of children's slippers. I looked at the mess and heard tutting. Was it me who had sent the slippers scuttling? Did I do it?

'Here, come and sit down.' I turned and saw someone in a shop uniform, someone who belonged there, someone to help me. 'You're as white as a sheet.'

I must have gone with her, because next I was sitting, sweating, on a blue plastic customer chair by a pillar. The Christmas music had receded and instead I thought I heard the gentle tap as a stylus dropped onto a vinyl record, and the black velvet hiss as a track began.

Another assistant materialised, interrupting: 'Is she drunk?'

Was I drunk?

There were people, faces, crowding round, arms full of clothes on hangers, gawping at me. Did I know any of them? *All* of them? Were they waiting for me to say something? But I couldn't remember what I was supposed to say.

'I'm ... I'm ...' I began, struggling to think of the next words and failing.

'Do you think you're going to be sick?' The voice sounded like we were underwater.

Why now? Why had Mark come now?

I heard someone suggest calling a first-aider, and I wondered if there had been an accident somewhere.

Another huge yawn.

Then someone was putting something into my mouth.

I tried to push them away with both hands. How dare they!

'Caroline. It's all right. They're just dextrose tablets. You're having a hypo.'

We were still underwater, but I knew this voice and tried to remember whose it was.

'Are you family?' someone asked, far away.

'Yes,' the familiar voice responded.

I peered out and recognised Eric Haffey, though I couldn't have told you his name for a while yet. Although he definitely wasn't family, he knew me and might understand what was happening. I heard him tell the small crowd that I was Type 1 diabetic and was experiencing an episode of low blood sugar. Meanwhile, he continued to stuff me with dextrose tablets.

Woozily, I knew he was right. That was the thing I needed to do – boost my blood sugar, quickly. I crunched up the tablets and held out my hand for more.

I don't know how long it took, though it's usually not very long, until, gradually, I felt my awareness return and smiled apologetically at the remaining concerned faces. 'Sorry. Did I give everyone a fright?'

A more senior assistant had arrived. She quizzed me slightly and told me her mother had Type 2 before inviting me to rest in their in-store café – in other words, please take this sideshow elsewhere as you're impeding the happy march of capitalism.

'Can you stay with her?' she asked Eric.

'Of course,' Eric replied. 'Caroline, you need to eat something.'

Now it all made sense. Everything dropped into place. I'd had a hypoglycaemic attack. I had taken my insulin but hadn't followed up quickly enough with food to balance it. Stupid of me. Really stupid. You'd think I would know better after more than forty years of managing the condition.

This also explained the so-called sighting of Mark. I had imagined all sorts of things, when my blood sugar had fallen really low – ghosts, talking walls, tigers in the house. Silly stuff. Something about a hypo brought a rush of creative thought, little of it reliable. I could easily have imagined spotting an old flame in a crowd.

Oh, but what a flame.

'Would you like a doughnut?' Eric asked, lifting a pair of silver tongs at the self-service counter.

'I'd prefer a croissant,' I told him, and he grabbed one for me.

'Tea or coffee?'

'Coffee, please. And since when did you start carrying dextrose tablets with you?'

'Since you told me you were diabetic.'

I had promised myself a few days earlier that I would attend the Chamber of Trade Christmas dinner dance with Eric, as I had agreed, but wouldn't see any more of him after that. Eric was all right, but we had no chemistry – at least, not as far as I was concerned. Now that he had so obviously come to my rescue, however, letting him down would be harder.

'Did you miss a meal?' he asked, as we sat opposite each other at a Formica-topped table by the Christmas tree.

'I suppose I did. I popped in for one item, but then I got sidetracked. I was probably already dipping by that stage, or my judgement would have been better.'

An in-store television was switched on across from us, playing an infomercial for a battery-operated toy with which to entertain a cat.

'I'm thinking of getting a kitten,' Eric suddenly announced.

'Really?' Eric was serious and measured. I couldn't imagine him with such a little bundle of fun and claws and teeth.

'Barry in work, his cat's just had a litter and he's trying to find homes for them. He's got two black-and-whites, one tortoiseshell and one marmalade.'

'I've always wondered how a single litter can contain so many different varieties. Human families all tend to look pretty much the same.'

'Although when you're a child, people like to say, "You look just like your dad," or "You take after your mum." Who did they say you looked like?'

'Oh, always Mum. She was petite, like me, and I've got the same eyes.'

'If you don't mind me asking, are you just speaking in the past tense, or have both your parents passed away, Caroline? You've never talked about them, and I've often wondered.'

'Mmm.' I sipped my flat white. 'They were very young. Dad was just forty-three and Mum was forty-one.'

'You can't have been very old when you lost them.'

When I lost them. Mum and Dad were always a little bit lost to us kids, but the thing was, we didn't actually mind. They made up for it by being so ... special. And then they died.

'Seventeen. But let's change the subject. What are your plans for Christmas?'

'Oh, just a quiet one, you know. I'll cook for Mum and me at our place.'

'Turkey and all the trimmings?'

'No, no. You need a family to enjoy a turkey – now there's just the two of us, it'd only be a reminder of happier times. We've tried goose, and last year we had a leg of lamb, but this year it's going to be fish. Confit salmon with lemon and parsley salsa. It's a festive southern-hemisphere recipe my sister sent me.'

'Sounds delicious.'

'You'd be very welcome to join us. And bring your daughter, of course.'

His eagerness tugged at my heart.

'Sorry, Eric – Tabby and I have a standing arrangement.'

'Don't be sorry. It was just a thought.'

Eric insisted on walking me to my car. 'Sure you're OK to drive?'

'I'm fine now, thanks.'

People are often amazed at how quickly I bounce back from a hypo. One minute they're wondering whether to call an ambulance, the next I've wolfed a bar of chocolate and I'm as sharp as anyone. Eric had seen it once before, when we went for a pub lunch and the food took a ridiculously long time to arrive, so he had witnessed the speed and completeness of my recovery and wasn't overly anxious this time. Good for him.

'I've booked a taxi to take us to the hotel on Wednesday,' he said. 'The Christmas dinner.'

'I'm looking forward to it.' I'm not.

'Safe home.'

'Thanks.'

I slammed my door and Eric stood aside, but did not walk away, instead holding up one hand in something between a wave and a salute.

For just a moment, I wished I liked him more. But then I retracted the thought. My life mightn't suit everyone, but it pleased me very much just as it was, and there wasn't room in it for Eric.

I would go home and cook something quick. I would be happy with a toasted sandwich from the sandwich press Tabby had bought me for Mothers' Day – a clever model where the non-stick plates popped out. I never used our old one due entirely to the deadly chore of trying to clean it.

When I pulled into my driveway, Gareth and Elaine were attaching fairy lights to the outside of their house. Gareth was up the stepladder and Elaine was feeding the lights to him.

'Hi, Caroline!' Elaine called. 'Have you been shopping?'

'That was the plan,' I replied. 'But I got derailed.'

Elaine and Gareth did their Christmas shopping early, I knew, because they led very busy lives, especially at this time of year. Elaine would have all their presents wrapped and labelled already, I was quite sure.

Gareth was a Scout leader and Elaine took Brownies. Gareth bivouacked and whittled and walked for miles and engaged dozens of children for hours, sometimes days. Elaine encouraged hordes of little girls to bake buns and mount climbing walls and grow vegetables. And all the two of them really wanted was to have their own baby. Bab*ies*. And somehow they couldn't.

Gareth turned on the steps to me. 'Ever wished you hadn't started something?' he said.

'It'll look great when it's finished,' I told him. 'Very festive.'

I'd have to get my tree soon. The man from the garden centre delivered, and had even been known to bring mine into the house and erect it for me, which was a huge boost. Standing a Christmas tree upright and tightening the screws to hold it there wasn't a job for a five-feet-two woman in her early fifties.

'Why on earth do you insist on a real tree?' Ray's wife, Jodie, would always ask, as if I were completely mad.

Maybe it was because we'd always had an artificial one when we were kids. Mum wouldn't stand for the mess of a real tree, and Dad wasn't going to contradict her on matters of décor.

I don't think we bothered with a tree at all, when we were first married. Christmas Day was spent with my in-laws.

Doris reigned in the kitchen, Bob kept the coal fire stoked like a furnace, and Auntie Jean perched in the corner in fear of Shane, Bob and Doris's mild-mannered rough collie. We would get there in time for Janice's call from New Zealand, where she had already had Christmas Day and was winding down, and then it was lunch, crackers, paper hats and wine, thank God. Doris would insist on us staying for the big salad tea at six o'clock, and then we would get out of there, race home and jump into bed.

I've made it sound like an ordeal, going to Doris and Bob's, and it wasn't. It was good to have somewhere to belong on Christmas Day. I'd had a few where I had been quite alone, and that was no fun at all.

Anyway, as soon as we'd had Tabby, Christmas moved to our place. Doris and Bob and Auntie Jean came to us. We didn't have a big house, but we had chosen an early seventies build, with one 'through-room' precisely because we wanted to have space to entertain. My parents had made exactly the same choice, but in their case it was to accommodate friends their own age, whose parties my brother and I used to spy on delightedly from the stairs. My house was more family-oriented.

For Tabby, we always had a real tree, one far too big for such a house, but I loved the size of it and the smell, and it didn't bother me one bit that it shed a few needles. That was why we had a vacuum cleaner. Tabby brought home little things she had made to decorate it, at school and at Brownies, and these were the decorations I loved most – a tiny, painted clay angel, a gold star made of carefully folded paper, a bauble covered with patterned fabric and a length of colourful paper-chain.

This year, I expected Tabby and I would kick off with the usual drinks invitation to Gareth and Elaine's. They filled their house with neighbours first thing on Christmas morning because, I thought, it pushed away the emptiness of no little children in pyjamas running round tearing open presents from Santa.

Indoors, I threw my bag down in the hall, hung my coat on the newel post and picked up the mail from the mat. A couple of cards, which I would get around to, and two brown envelopes, which I would open when I'd got my sandwich on.

Bread was difficult to manage, when you lived alone. A whole loaf meant you were stuck with exactly the same thing for days. A smaller loaf cost almost as much as a large one, so seemed like bad value. In my bread bin I had the tail end of a sliced wholemeal and a couple of brioche rolls that never seemed to go hard. I switched on the sandwich toaster and went to the fridge. There was some cheddar cheese, which I could brighten up with a spread of Branston pickle, and a new bottle of Sauvignon Blanc. It might not sound much, but there was pleasure to be found in little things like something appetising to eat and drink.

I poured a glass of wine and switched on the radio to keep me company as I prepared my sandwich, but the music was too abrasive and I soon went looking for a CD of carols, instead. I chose the recording from Trinity College, Cambridge. Most people went for King's, but in our house, we knew better. One year, when Tabby had been two or three, this had been her going-to-sleep music, for months after Christmas. At Easter, I had put my foot down and said she had to choose something else or carols wouldn't feel special and Christmassy any more.

I wasn't superstitious, or even particularly spiritual, but this scenario had happened so often: I would be thinking about Tabby and at that exact moment my phone would ring and it would be her. That evening it happened just like that.

'Hi, Mum. What're you up to?'

'Just grabbing some food.'

'You haven't eaten yet? It's late.'

She means 'Be careful'. Tabby worries that I'll have a hypo in the house on my own some day with no one to notice and feed me sugar.

'It's fine. I had a croissant earlier, when I was out shopping.'

'Ooh. Buy anything nice?'

'Nope. Nothing. Sorry. How are you, anyway? Were you ringing for anything in particular, or just for a chat?'

'No chat tonight, I'm afraid. I've got a date! So I'm just about to jump in the shower, but I wondered if you super-quickly had any bright ideas of what I might get Noah and Lucas for Christmas. Do you know what Santa's bringing them?'

'Now hang on a minute, you can't just drop "I've got a date" into the conversation and change the subject! Tell me more.'

'There's not much to tell yet. Let me see how tonight goes.'

'How did you meet?'

'No "meet-cute", I'm afraid. A few of us from work went to Foxy's for Carla's birthday.'

'So you've danced with him!'

'He saw me home on the night bus.'

'Are you saying he stayed over?'

'Mum, I am not doing this. Don't make me sorry I mentioned it. And I haven't got time to talk, anyway. It's a first date, and that's all I'm saying. If it starts to look promising, you'll be the first to know.'

'Just tell me he's not Australian. I don't want him taking you away to the other side of the world where I can never see you.'

'He's not Australian.'

'Good. Well, in that case, I hope you have a lovely time. Are you going for a meal, or ...'

'It's just a drink, Mum. Now leave it. But I have tomorrow morning off, and I thought I'd get some Christmas shopping done – I just don't know what to get anyone, this year.'

'I'm struggling myself. I thought I might buy the boys an "experience" rather than a thing – maybe theme-park tickets, or something like that. They're a bit old for dressing-up costumes, and I don't want to be a bore and give them clothes. Art stuff, maybe? They both still draw a lot.'

'OK. That's food for thought. Now I really have to run, so tell me, quickly – how are you? And the boys? And work? Everything all right?'

'All fine,' I replied. 'Everything's fine.'

But it wasn't.

2

Time to do the Friday dance. I quite liked my job at the *Gazette.* In fact, I liked it a lot. I must have done, to stay at the same desk for thirty years. But everybody loved a weekend. That morning, I had the softest of starts – Fergus, the editor, wanted a colour piece on a Christmas craft sale and coffee morning being held at a church hall in one of our outlying villages.

'Jamie can take you, and if Lesley Lunt is there – as she surely will be – tell him to put her on the end of a row in the photographs so we can cut her out.'

Jamie was the staff photographer who had replaced Ray. He wasn't half as good, or half as nice. Lesley Lunt was a local councillor who seemed to do nothing but get herself photographed at local events. She would be grinning out of every page of the *Gazette*, if we didn't curtail her.

'Bring us back some goodies from the cake stall,' Madeleine on the front desk said, as I burrowed into the small stationery cupboard at her feet for a new notebook.

'Ow!' I banged my head as I rose.

'Honestly, Caroline – you do that every time! I'm going to buy you a helmet.'

Jamie appeared, grumpy as usual, and paused to look at the diary for the day's markings, the local term for his booked assignments. 'Aw, this is a joke,' he moaned. 'How am I supposed to get from St Colman's to fucking Riding for the Disabled in five minutes? That's a half-hour drive.'

This happened a lot – people phoned in their requests for a photographer and they all got written down in the diary, but no one really bothered to look at it from the photographer's point of view. Consequently, he got a list of appointments that criss-crossed the borough. He couldn't possibly service them all. Everyone agreed there should be a better system, but nobody ever came up with one.

'Let me see,' I said, pulling the diary towards me. I didn't much like Jamie, but I could understand his annoyance. 'OK. I'm going to pick out the ones that'll make a big impact on the page, and those are for you,' I told him. 'Everyone else, I'll ring round and explain that we simply can't make it, but we'll happily use their pics, if they take their own and email them to us by Monday evening.'

'And you're taking responsibility for that?' Jamie was wary

of Fergus, who sometimes seemed to expect miracles of his photographers.

'I am.'

'And I'm a witness,' Madeleine added.

'OK.' Jamie seemed satisfied. 'You ready?'

I loathed the drive to the church hall. As well as being taciturn, Jamie went much too fast up the dual carriageway. I asked him to slow down. I asked politely but made my discomfort unmistakably clear. He ignored me. Ray would never have done that.

When we arrived, I did a quick check of my blood sugar with my trusty old glucometer – if I wasn't running high, I could enjoy myself and have tea and something sweet while Jamie took his pictures.

'Don't drip blood on my seats,' Jamie said.

I licked my finger.

4.2: excellent. I could have something nice.

'Caroline! Thanks for coming. And you've brought your lovely photographer – aren't we lucky?'

That was June Black, stalwart of the Women's Institute, the ladies' choir and the Blooming Marvellous committee, which kept the towns and villages of the borough in seasonal colour. She was sitting in the lobby with a companion at a green-felted card table upon which rested a battered Quality Street tin full of pound coins.

'I like your headgear,' I said, smiling at her flashing antlers.

'Oh, thank you. We have a really great event, this year,

with half the proceeds going to Médecins Sans Frontières –
Dr Nelson's daughter is working for them out in Yemen, the
brave girl – and the other half going to the church's fund for
a new heating system. But of course there's no charge for the
press.'

Jamie shifted his weight impatiently.

'We'd better go and take a look,' I said.

'Please do. Refreshments are being served in the Watson
room.'

There were knitted hats and scarves on offer, crocheted
animals and felted jewellery. A noble fir dressed in red
gingham decorations, each for sale individually, caught my eye,
and I stopped to try a sample of the spiced apple juice that
was produced at the micro-brewery up the road. 'I'll take two
bottles,' I said, pulling out my purse. It would be a festive treat
when Tabby came home.

I bought half a dozen packs of shortbread stars and chocolate
crispy things for my colleagues, then ventured into the Watson
room, found an empty table and set down my notebook. I
would scribble a few of my impressions while they were still
fresh in my mind.

'Mind if I join you?' It was Emma, a friend of Tabby's from
school.

'Sure,' I said, lifting my handbag off the chair next to me and
setting it on the floor. 'It's nice to see you.'

A matronly woman with a flushed throat came along and
placed a three-tiered cake stand stacked with bite-sized scones
and pastries on our table. 'Help yourselves, ladies,' she said.
'Would you prefer tea or coffee?'

Church-hall tea was the absolute best, in my opinion. Something divine at work in the water.

'So what's Tabby doing, these days?' Emma asked. 'I haven't seen her for ages.'

I explained that she had secured permanent but part-time speech-therapy hours at a special-education school, and boosted her income with shifts in a coffee shop.

'Still, it's great that she's got a permanent position,' Emma said.

'It is. How about you? Have you found a permanent teaching post yet, or are you still subbing?'

'Still subbing. But I'm getting plenty of work. This is my first day off in weeks. The money's good – just a pity there's no holiday pay. I've covered two maternities in the past couple of years and they're great – it's steady and there's time to get to know the kids. Otherwise, it's just getting up in the morning, hoping for a phone call.'

'You're building up your experience, though – that must be a good thing.'

'It is and it isn't. The more experienced I get, the more I rise through the pay grades, and a newly qualified teacher can look a whole lot more attractive to a board of governors than a more expensive one. My big news, though, is that I'm getting married.' She'd been sitting on her hands, but now pulled out the left to flash me the ring.

'Oh, that's beautiful,' I said. 'I'm sorry, I don't know who your other half is.'

'Stefan Moorhead. You probably don't remember him – he was at school with us.'

I remembered Stefan. Tabby had had a huge crush on him but he never gave her a second glance. It had been heart-breaking.

'So, is Tabby seeing anyone?'

I was delighted to report that my daughter had been on a date the night before, though I hadn't had any details yet. I wasn't going to divulge to Emma that, if anything came of it, this would be the first boyfriend Tabby had had for over a year.

'Maybe you'll meet him at Christmas,' Emma said, with the ease of a girl who'd had boys chasing her all through school and uni while Tabby had sat at home wishing, sometimes weeping, and furiously lashing black mascara onto her stubbornly blonde eyelashes.

Jamie dropped me back at the parking spaces in front of the office. There were only two – one was for Fergus, naturally, and the other was labelled 'Photographer' because he or, possibly in the future, she had to come and go with haste. The rest of us parked a short walk away in the free car park.

'You coming in for some of these treats?' I asked.

'No time,' Jamie replied.

'But you didn't get anything at the hall, either.'

'I'll get a McDonald's later.'

As I entered Reception my tread on the carpet must have been silent, because Suzanne, the *Gazette*'s junior reporter, though she was in her thirties, was leaning over Madeleine's desk, talking, with her back to me.

'I'm just saying, she can't go on being so choosy at her age. She could do worse than Eric Haffey. He's got a good job, no ex and no kids, probably a nice fat pension, thank you very much, and, for some reason, he dotes on her. Who does she think she is anyway? And who does she think's going to roll up who's any better? George Clooney's taken.'

Madeleine grimaced and Suzanne swung round. She couldn't hide her embarrassment at being overheard gossiping about me, but she would never admit it.

I could understand Suzanne. She was selfish, prone to jealousy and had a nasty streak. But Madeleine shouldn't have been spreading what I had told her privately about ending the little relationship between me and Eric right after the Chamber of Trade dinner. She was my friend and she had known it wasn't for common consumption.

'Kylie Minogue's fifty-four,' Madeleine offered, presumably by way of compensation. 'Nicole Kidman's fifty-five!'

'I brought treats,' I said, not bothered enough to sulk. 'Shall I put the kettle on?'

'Let Madeleine do that,' Fergus said, coming down the stairs. 'I want to talk to you about what else you've got lined up for next week's paper. You too, Suzanne.'

'There's nothing happening, boss,' Suzanne said. 'This place is so sleepy. We can't make up news if there isn't any.'

'That's not how it works. Tell her, Caroline.'

'Fergus expects us to nose out something, however quiet it seems,' I said. 'For example, we're having a cold snap, so he'll have us running to the shopkeepers – are sales of warm coats or hats and gloves up? What about oil? Are deliveries booming, and have prices risen, too?'

Suzanne scowled.

'And if you don't like that, there's all the Christmas stuff,' I continued. 'Are people buying real trees this year, or artificial ones? What about sales of Christmas puds and mince pies? Are orders for turkeys as popular as ever or are people trying something different – like goose? Ask the butchers.'

'See what I mean, Suzanne?' Fergus said. 'There's always a nice feature to be had at the dog pound, too, if you get in quick – Christmas is the wrong time to take in a dog, because everyone knows that new pets need a lot of patience for the first couple of weeks, and that's sadly lacking on Christmas Day and Boxing Day. But if you go up there now, with Jamie, and get him to photograph the pooches' parade, then we can print the photos in next week's issue and help the pound to rehome them while there's still time before the madness starts. You'll get some great pics and possibly even save a few doggy lives.'

'Fancy popping out for a coffee at lunchtime?' Madeleine asked, as Suzanne slouched off. 'We haven't had a catch-up in a while. I can ask her ladyship to mind the front desk.'

'She won't like it,' I said.

As junior reporter, Suzanne was expected to muck in and help out anywhere she was needed. She wasn't happy about this, and answering the reception phone and taking details for births, marriages and deaths notices ranked among her pet peeves. Still, Madeleine had the confidence of a woman who had pretty much run the office for three decades and had seen considerably bigger fish than Suzanne come and go, and she wasn't put off.

'She can lump it,' Madeleine said. 'See you at one.'

'You ready?' Madeleine stuck her head round the editorial office door. 'Suzanne, be a pet and keep my seat warm for half an hour while Caroline and I get ourselves a coffee.'

'Again?'

'Yes, again. Want us to bring you something back?'

'Where are you going?'

'Santino's.'

'Then I'll have a latte. Two sugars.'

I pulled on my coat and we trotted downstairs.

'In other words, you went Christmas shopping straight from work, without having anything to eat,' Madeleine said, as we faced each other across the table. 'Well that's asking for trouble. You need to be more careful, Caroline.'

'It was stupid, I know.'

'Lucky Eric was there. Maybe you should think about wearing one of those medical bracelets – one of these days you might need it.'

'I draw the line at that – they're hideous. But I promise to be more sensible from now on. No swanning around the shops on an empty stomach.'

'Did you even get the pyjamas in the end?'

'Nope. I didn't get anything.' I sighed. 'Every year I promise myself I'll start sorting the Christmas shopping in September, and beat the rush. Now here we are on the third of December and I haven't bought a thing.'

'I take it you're going to Ray and Jodie's for Christmas Day, as usual.'

'Yep.'

Madeleine rolled her eyes. 'You're like Rod Stewart's family,' she said. 'All his wives and children come to his place for Christmas dinner together, apparently.'

'Rod Stewart has rather more wives and exes than Ray – he only has me and Jodie.'

'And you really don't think it's odd, you spending Christmas with him and Jodie in their marital home with their children?'

'He's Tabby's dad – if she can celebrate Christmas with both of us in the same place at the same time that has to be a good thing. As well as which, I don't have a problem with Jodie. I'm happy to let her feed me – I get to quaff prosecco and play with the boys while she does all the sweating in the kitchen.'

'You're insanely fond of your ex's children.'

'They're Tabby's little brothers.'

'But it's not just that.'

'No, it's not. What can I say? They're lovely kids.'

'It's too weird, the way you even babysit them so that Ray can take Jodie for a night out. Most women whose husbands dumped them for a younger model would want to cut his gonads off – but you actually care for his progeny.'

I chuckled. 'I loved him, I lost him. It's old news, Mads.'

'But doesn't it make you sick that he only got rich after the divorce?'

I had thought about that sometimes. When I had first met Ray, he had been the staff photographer at the newspaper and I had been the junior reporter. In fact, when I had *very* first met him, it had been on the phone – he had rung through some caption details as he had too many markings to make it back to the office. No email, in those days. He had a lazy local drawl, and I'd thought his voice sounded like warm honey dripping off a spoon. I couldn't wait to meet him. I knew I'd find him attractive.

'Is he your type?' a young Madeleine had asked me, her curiosity piqued.

Did I even have a type? Mark, who was already history by that time, had been tall and lithe, despite his limp, mercurial, with floppy dark hair and blue eyes. Ray was stocky and sandy-haired and deliciously languid. If there was a characteristic shared by the men to whom I was attracted, it was only that I liked them sexy. 'There's no point dwelling on it,' I told Madeleine now. 'When Ray and I worked on the *Gazette* together, we didn't earn much because we weren't ambitious, but we were content. It's down to Jodie that he's running his own picture agency – she saw his potential and swooped in. She managed him to success, so the fact that he's doing very nicely is down to them. Anyway, they're good to Tabby.'

Madeleine dabbed her mouth with her paper napkin.

'Actually, I might pop up the street to Jodie's shop, now,

while I'm out,' she said. 'I need a baby gift for yet another of my ludicrously fecund nieces and Jodie always has the nicest things. Sorry if that's disloyal.'

'Haven't you been listening? I'm not anti-Jodie. Not any more. I've been over all that for a long time.'

I left Madeleine at the coffee shop and wandered back to the office with Suzanne's latte.

Fergus had once admitted to me that he had made a mistake in appointing her. 'I took her on over a young guy who'd done his NCTJ course because she seemed so hungry,' he had said – or something like that. 'Ten years in the civil service had left her bored out of her mind and she was champing at the bit for a change. I should have told her to go away, take the course and come back when she'd nailed her shorthand and typing and had a basic grasp of libel law.'

I could see what he meant. What Suzanne really wanted was to cover murders and corruption, but she wasn't so keen on sitting with her notebook night after night trying to take down the ten o'clock news verbatim and then transcribe it, word for word. That was how you got your shorthand up to a hundred words a minute and deadly accurate.

She was supposed to be learning touch-typing online, too, which I didn't think could be a patch on the classes I'd attended, hammering the home keys of an old upright typewriter over and over again without looking, learning where each finger reached across, up and down to cover the entire alphabet without thinking. *Now is the time for all good men to come to the aid of the party.*

I was still raw, back then, from the whole Mark thing. It was probably the reason I focused so intensely on getting good.

If Mark ever did find me, if he ever came back for me, it was unthinkable that he should meet Tabby. I heard the gentle tap as the stylus dropped onto the vinyl record and the soft hiss as the track began. I didn't know what Mark might tell her. Tabby must never, ever know what we did.

3

It was Saturday morning and Ray, Jodie and the boys were picking me up at ten. We were going to see Santa. Not just the one in the shopping centre, though. Jodie had found a special winter-wonderland experience, with live animals in the nativity scene, an elves' workshop and marshmallow-toasting. It was a fifty-mile round trip, but she had a nice big comfortable 4x4 and she was a good driver. Plus, with Lucas now seven and Noah nine, this might conceivably be the last year they both truly believed.

I washed up my breakfast dishes, emptied the compost caddy, wondered if I had time for a quick trip to the bottle bank and decided I did.

'Clearing the decks before Christmas?' It was Fergus,

feeding assorted jars and bottles into one of the huge recycling bins in the pub car park.

'You too?' I asked.

'Something like that.'

I started lobbing bottles through the slot in the next container.

'Had a party?' Fergus enquired.

'No, no. I just haven't had a clear-out in a while.'

'I hate doing this. I'm the same with posting letters. I'm always afraid I'll post something I'm not meant to by mistake – like my car keys, or my wallet.'

'And have you?'

'No.'

'Well, then, it's not very likely, is it? What are you and Marina up to, today?'

'Writing our Christmas cards is the plan.'

'Oh, well, that's nice.'

'Is it? Every year the address book has more and more names crossed out where somebody else has died. It's depressing.' Fergus's last jar crashed and he folded his carrier bags neatly inside each other. 'Fancy grabbing a coffee somewhere?' he asked.

Fergus was a different person away from the *Gazette* office. At work, he was busy, efficient, in control. Elsewhere, he sometimes seemed a bit lost. None of us could quite fathom his marriage. Marina had problems. She was neurotic, very religious, anxious and demanding. She rarely left the house and seemed to expect Fergus to do the same when he wasn't working. She rang him at the office a lot, and he almost always took her calls with great patience. But occasionally, according to Madeleine, who transferred callers to our extensions, if he happened to be downstairs with the advertising staff, he shook his head wearily at her and signalled not to put his wife through.

The invitation for a coffee, I sensed, was because he didn't want to go home. Not just yet. I wished I could say yes, but I didn't have time. 'I'm afraid I have a date with Santa.'

'Ah. Well, it is that time of year. Anything you can get a story out of for the paper?'

'It's out of our circulation area. Sorry.'

'No worries. That was a nice piece you did about the craft fair.'

'Thanks.'

'Jamie got a few good pics, too. He's getting more creative. About time.'

'I really do have to shoot off, now, Fergus, or I'll be keeping everybody waiting.'

'Sure! Have fun with Father Christmas.'

'See you Monday.'

For a moment, I thought about kissing him, but you never knew who was watching and I didn't want Marina hearing that her husband had been seen kissing some woman in a pub car-park, so I just smiled and went back to my car.

Jodie, Ray and the boys arrived right on time. Before I could grab my bag, Jodie was on the front doorstep, holding Noah's hand.

'Hi, guys. Excited about seeing Santa?'

'Sorry, Caroline. Can this one just pop in and use your loo?'

I stood aside. 'No problem. You know where it is, Noah.'

As he scooted off upstairs, Jodie sighed. 'I'm going to have to take him to the doctor, Caroline. He needs to pee all the time. I mean, constantly. What do you think it is?'

'What do *you* think it is?'

'A urinary tract infection, I suppose.'

'I guess it could be. Or just coming out in the cold?'

'But he's been doing it for days.'

'Excitement maybe? Over Christmas?'

'So you don't think I should take him to the doctor?'

'I'm not saying that at all, Jodie. If you're worried about him then you've got to make him an appointment. I can give you a specimen jar, if you like, and you could bring a urine sample along with you, get the ball rolling.'

'If you've got a spare, that would be great.'

'Even if it is an infection, it'll just be a few days of antibiotic and he'll be sorted. Are you sure you want to do this Santa thing today? We could leave it for a week, if Noah's under the weather.'

'Ray's going to be working the next two Saturdays, so we really have to go today. Anyway, I've bought the tickets.'

The toilet flushed, and Jodie called: 'Big soapy hands-wash, Noah!'

When he came back downstairs, I felt his forehead and the back of his neck. No temperature, at least. 'You up for this?' I asked him.

'Yes.'

Five minutes later, we were on our way.

The boys insisted I sit in the middle seat, so they were both beside me.

'I don't have any sweets,' I warned them. I was under strict instructions from Jodie.

Usually, when Noah and Lucas were out and about with their parents, Jodie dressed them as if they were going to a wedding – stiff trousers, good shoes and long-sleeved shirts. In a nod to today's occasion, however, and probably thinking of the photos Ray would take, she had put them in what looked like brand new jeans, wellies and Christmas jumpers. Noah's had a snowman with little white lights – how would you ever wash that? – and Lucas's sported a reindeer's face with a red pom-pom for its nose. On the parcel shelf behind us lay two pristine navy duffel coats with varnished wooden toggles.

'Can we play a game?' Noah asked me.

'Give Caroline a chance,' Ray said, from the front passenger seat, in his sleepy drawl. 'Just look out the window for a while. You'll have loads of fun when we get there.'

'Aw,' the two boys replied, but they hushed.

'Have you started rehearsing your Christmas play yet, at school?' I asked Noah.

'Yes. I'm the stupid inn-keeper,' he replied quietly.

'What's stupid about it?'

'I wanted to be something else.'

'Oh – what?'

Noah squirmed in his seat and didn't answer.

'Fairytale of New York' came on the radio and Jodie turned it up. 'I love this song,' she said.

I wondered what on earth in a tale of drug-addled disillusioned dreamers spoke to Jodie, who had been brought up in a bungalow in the country and ferried in her full-time mother's runabout to ballet, music and speech-and-drama. She had bounced from a good, middle-class life with her parents to a good, middle-class life with Ray.

'I love it too,' Lucas announced. 'You scumbag, you faggot!' he cried, addressing no one in particular, and collapsed into giggles.

'Lucas, don't be rude,' Jodie snapped, making me wonder afresh how this could really be the song for her.

'Has Tabby said when she's coming home for Christmas?' Ray asked.

'Not yet,' I replied. 'School finishes on the twenty-second, but I think she'll still be expected to work at the coffee shop.'

'Will you be buying her another Pandora charm this year?' Jodie asked. 'The boys were each going to get her one and we don't want to end up choosing the same one as you.'

I had bought Tabby a charm bracelet for her twenty-first and it pleased me to add to it when the occasion arose. I wasn't sure I loved the idea of Jodie muscling in on it, but if the charms came from Noah and Lucas, that felt all right.

'I've already got mine – it's a little cat, in acknowledgement of Lennie's arrival.' Lennie was the rescue cat Tabby had adopted a few months ago. He was coming to my place for Christmas, too.

'So anything else from this season's range would be all right?' Jodie checked.

It would.

There was a long queue to get into the winter-wonderland car-park.

'This is ridiculous,' Jodie said. 'If you buy tickets in advance, there should be a fast-track. Or, at least, they should know how many people are coming and be ready for them.'

'I need to go to the toilet,' Noah said.

'Well, you'll just have to hold it.' Jodie sounded firm.

'I can't.'

'I'll take him,' Ray said. 'We'll find a hedge to go behind.'

'He is not peeing behind a hedge,' Jodie replied.

'Actually, I could do with finding a loo myself,' I fibbed. 'I can take Noah with me.'

'Are you sure?' Jodie asked, though I think she was relieved. 'Look, this queue is creeping along. Ring Ray when you're finished and he can tell you where we are.'

As the two of us went in search of a toilet, Noah slipped his hand into mine. I was touched. Now that he was nine, I didn't know if he still wanted to hold anyone's hand.

The Santa experience was attached to a large garden centre, with its own coffee shop, and after some hunting we found toilets at the rear. There was another queue, of course, but I chose not to worry because there was absolutely no point and we waited in line until it was our turn.

'Will you come in with me?' Noah asked. 'I'm afraid of getting locked in.'

When he had finished, and washed every facet of his hands, he said, 'I wanted to be an angel.'

The live nativity scene was sweet. There were three imperturbable woolly sheep, two Jersey cattle, a donkey that looked as sad as donkeys always seemed to look, but didn't mind children petting it, some chickens I didn't recall being mentioned in the gospels and, for even more unfathomable reasons, a llama.

'Can we touch them?' Noah asked, although Lucas was already rubbing one of the sheep's backs vigorously.

'Yes. But don't touch your mouth and nose afterwards,' Jodie said.

I noticed the other parents looking admiringly at Ray's camera, while they snapped away on their phones, and felt a familiar surge of pride. He might not be my husband now but, thanks to him, I had a beautiful professional collection of photographs of Tabby on every occasion. We had bought her clothes in Woolworths and Adams and not the expensive children's outfitters Jodie used, but I adored her in those pictures.

'That boy is going to let the donkey out!' a girl's voice suddenly cried. I turned. It was Lucas, tugging at the gate's bar.

'He wants to go for a walk,' Lucas said.

'Don't worry – he won't be able to open it,' a man in a garden-centre fleece jacket said confidently, just before the gate swung open and Lucas cried, 'I'm strong! I could do the monkey bars when I was three – couldn't I, Noah?'

A nearby woman grabbed the gate and pushed it closed, but really we shouldn't have been surprised – Lucas could open his stair-gate from the day it was fitted; we all called him 'Houdini'.

'Not cool, Lucas,' Ray drawled. 'People could get hurt if the animals escaped. The animals could get hurt.'

'Remember who you've come here to see,' Jodie added. 'You don't want to end up on his naughty list.'

We were standing back while Noah and Lucas made penguins from yogurt pots in the elves' workshop.

'How's the gift shop doing?' I asked Jodie. 'Having a good Christmas?'

'Unbelievable,' Jodie said. 'I've had to make my two part-timers full-time for the foreseeable and I'm desperately trying to get more stock.'

'That's great!'

'Actually, don't breathe a word, but I'm thinking of opening a second place.'

'Where?'

'Just the next-door unit. It's been empty since the electricals showroom went. I could expand the baby end of things into the new premises and keep the other home and gifty stuff where I am now.'

'Exciting.'

'It is. Getting that new free short-stay car park practically on my doorstep has been a potential game-changer.'

'I know we reported the Chamber of Trade welcoming it.'

'If I don't take the plunge quickly, someone else is going to snap up that unit, and there's no way of knowing what they might be selling – they could be competition.'

'What does Leanne think?' Leanne was Jodie's shop manager.

'It's not up to her. It's my investment. My risk.'

'Well, good luck, if you decide to go ahead.'

'Thanks. I'll be asking you to do me a write-up in the paper, if I go for it.'

The last time I had written a piece launching Jodie's new business, it had been the original gift shop. Ray had taken the photographs. And Jodie had taken Ray.

'I'd be glad to.'

We snaked up through the enchanted forest, decorated with multitudes of white fairy lights that lit up the wintry sky, eventually arriving at Santa's grotto.

Santa was suitably rotund and seated in a rocking chair by a wood-burning stove. He clapped his big hands in welcome when he saw Noah and Lucas, as if they were the very children he had been waiting all day to meet.

Ray took a picture of the boys standing either side of Santa with their gifts, and another of them whispering into Santa's ears as they put in their requests for his Christmas delivery.

Santa allowed the staging, but then explained that when two

boys talked at once, he couldn't hear what they were saying, and could they please tell him again what they wanted, one at a time.

Lucas didn't hesitate. 'I want Lego Super Mario Adventures and a Gotta Go Flamingo.'

Santa nodded and glanced almost imperceptibly at Jodie, who tilted her head ever so subtly in assent.

'I think we should be able to manage that,' Santa told Lucas. 'And how about you?' He turned to Noah, who said nothing.

'Tell Santa what you want, Noah,' Jodie instructed.

Noah shrugged.

'You don't know?' Santa asked. 'Well, have a think, and you can write me a letter. But don't take too long – the elves need a chance to get your present ready.'

'Lucas, jump up on Santa's knee,' Ray drawled, looking for the next shot.

'No!' Jodie barked. 'Santa's very busy, Lucas. He has lots more boys and girls to see. Thank you, Santa. Merry Christmas.'

Bundling the boys out, she whispered to me: 'He seems very nice and I'm sure he's been vetted, but you never know.'

On the way back to the car, Jodie said: 'Did anyone notice that roadside place on the way here – the High Hedges Inn? How about stopping off for lunch?'

'Actually, I've heard bad things about their food,' I lied. 'And someone told me they're not very welcoming to kids. But there's a family diner between there and home that has a good rep.'

'Really?' Jodie said. 'OK, then, we'll stop there. Coats

off, boys, and jump in. But keep those wellie boots off the upholstery.'

Noah, who had used the toilet twice at the winter wonderland and also at the diner, was in need again when we got as far as my place.

'Why don't you all come in for a sit-down, and the boys can draw?' I said.

'Say yes, Mummy,' Lucas pleaded. 'I love drawing.'

'Just for half an hour,' Jodie said. 'I want to go for a run before it gets dark.'

I went to the cupboard under the stairs and rummaged for the boys' drawing pads and the old biscuit tin full of markers, inevitably banging my head as I withdrew.

When I returned to the front room, Jodie was sitting with her usual poise on the sofa, flipping through my *Radio Times*.

'Ray in the kitchen?' I asked.

Jodie looked up. 'Ray?' she called.

'Yeah.'

Jodie smoothed the magazine with her long fingers. 'Ray, you can't just walk into Caroline's kitchen like you own the place.'

He had done, once, with me.

'I'm being helpful, making coffee.' That drawl again.

'Well, don't. Caroline could have personal correspondence sitting about or anything. You should respect her privacy.'

Ray stepped into the lounge. 'Caroline, can I please have

your permission to be in your kitchen and make everyone a cup of coffee?'

'Be my guest.'

'Got anything the kids could drink?'

'Not fizzy,' Jodie said quickly.

'There's orange juice in the fridge. Or milkshake syrup in the cupboard above the kettle.'

Ray made a face. 'You don't have a whole lot of milk.'

'It'll have to be juice, then.'

As with bread, it was hard to manage the supply of milk when you lived alone. A litre didn't last, and two litres could be too much. I regularly ended up either tipping half a carton down the sink or finding myself running out completely.

'You should keep a couple of packs of long-life in the larder,' Jodie said. 'It tastes OK on cereal or in coffee.' Her suggestion irritated me slightly. I admired Jodie in many ways – she was focused, energetic, productive – but she tended to presume that her priorities were everyone's, or should be. She had a less than healthy amount of self-doubt.

Ray brought in the tray and I cleared a space on the coffee-table.

'I must leave you in a copy of *Tatler*,' Jodie said. 'That shoot Ray did at the manor house back in July looks amazing. You'd really believe it was Christmas. Thumb out, Lucas.'

I asked Noah and Lucas if they wanted me to set up their art stuff at the dining table. Usually, I'd let them lie on the lounge floor to draw, but I suspected Jodie would object.

Once the boys were engrossed, I whispered: 'What can I get

them for Christmas? Any suggestions? Tabby was asking me for a steer, too.'

'You always get them their Christmas pyjamas, Caroline – that's enough,' Jodie said.

'But that's for Christmas Eve. I want them to have something from me to open on the day.'

'Get them a selection box and they'll love you for ever,' Ray said.

'*Don't* get them selection boxes. If you're really sure, let me have a think and I'll get back to you.'

Ray had a look through that week's *Gazette*, Jodie examined the three Christmas cards on my mantelpiece and, in exactly half an hour, the four Rankins said their goodbyes, thanked me for joining them and for the coffee, lined up to kiss me and went on their way.

When they had gone, I piled the dirty cups and glasses into the sink and left them for later. I should really have caught up on the week's post, but I didn't feel in the mood. Instead, I texted Tabby and told her about my trip with the boys.

She immediately texted back: *And was he a sexy Santa?*

I replied: *No. Like all good Father Christmases, he was fat, bearded and asexual. I know they say there's someone out there for everyone, but Santa and I are definitely not a match.*

I told her about my plans to let Eric Haffey down gently, but firmly enough for him to get the message that I wasn't interested.

How many times did you actually go out with him? Tabby texted.

Three. Suzanne thinks I should be grateful for his suit and marry him ASAP.

But you don't lurve him.

Nope. How about you – are you seeing this guy again?

Yes! We're cooking at his place. His mum gave him Rachel Allen's Recipes From My Mother *for his birthday and we're going to try something out of that. He says it's somewhat ironic as the only recipes his actual mother had to share were fish-finger sandwiches with the fish fingers black on one side and frozen on the other, and Heinz Scotch Broth.*

Sounds like a woman after my own heart. Do you really like him?

I do like him. But I'm punching above my weight – he's a looker.

Oh, Tabby. When would she ever start to love herself?

Don't say that. You're as good as anyone. You're beautiful.

Yes, Mum. Here comes my stop, so I'm off to the shops to get some pressie ideas. Speak soon.

And she was gone.

I consulted the *Radio Times* and found a channel doing wall-to-wall Christmas cooking programmes. I would light the fire, put my feet up and get in the mood, knowing perfectly well that I would very likely *not* be stuffing a turkey with a goose, or baking my own *Stollen* or making date-blue-cheese-pancetta-and-polenta-stacked canapés to delight my friends.

As I carted my sticks and logs in from the shed, I remembered Jodie suggesting we stop at the High Hedges Inn. I had got out of it without making a fuss, because I couldn't possibly go there. It was out of the question. Utterly. Because the High Hedges was where I regularly went to meet my lover.

4

'**O**f course, we were children in the seventies, which was the best time to be a kid,' Madeleine said. It was Sunday morning and she had brought round the holly wreath for Mum and Dad's grave. Her brother-in-law made them at this time every year and they were nicer by far than the ones in the grocer's or the market – which were mostly fir and had nasty red plastic flowers attached – and cheaper than the ones in the florist's.

'Do you think so?' I asked.

'Certainly.' She set down the Christmas card she had picked up from my mantelpiece and flopped onto the sofa. 'Everybody had a bike, even if about six members of your extended family had owned it before you, and the paint was almost worn off. Everybody had a TV – you could rent them, if you remember. Everybody had 10p to go to the shop for sweets. Kids played out, there were no eating disorders and no families living in B&Bs.'

'There was still poverty, Madeleine. There was still deprivation. And other problems.'

'Not like these days. And people's expectations weren't as high – having a chicken in the fridge meant it was a special occasion. Fridges were just little cold boxes that fitted under the counter, too – not like the spaceships they are now. We lived on stewed steak, sausages and corned beef.'

'You just remember those times as carefree because you were young and had no responsibilities.'

'Wrong, Caroline! Wrong! Kids these days are still young, but they're stressed out of their heads with SATs and social media and scheduled after-school activities every day instead of going home and lying on the sofa with a bag of Hula Hoops, watching *Scooby Doo*.'

I smiled. I had to. I partly agreed with her, although maybe my view wasn't quite as rose-tinted.

'Christmases were particularly fine, back then,' Madeleine continued, clearly enjoying herself. 'Do you remember the *Blue Peter* Advent crown, made from wire coat hangers and tinsel? They lit another candle on it for each of the last shows before the big day. It could only have been more of a fire hazard if they'd doused it in petrol, but nobody minded.'

We lost ourselves in memories of the old ad campaigns for Hai Karate aftershave and Shaker Makers, agreeing that, when we were children, seasonal aspirations had been much more modest.

'All you required for a family Christmas was a tree, a turkey, a tin of Quality Street and a few presents,' I conceded. 'You didn't need hand-tied blooms as your centrepiece, or three different luxury desserts, and you certainly didn't undertake the complete redecoration of your living room, which Ray and I did one December and vowed never again.'

'I have to plead guilty there,' Madeleine said, holding up her hand. 'I persuaded myself that we couldn't do Christmas this year without a double-oven, and then I decided that, if we wanted a double-oven, we might as well go the whole hog and replace the old one plus the hob with a range cooker, and now it's coming on Wednesday.'

'But how will you fit it into the gaps left by the old things?'

'Good question. That's what Jimmy said. So we're getting a whole new kitchen starting next week.'

'Oh, Madeleine.' I couldn't imagine a worse time to have workmen in the house and nowhere to cook until the job was done.

'I know. I wish I'd left it until January now, but I got carried away.'

'No wonder you're reminiscing about more relaxed times.'

'Let's change the subject – I don't want to think about my house. What were Christmases like in the Maxwell household?'

I smiled again. 'Great, actually.'

'So tell me.'

'Well, the excitement would start on Christmas Eve, when

Mum and Dad would let us have a Martini after tea – I'm talking about the stuff in the ads you mixed with lemonade, not the kind James Bond drinks. We thought this was absolutely thrilling, although, with hindsight, I reckon it was to make sure we slept soundly while Santa went about his business. We'd wake up when it was still dark, see what we'd been brought and start to play.'

'Did you bounce in and wake your parents?'

'No. Never.'

'They had you well trained.'

'Then, in the morning, Mum and Dad had the neighbours in for drinks, which sounds posh, but we definitely weren't. We lived in a new-build terrace – I'm sure I've told you this before ...'

'You have, but continue. I want to hear it again.'

'Well, ours was the best house in the row for entertaining because Mum and Dad had gone for an open-plan living-dining room, whereas everyone else had opted for two smaller rooms. It was Harveys Bristol Cream and Ritz crackers and the Elvis Christmas album until the neighbours went home. Then we piled into the car and went to our grandparents' for Christmas dinner.'

'What did you make of that? Didn't you wish you could stay in your own house?'

'I never thought about it.'

Granny Jackson cooked a superb lunch and Mum and Auntie Alex helped with the washing-up, so we kids didn't have to do a tap. Then, while the adults drank and laughed about things we barely understood in the sitting room, we retreated to

Mum's old bedroom, where Granddad had rigged up a portable black-and-white television, and watched whatever film or pantomime was showing. In the evening we were summoned back to the dining room for salad and trifle, and then we fell asleep in Mum's old bed, to the sounds of music and revelry from downstairs.

'This is nice to hear. You hardly ever talk about your mum and dad,' Madeleine said, her head on one side. 'Is it because of what happened?'

'And you hardly ever ask about them,' I replied, raising my eyebrows for emphasis. 'Which is one of the main reasons I like you.'

It's not that I've forgotten them. Far from it. I can still smell Mum's almond blossom hand cream like it was yesterday, and Dad's spicy aftershave. They were beautiful. Glamorous. Dancers. Lovers. Roy and Josephine Maxwell. Maxie and Josie. The king and queen.

I filled the car with petrol and bought a bottle of Lucozade at the garage shop. The drive to the graveyard would take me the best part of two hours, even on a Sunday.

Usually, Tabby made the trip with me. It was the only time we went. Sometimes, if no one had removed it for me, we found the skeletal remains of last year's wreath, which we dumped in the bin. No other maintenance was required. I paid a small annual sum to the church for the privilege of the graveyard grass being cut, and the headstone needed no work.

My parents were buried in the same graveyard as Granny

and Granddad Jackson, at the church Granny had attended. I think both Mum and Dad were closer to the Jacksons than to Nanny and Papa, as we knew Dad's parents. Dad's family was the more religious – even after Dad left home, married Mum and moved away, he still went to church most Sunday mornings. I don't know whether he believed. I sensed it was more a matter of honouring the parents he loved, but felt bad about not relating to. Nanny and Papa gave us Bibles and hymn books and school socks for Christmas, whereas the Jacksons gave me a Sindy doll and my brother an Action Man. Nanny and Papa and Granny loved Jesus. Maxie and Josie loved Elvis.

I missed having Tabby with me, and knew she would be sorry not to have taken part in this annual ritual. When she was little, she loved to hear stories about when I'd been a child. She always wanted me to tell her about the pussycat wallpaper in my bedroom, which Josie put up, and Maxie teaching me to swim in the sea and to ride a bike.

'What did you say when you were learning to ride your bike?' a young Tabby would ask.

'I'd say: "Promise you won't let go!"'

'But he did let go, didn't he, Mummy? And you still didn't fall off.'

Ray taught Tabby to ride her bicycle – if it had been down to me I'd be holding it still.

I listened to Radio 2 all the way along the motorway, but as I joined the country roads I changed to Classic FM. They were playing 'In the Bleak Midwinter', the Darke version – the 'wrong' version: I preferred the Holst.

A cold winter sun made the trees and hedgerows look stark,

but at least it wasn't raining. There was something desperately gloomy about standing in a graveyard getting soaked.

How many years had I been doing this? Maxie and Josie had died in 1985, so that made this – what? – my thirty-seventh visit.

Those first years, all my grandparents had still been alive, but I don't think they ever got over being predeceased by their children. Granny lost her sparkle, Granddad retreated into himself, while Nanny and Papa were both diagnosed with dementia, which I suppose was an escape of sorts, and went to live in a home. Within four years, they were all gone. Uncle Johnny and Auntie Alex inherited the Jackson farm, but sold it after a couple of years and bought a place in Canada. As far as I knew they never came back.

Madeleine thought, after all of the losses, I should make a greater effort to keep up with my brother. She thought it was bad for me to have no family support.

'Tell you what, to keep you happy I'll put one of those awful boasty newsletters in his Christmas card,' I'd said. 'I'll tell him I've been elected to the parish council and won the annual table-tennis tournament, and Tabby has taken up the trombone. See if he can match that.'

'There's no need to be flippant, Caroline. And you don't have to make stuff up – you're doing very well, you *and* Tabby. Some of us actually enjoy getting those "awful newsletters", as you call them. I like hearing what everyone's up to. Why don't you suggest he comes over, this year? You've got room.'

'I'm afraid they'd find my little house very humble, after what they're used to. And Amina has a fear of flying.'

'Then you go to them. If you book now, you could be out there in April, before it gets too hot.'

'Maybe.'

'Oh, you always say that, and you never go.'

'I'm a homebird, Mads.'

'We're all homebirds, really. But free accommodation in a jet-set tourist destination is not to be sniffed at. If you're worried about leaving Tabby, why don't you both go?'

'I suppose she does get time off school at Easter.'

'Well, then ...' Madeleine hesitated. 'Unless there's some other reason you don't want to go.'

I'd given her a little smile. 'You got me.'

All in all, having lost so many people, was it really so surprising that I inclined away from the past and allowed my brother to do the same, preferring our entirely tragedy-free new families, courtesy of Ray and Amina? As I might have said before, my life wouldn't suit everyone, but it worked for me. I did wish Tabby would find love, but apart from that, I was perfectly content. So leave me alone.

'I'll send them a nice card. But I've almost certainly missed the last posting date, as per usual. I think they must get my Christmas cards about February.'

I was coming to Kerr's corner. If I turned right, the road would take me straight to the churchyard. If I went left, it would lead me past Granny and Granddad's farm. I hadn't been up for a look for years and, since I was in no hurry, decided to make the detour.

The way was narrow and twisting and I had to go right down to second gear to take some of the tight bends. I passed the Tullivers' place and the Martins', and the gate-posts where old Mr and Mrs McGrath used to hang their shopping basket, with grocery list and money tucked inside, so Mum, as a girl, could take it with her on the bus to town.

I came to the foot of my grandparents' lane and turned in. It had always been surfaced with rough gravel, marred by potholes, which Granddad was constantly filling in using a shovel and more stones. The gravel was gone, I noted, replaced by concrete. What had been a rattling drive in our old Hillman Minx was now much smoother. I took a bend in the lane, then another, and the house came into view.

Except it didn't. Where I had always known a delightful farmhouse, two storeys dashed with real pebbles and a painted wooden front door, there now stood a red-brick bungalow with white uPVC windows and plastic pillars on each side of the entrance. It didn't even look that new – it might have been there ten years, or twelve. It was quite possible that was how long it was since I had made a visit.

A face appeared at a window and I suddenly felt like an intruder. I turned the car in the front yard and went back down the lane.

A dozen vehicles were parked at the church – all for the graveyard, I presumed, as there weren't enough people for a service. I passed an elderly man filling his grave-vase at an outside tap and a woman on her knees in front of a headstone, with a large pair of scissors, snipping the ends off stems and dropping them onto a torn sheet of cellophane.

The graveyard was looking well, as Granny would have been pleased to announce. The grass and footpaths were tidy and the graves well tended, many with what looked like fresh seasonal colour. I got to see the whole thing, as my family's plot was located in a small, enclosed section right at the back, which necessitated walking past everyone else's.

Ray had once asked me where we would be buried, and I had told him I had no intention of ending up in the ground. If I went first, he was to cremate me, clutch my ashes to his bosom for a full year and finally release me into the waves some place wild where we had been on holiday. If Ray went first, I would simply have to live for ever because it was unthinkable to leave Tabby all alone.

Still, I was glad to have this quiet country churchyard to which to make my pilgrimage, even though I did it only once a year. It was a place and a moment in time around which my loss could coalesce annually, briefly.

When I was almost at the grave, I met an elderly woman, slightly stooped, carrying the kind of handbag the Queen wears over her arm. 'I don't need to ask who you are,' she said, giving me a big smile. 'You're the spit of your mother.'

It's something I used to hear all the time, but had to come back here for someone to say it to me now.

'I taught Josie at Sunday school,' the woman said. 'She wasn't one bit interested, but I loved her anyway. You had to love Josie. It was very sad, what happened.'

'I'm just putting this on, for Christmas,' I said, holding up the wreath by its vinyl ribbon. 'I'm afraid I don't come very often – it's quite a long drive from where I live now.'

'That's a lovely one. Well, don't you worry. My late husband's buried beside your mother and father, so I'll keep an eye on things for you.'

The little back place where Mum and Dad's graves were was in a hollow, and the sun didn't seem to have reached it. I thought the path looked icy and was watching where I was going. This was why it took me completely by surprise to look over and suddenly see the red roses. No one else ever came to this spot. It was only ever Tabby and me, and she wouldn't have come without telling me. Plus it was so far out of her way and she didn't have a car.

At first I was curious, but then I saw the card. Who left a card on grave flowers? Nobody.

The card read: *Count them.*

Crashing down on my knees on the white pebbles, I dropped the wreath.

Trembling, I began to count the blooms, but I already knew exactly how many there would be. Seventeen. This wasn't a tribute to my parents, but a message to me. This was Mark.

5

'**M**orning, Caroline. You look like shit.'

'Thanks, Michael.'

It was Monday, and time for the magistrates' court sitting. I had been taking my place in the press box there since for ever, and for the past ten years Michael from the *Chronicle* had been keeping me company. The *Chronicle* was the newer paper in town, and it wasn't as good as the *Gazette*, but Fergus hurt any time they got a story we had missed, and knowing they were sniffing about kept us on our toes. Despite working for rival publications, Michael and I helped each other over court matters. If I got back to my desk and discovered I couldn't read my shorthand, or had omitted to note down an address, I could ring Michael and he would fill in the blanks, and vice versa. Once or twice, when a very young person had done something stupid that could mar their whole future if it appeared in print, we had agreed to 'lose' our notes. While I knew this was playing God, and Fergus would have killed me if he had found out, I didn't really regret it.

'You're not going to pass out on me,' Michael checked.

'It's not a diabetic issue,' I said. 'I'm just a bit off-colour.'

'Well, it's not too long a list, and there's nothing contested. We'll be out by twelve.'

He passed me a pile of charge sheets and I noted down names and addresses. Most of the list was motoring offences – driving without insurance, driving over the limit, taking and driving away. These were the types of thing that appeared in our pages every week.

I had barely handed the bundle of papers back to the clerk when the resident magistrate strode in and everyone rose. Judge Ralph Nicholson was tall and tanned, with pewter hair he wore a little long, and blue, blue eyes. He had been our RM for about five years and I enjoyed watching him work. On my fiftieth birthday, he had asked me out for a drink and, possibly because it was my fiftieth birthday, and thus loaded with all sorts of emotions, I had said yes. We had gone to a swanky hotel the following evening and we had stayed the night. He had called me afterwards, talked to me, listened to me, asked about Tabby and work. He had lent me a book, sent flowers to my home. I had enjoyed the attention. But we were seen, and word got back to Fergus, who took me aside and told me I should stop: Ralph Nicholson was married, he would never put me first, his wife and family would always be his priority, and I deserved better.

I took down the particulars of each case, solicitors stating the usual mitigating circumstances. 'Your honour, the defendant has been driving for twelve years with no previous convictions' and 'The defendant requires her licence for work'.

A shop-lifting gang who were stealing to order was passed up to a higher court, and a man who had made thirty-two hoax calls to the emergency services was given a suspended sentence and a stern warning.

'Fancy grabbing some lunch?' Michael asked, as we folded up our notebooks. 'I'm buying.'

'I'll pass, I think. I'm still not feeling great.'

'You should have taken the day off.'

'And who would have covered court?'

'Is Fergus ever going to give Suzanne a crack at it?'

'I wish. She's itching to have a go, and I'd be more than happy to let her take over, but Fergus doesn't think her shorthand's up to speed yet, and he's terrified she'll make a mistake and get us sued.'

Walking back to the office, I felt light-headed. I'd barely slept the previous night. Finding the roses had rocked me. Since Thursday, I'd more or less decided that I had not, in fact, seen Mark in the shopping centre, just someone who looked a bit like him, which my hypoglycaemic imagination had conjured into more. But the flowers were real. And the message on the card was clearly meant for me.

When Mark and I had split – and split was the right word, agonisingly, sickeningly, like a fingernail, all the way from the free edge to the cuticle, or cleaved through the heart with a butcher's knife, leaving us one severed, useless ventricle and one gasping atrium each – we had both moved away. I didn't know where Mark had gone and I had come here. I had cut my hair, met and married Ray and changed my name to Rankin, which I still retained, as I wanted to be called the same thing as Tabby. When asked, I was vague about my past and where I had come from, and because most people thought I had an interesting job they were happy to chat about that instead and seldom enquired too deeply into what I had done before.

Madeleine, who had started at the *Gazette* a month before me, would have liked me to let her in more, but over the years she had got used to me keeping some things to myself. I, in turn, never mentioned her weight, or nagged her to do something about it, or undermined her when she announced yet another new diet she wouldn't stick to. Maybe one day she would.

Lying in bed, I had gone round and round in circles for hours, before finally deciding that, if Mark had had an address for me, or had known where I worked, he would have come to one of those places. Instead he had left the roses somewhere he had guessed I would show up. So he might have an idea where to look for me, but he hadn't actually found me.

This had given me just enough confidence to get into my car and drive to the office, in a semblance of a normal day. But it also prompted me to take one obvious practical measure.

'Anybody in with Fergus?' I asked Madeleine, when I returned.

'No callers,' she said. 'How was court?'

'Same old, same old.'

I went upstairs, where both Suzanne and Richie, our sports editor, were on their phones. I dropped my bag on my chair and continued to Fergus's office.

'Caroline. What can I do for you?'

I closed the door and sat down. 'I'm looking for a favour. And you're going to think it's a bit strange.'

'Oh?'

'I'd like you to stop bylining my stories. Just for a bit. A few weeks, probably. Maybe until after Christmas.'

'Can I ask why?'

Because if Mark picks up a paper and sees my picture, he could track me down here in a blink. 'It's a bit delicate.'

'Your name sells papers, Caroline. Readers like your work. Women in particular.' Fergus sighed and tapped his pen on his desk. 'You're part of the fabric of this newspaper. If you want me to remove your name and picture you're going to have to give me a good reason.'

'It's ... sort of a stalker situation.'

'A stalker! Jesus, Caroline. Have you gone to the police?'

'No. At least, not yet. I mean, I'm exaggerating. It's not a stalker, exactly. He's probably harmless. He hasn't really done anything I could report. And the thing is, I'm sure he doesn't know where I live or where I work, and if I can keep those things to myself, then he'll most likely just give up and go away.'

'On a scale of one to ten, how frightened are you of this person?'

Ten. 'Two? If even that? This is what I'm trying to say – I'm not scared, Fergus, I could just do without the hassle, by nipping it in the bud.'

Fergus paused, set his pen down, picked it up again. 'Let me think about it.'

'OK. Well, let me know. And if you don't mind I'd prefer to keep this conversation between ourselves.'

'Your colleagues are going to notice.'

'Richie won't – he doesn't even read the news section. He's only interested in his sports pages. And Suzanne will be delighted, so she won't want to rock the boat.'

'It's not Eric Haffey who's bothering you?'

'Seriously? Eric knows exactly where to find me. No – it's not him.'

'All right. I'll give it some thought. Caroline, if you're ever worried about anything ... I'm here.'

Don't be kind to me or I'll cry, and I have *never* cried at work. Not even when Ray left and I had to tell everyone, face them, and carry on working alongside him. *Bloody* Mark.

'Moving on, the Christmas Tree Festival at St Gregory's opens on Thursday – will you give them a call and arrange to see round?'

'Sure.'

'We also have a potentially nice lead about twins with cerebral palsy who've had a wish granted to fly out and see Santa in Lapland at the weekend – problem is, as of yet, there's no snow, so just keep an eye on that one and cross your fingers.'

'Anything else?'

'That's it for now. Nothing juicy in court, I suppose?'

'Nothing unusual.'

'Right. Well, while you get on with writing that up, send

Suzanne in. I need a bundle of Christmas-shopping ad features done this week.'

'She won't like that. Eight million stories in the naked city and you want her to write about the butcher's and dry-cleaner's in Abbott Street.'

'Too bad.'

'I'll tell her you want a word.'

Starting to write up court kept me busy until lunchtime, when Madeleine appeared in Editorial and asked Suzanne to mind the desk while she took a break, as the ad-sales staff had all been called to a meeting at head office.

'Could this day get any worse?' said Suzanne, who was, as predicted, not pleased to be spending her day writing Christmas 'advertorial'.

'There's a box of Roses on the counter. Help yourself,' Madeleine called after her. To me she added: 'Mary brought them in for Christmas.' Mary called us every week to place a classified ad thanking St Jude for favours granted.

Richie had popped out to grab a sandwich, so it was just Madeleine and me.

'The kitchen fitters arrived at eight o'clock this morning,' she told me, sitting in Richie's seat and swivelling from side to side. 'I was still in the shower. I had it in my head that they'd bring everything in through the back door, but of course Jimmy let them in the front and the hall carpet's going to be ruined.'

'Oh, Mads, I'm sorry.'

'I must have been out of my mind, thinking this was a good idea so close to Christmas.'

'Well, it's too late now for regrets – focus on how pleased

you'll be when the work's done, roasting your turkey and spuds in the big ovens, having burners aplenty for all your pans.'

'Keep going. I need words of encouragement.'

'It'll add thousands to the value of your house.'

'Good. What else?'

'Because it's all new and shiny it'll be a pleasure to keep clean.'

'Thank you. You always know what to say, Caroline.'

My phone rang.

'Don't answer it. We're entitled to a lunch break,' Madeleine said.

The phone rang a few more times, then stopped.

Richie's phone rang.

'Suzanne knows we're up here – she'll just keep ringing,' I pointed out.

'And we'll just keep ignoring it.'

Richie's phone went quiet, but before we could resume our conversation there was the sound of someone clattering upstairs. It wasn't Richie's usual patter.

'Are you deaf?' Suzanne asked, bursting in.

'No. We're on our lunch break,' Madeleine said levelly.

'Jimmy rang to say the showroom called and there's a dent in your range cooker, so you can have it for seventy pounds off or wait until Friday for another one.'

'Where's the dent? Will you be able to see it when the cooker's in place?'

'How should I know? Ring your husband.'

Suzanne stomped back downstairs and Madeleine raised her eyebrows. 'When we first worked here, we wouldn't have dared speak to a senior member of staff like that. Shall we go for a walk round the block – brighten ourselves up a bit?'

I shook my head. 'Too much on – I'll have to eat my sandwich at my desk and work through.' The truth was, I felt better tucked up in our office, out of the way, instead of roaming about, where anyone could see me.

'Suit yourself.'

After she went, and I was alone in the room, I found myself thinking about the past again, going over the same thoughts that had kept me awake most of the night.

Mark. He had been my first real love affair. When it happened, I couldn't imagine anything or anyone else. I was absorbed, completely. And a little deranged, I think. I dropped my friends to be with him. Stopped caring about school and Guides, about everything.

Mark loved me just as much, I was sure. There was no game with us, no preening or playing hard to get or coquetry. I didn't share tales with my girlfriends in the sixth form, didn't discuss with anyone what we were doing. There was no going shopping on Saturdays for something to wear to impress him. Mark didn't give two hoots about my clothes. He liked me naked.

The first time it was, I think, a mutual seduction, wordless and instinctive and, I now know, more graceful than two teenagers had any right to expect. It was, in a word, exquisite.

It would have seemed unfathomable, back then, that we would ever be apart. How could we be? What on earth could possibly come between us? People who've been together for a long time speak so casually about 'my other half' but we really were each other's other halves and there was nothing casual about it.

I knew what love between a man and a woman looked like, and this was it.

This was it.

When Mark ended things between us, it felt like the end of everything – all happiness, ambition, hope. I couldn't taste food, I couldn't leave the house, I couldn't talk to anyone. My heart was sick.

I didn't look at another man for years, I wanted to tell him. I'd lived alone, eaten alone, slept alone for the longest time.

Eventually, I woke up one day and thought: This has to stop. I'm in my twenties and I have to begin living again. I started to flirt to see where that got me. But I needed to be drunk and giddy to enjoy so much as a kiss. It wasn't like it had been with you, Mark.

Then I met Ray. Sunny, languid, sexy Ray. The two of them couldn't have been more different, yet for the first time since Mark, I felt a genuine attraction.

As I had no parents of my own, it was a definite bonus that Ray came with lovely Doris and Bob, who fed me and warmed me and treated me like a beloved daughter. Even their dog, Shane, welcomed me into the fold. Being with Ray and his circle felt like being somewhere no winter would ever come. Ray was sensual and tender, but he was also safe.

The morning of our wedding, I thought of Mark. Of course I did. No matter that he was the one who'd broken up with me, no matter that years had passed and he'd never, so far as I'd been aware, tried to get in touch, marrying Ray still meant

I was betraying him. I knew it then and I knew it now, and I didn't doubt that Mark would see it that way, too.

But I pushed the thought down, on my wedding day, packed it deep in my chest where I wouldn't have to look at it and drove with Ray to the registry office. Our first dance was to Roberta Flack singing 'The First Time Ever I Saw Your Face' and everyone said we made a lovely couple, though Ray told me later that his friends reckoned they couldn't believe his luck. They were wrong. I was the lucky one. Ray saved me.

Then it was parenthood and Tabby was the apple of our eyes. She looked like Ray – solidly built with sandy hair and those pale eyelashes that I thought were sweet but which would cause her so much grief as a teenager. Someone at school said they made her look like a cow. I could have slapped them. Tabby wanted to get them salon-dyed, but every time she had a skin test the patch reacted badly so she had to make do with loads of hypo-allergenic mascara.

'Why couldn't I have taken after you, Mum?' she'd wail. And once she'd fallen out with me completely and wouldn't say why. Only months later, when we were friends again, did she tell me it was because the boys at school – the same boys whose approval she craved – had put me at the top of a list of mums they'd most like to fuck. I reeled at her spitting that word at me, about me.

'They're not worth it, Tabby,' I told her repeatedly. 'They don't deserve a single moment of your time.'

'You don't understand,' she'd reply. 'You can never understand, because you've always been beautiful.'

If by some fairy-tale magic I could have become an old

crone, in exchange for Tabby looking however she chose, I'd have done it in a heartbeat. As it was, I was powerless to make any material difference to the person I loved more than anyone in the world.

Since leaving my past behind, I had built a whole new life for myself. I'd forged a career, made friends and acquired a family, albeit an unusual one. I had earned myself a place among the respectable. Mark could take all that away in a single stroke, simply by telling the truth. And although that would be a huge price, I could deal with it, if I had to. Just so long as I could keep him and his poisonous veracity away from my girl. Just so long as he didn't get to Tabby.

'Caroline?'

Bang! I'd forgotten where I was, momentarily, and was suddenly surprised to find myself still sitting at my desk, looking at the wall. 'Yes, Madeleine?'

'I said there's a woman downstairs who wants to talk to someone about speed bumps. Are you or are you not available?'

You are no mere bump in the road, Mark. You are a checkpoint manned by a madman with a machine-gun. And I'm frightened.

6

I changed my landline to ex-directory. I couldn't know if I had done so in time, but it seemed sensible to try. They offered to change my number at the same time so I did that, too. All it meant was that, if Mark called Directory Enquiries, they wouldn't release my number. If he got his hands on an existing or old printed local directory, though, my address would be there with my name, even though the phone number was no longer valid. So the question was, did he know I was Rankin, C., these days? Did he know I'd been married? Did he know I was divorced? Did he know where I worked? Not yet, I didn't think. And did he know I had a daughter? That was the million-dollar question, but also the one I was most confident about – Mark had only just shown up, and Tabby hadn't been home for weeks. There was no good reason to think he was aware of her at all.

The day's big excitement at work was a visit from Paddy Madden. Paddy was our much-loved deputy editor, but we didn't see much of him as he had been working from home for the past three years. This was because his daughter had broken her back when she fell from her horse and was now tetraplegic, and Paddy and his wife, Amy, shared her constant care. Their home was specially adapted and professional carers came in and out all the time, but this only slightly eased the burden, I thought.

'Caroline! Look who's here!' Madeleine called, as I came downstairs. 'I was just going to buzz you.'

Paddy stepped forward and kissed my cheek, then raked his fingers through his hair.

'Are you staying a while?' I asked. Occasionally, Paddy would do a few hours in the office. Reasons were unclear, but I suspected sometimes it was just something he needed.

'Sadly, no. I had to come into town and I hadn't paid Madeleine for the Christmas party yet, so I thought I'd pop in.'

'Then you're coming?'

'That's the plan.'

Paddy used to be the life and soul at Christmastime, at any time. He was the one who rounded us all up for Friday drinks every week once the paper was published. He persuaded us all into a day at the races one Easter Monday, a riotous trip to the karting track and the now-famous staff weekend on the Isle of Man. He had seemingly boundless energy and could have squeezed laughter from a stone.

Now it was hard to believe he was the same man. His face was lined, his hands trembled. He and Amy moved around the daughter and the hoist and the chair and each other like hollowed-out casings of their former selves. Everyone sympathised with them – all three of them. Everyone admired their courage – all three of them. None of this did a damn thing to help any one of them.

'Bringing your dancing shoes, I hope,' I said. Paddy and I had always danced well together. Not for us the foot-to-foot shuffle – we really moved. Maxie and Josie had been dancers, of course, and when I was nine or ten and begged her to show me, Josie had taught me to jive. It had felt like learning to fly – and I mean actually fly, on your own wings. I don't mean piloting a plane.

'I fear I may have hung them up,' Paddy said, taking a Roses, without really looking, from the tub Madeleine proffered. 'So all I know so far is that it's next Tuesday, but what's the venue, and what time's the meal?'

'Seven forty-five p.m. at the Arlington,' Madeleine said. 'Actually, since you're here, you can tell me what you want to eat. Where did I put my pen? Caroline, make sure I find out what everybody upstairs wants before they go home – the hotel needs our choices by Thursday.' Madeleine rummaged through a pile of paper on her desk, found something, and read from it. 'Paddy, you can have turkey and ham, roast beef, salmon or vegan wellington. The vegan wellington is, quote, "packed with roasted red peppers, beetroot and kale ..."'

'Think I'll have the roast beef.'

'Caroline?'

'The salmon, please, Madeleine.'

As Madeleine wrote down what the ad-sales team wanted to eat, Paddy turned to me. 'So how are things?'

'Things are fine.'

'Doing much freelancing?'

'Not a lot. This place keeps me busy. Plus the occasional piece in the *Tribune*.'

'But you could do so much more, Caroline. You've always been too good to be stuck in a local weekly. Don't you ever want to go bigger?'

I could understand Paddy asking, from his perspective. He was unable to get out and about, scouting for stories, making contacts, roaming at large. My freedom must seem wasted on me. And yet my answer was no. In a nutshell, no. My life was small, and I liked it that way. I was small, my family of one daughter was a small family. I drove a small car, worked in a small office for a small publication in a small town, had small overheads and a small number of friends. This suited me. I didn't want something big to happen. In fact, something big was the opposite of what I wanted.

'I've never been the ambitious type.'

'Hmm. Fergus tells me the new girl is all ambition, as yet to be justified. How's she coming on?'

'Suzanne's all right. She just needs experience.'

'I sub her copy every week – she needs more than that.'

'Then help her – give her feedback. Call her and tell her why you're making changes to her work so she'll know for next time.'

Madeleine returned and asked if Paddy was staying for a coffee.

'Can't, I'm afraid.' He patted a large paper pharmacy bag. 'I was picking up Katrina's prescription.'

When the front door closed behind him, Madeleine said: 'It's absolutely tragic what happened to that family. Not just to Katrina – to all of them.'

'I see you drive a Volvo, yourself,' Harold Kirkpatrick (sixty-four) of Glebe Terrace said. He was the proud owner of a brand new Ford Fiesta, thanks to holding the winning ticket in the cardiac-care Christmas draw.

Ray and I had bought our first Volvo when Tabby was a baby and our primary concern was her safety. It was one of those big boxy things, like a hearse, only it was blue, and I believed it would withstand any misadventure. We had never had an accident in it, or in any of the subsequent models, so maybe it had been an unnecessary precaution, but worth it to have had peace of mind for all that time.

Now I drove a much smaller Volvo, almost out of habit, although it was still reckoned to be extraordinarily safe, which gave me confidence when I was transporting Noah and Lucas. Ray had a racing green two-seater for him and Jodie, and Jodie had the big 4x4 as the family car.

'She has a lot more miles on the clock than your lovely prize,' I said, taking out my notebook. 'So tell me how it happened. Where and when did you buy your ticket? And do you buy one every year, or was this the first time?'

Harold was delighted to fill me in on his story. He had always been a supporter of the famous Christmas draw, but this year his wife had had stents fitted, so it brought it closer to home. Consequently, they had spent twenty pounds on tickets from the stall in the hospital foyer. They had seen it as an act of charity, never expecting to hear any more about it. And then the phone call had come last week, telling them they'd won first prize.

'I thought it was a wind-up,' Harold said, with a chuckle, 'somebody having a laugh, or else a scammer who was going to ask me for my bank account number. But they didn't want anything except my address, plus a time to come round so they could make the presentation.'

'So when did you start to believe it?'

'Not until they pulled up outside the house and his worship the mayor, in full regalia, handed me the keys! I began to say to myself: "Harold, I think you've maybe just won a car!"'

'What's your wife's name, Harold?'

'Norma.'

'And was Norma at home, too, when the car arrived?'

'She was here, yes. And I hadn't mentioned the phone call to her, because, like I say, I thought it was a wind-up.'

'So she was surprised.'

'She was gobsmacked.'

'Is she here now? Can I speak to her?'

'She won't come out in case you take her photograph.'

'Ah, well, we would really love to get a picture of the two of you with the car, but our photographer won't be here until after lunch. I'm keen to hear what she has to say, though.'

'Come inside and have a cup of tea. She might listen to you.'

I got my story and I persuaded Norma to be in Jamie's photo – well, I had been doing the job for a long time.

In the afternoon, I visited a minister who was sitting outside on his town-centre church steps for a week, collecting for the homeless. Despite his big, hooded cloak and leather gloves, it was colder than he'd expected, he admitted.

Back at the office, Madeleine came into Editorial and rested her rump on my desk. 'Fergus wants to buy everyone coffee and treats from Santino's, so I'm taking orders. Suzanne?'

'Gingerbread latte.'

'Anything to eat?'

'Caramel square, if they have one. Failing that, a chocolate brownie.'

'Caroline? Do you want to check your blood sugar first?'

I took out my kit and pricked my finger: 6.2. 'A coffee will be plenty for me.'

'Flat white?'

'You know me so well.'

When Madeleine rang to say our refreshments had arrived, Suzanne and I went downstairs to join the ad staff.

'What's the occasion, boss?' Suzanne asked.

'Nothing in particular. You've all been working hard, that's all. And it's nearly Christmas.'

'Thanks, Fergus,' I said, taking the lid off my cup to let the contents cool.

'You're welcome.'

'Anyone doing anything good at the weekend?' Suzanne asked, with her mouth full.

'I'm going to the Railway Players' production of *Aladdin*, on Friday, with some of the girls,' Madeleine said.

'Does that include you?' Suzanne asked, turning to me.

'You *should* come! It'll be a laugh, and I'm sure we could get you a ticket,' Madeleine said, and sounded like she meant it.

But I had the High Hedges. 'It's OK. They've offered me freebies and I was thinking of taking Noah and Lucas on Saturday.'

'Then meet up with us for a drink afterwards. You hang out on your own too much. And spending time with Ray and Jodie's kids doesn't count.'

'All the same, I think I'll pass.'

'I'm sure Caroline has no problem finding company, if she wants it,' Fergus said gently. 'How about you, Suzanne? Going anywhere?'

'Pub.' She licked her fingers and brushed the crumbs off her top.

My mobile rang at seven and I hoped it would be Tabby. It was Jodie.

'Hello, missus. Just calling for a chat or is something up?'

'Caroline. Thanks for picking up – I know you're barely home from work, but I just didn't want to leave this any longer.'

'Leave what? What's wrong, Jodie?'

'It's Noah. I think he might be diabetic.'

'Diabetic?'

'Well, all this running to the loo – there has to be a reason for it. I googled it, and it said it was a common symptom of diabetes, so obviously I thought of you.'

'OK. But you were going to leave in a urine sample at the doctor's – did you do that?'

'Yes, but that was when I thought he just had an infection – so they weren't looking for diabetes then, were they?'

It wasn't like Jodie to sound so flustered.

'I think it's likely, if a child presented with excessive peeing, they'd check for sugar in the sample.'

'Would they?'

'When you say Noah is running to the loo all the time – when he gets there, is he weeing a little or a lot?'

'Sometimes a normal amount, other times just a few drops.'

'And is he getting up in the night to pee, or wetting his pyjamas?'

'No.'

'Is he constantly asking for drinks, or getting up and asking you for a drink after he's gone to bed?'

'No.'

'Is he off his food?'

'No.'

'Has he lost weight? I don't think he has, Jodie, but you're the best judge. Are his ribs sticking out more than they used to?'

'I don't think so.'

'Then he doesn't really have the symptoms of diabetes. If his blood was full of sugar, his little body would be trying to flush it out like crazy – he'd be drinking and peeing *a lot* – so much you couldn't miss it. When he got to the toilet, it would be a flood, not just a trickle. And he'd be getting thinner.'

'So you don't think it's diabetes.'

'Of course you must check it out with the doctor, but it doesn't sound like it.'

'All right. It must just be an infection, then.'

'Since you're on, would Noah and Lucas like to come to a Christmas tree festival with me after school on Thursday? I'm covering it for the paper and I thought they might enjoy it. About four o'clock. It's in St Gregory's.'

'Are you sure they wouldn't get in your way?'

'Not at all – it would be nice to hear their points of view.'

'I'll let you into a little secret – I was invited to do a tree, to represent the shop. But Christmas is such a busy time for us, I said no. I might pop across, though, and take a look myself, maybe enter a tree next year.'

I put my feet up with a glass of wine and the Christmas cards I'd scooped up from the hall mat when I first came home. One hand-delivered from Gareth and Elaine, featuring a jolly Santa with rosy cheeks and a sack of toys. It was obvious to anyone that they'd make brilliant parents – and hard, sometimes, to believe that God had any say in who got to conceive and who didn't. There was a card from Doris and Bob of two little boys building a snowman. And one from the clean-water charity I supported.

I'd have to get around to writing my own cards soon. I'd picked up some packets at the coffee morning in aid of Médecins Sans Frontières. Now that I looked at them, I realised I didn't really like the design, but they were in a good cause, and Tabby would be in favour.

I hoped her new romance was going somewhere. While I

believed Tabby was very lovable, I feared that after so many years of trying her hardest and getting nowhere, she now carried something of an aura of desperation – precisely the kind of thing to put people off. Parents worried about their children. It was natural. That was why I understood Jodie's concerns about Noah and didn't mind her calling. I remembered the day my diabetes was diagnosed. I was five years old, and before we went to the hospital Mum put me in my best clothes, which were hanging off me because I had lost so much weight, and Dad took a photograph of me in front of the roses in the garden. I still had the photo. I was wearing a little kilt, with a big decorative pin that fascinated me, but which I was afraid to open in case I couldn't close it again and Mum shouted at me. As he took the picture I saw that Maxie, my big, strong, indestructible dad, was tearful, and somewhere along the line I learned that he and Mum thought I had cancer, thought that when I went into hospital I'd never be home in our garden again.

I don't remember how or precisely when I came to know this, either, but somehow I discovered that Mum and Dad cried because they thought me being ill was a punishment for loving each other more than they loved us kids. It was a strange thing to find out, as children, but it didn't upset us. We were glad that Mum and Dad loved each other more than anyone else – even us. It made us feel safe.

The nurses in hospital were kind, but I had to have so many blood samples taken I thought I'd rather just die. Mum brought me my *Twinkle* comic and I was allowed to have my Sindy doll, who lay beside me in the bed. I don't honestly know how long I remained there – days? Weeks? The nurses began injecting me, which wasn't nearly as bad as the phlebotomy. Then they showed Mum how to do it, and I remember the concentration on her face that first time. One day, Mum and Dad were sitting on my bed and smiling and telling me I could come home – I was fixed. But Mum would have to inject me every day, and I wouldn't be allowed to eat sugary things any more. No sweets or chocolate, no cakes or biscuits. But I could have apples – they would buy them especially for me and give me my very own fruit bowl and no one would be allowed to take one of my apples, unless I said so.

Nobody used the term Type 1, which was so well known now. It was just diabetes, back then, which meant daily doses of insulin, a strict, sugar-free diet and regular checks on my urine. And I'd have it for the rest of my life.

I returned to primary school and none of the little kids batted an eyelid. Later, in high school, some of the girls said – behind my back – that no one would ever marry me, because I wouldn't be able to have children. Some of the boys, with their despicable cracking voices, loved to assure me that there was no sugar in a blow-job. Juveniles. No wonder I'd preferred Mark – at least he had class.

As much as I could, I had been managing thoughts of Mark with a tried and tested combination of small, practical acts (the byline, the landline), keeping busy and a well-honed practice of denial. This wasn't my first time dealing with the unbearable, don't forget.

But here, on my sofa, the busyness of the day gone, all alone in my findable, vulnerable little lair, I began to brood.

Where did I suppose Mark was now? The roses at the graveyard suggested he was back where it had all started, but when he didn't find me there, surely he would keep looking. He'd already turned up at the department store – by chance, or had he been acting on information? And, up until now, I'd been working on the assumption that I had seen him there, but he hadn't spotted me. Was this, in fact, wishful thinking? Had he tracked me down already? Was he *watching* me?

I poured another glass of wine and tried to think about something else. But I couldn't. A lump formed like a beach pebble in my throat as I began to see myself opening the bedroom curtains in the mornings from the point of view of someone down in the street. I observed myself leave home by the front door, jump into my car, drive to work. Why had I always done everything so predictably in the same way, day in, day out? I should have changed my routine, shaken things up, instead of acting like the perfect target – everyone should: you never knew who was out there.

What if, at the first inkling that I was in trouble, I had made an excuse to stay with Madeleine? But Madeleine had the *bloody* builders in. The band of my bra felt uncomfortably tight all of a sudden. It was constricting my breathing. I tugged at it. Would Suzanne have put me up if I'd asked her? Should I have gone to a hotel? Gone on holiday where he couldn't find me? But that might just vex him, and then what would he do? A growing bombardment of questions, and a hot, unpleasant sensation that the gears inside my head were all turning at once.

I was feeling disconcertingly aware of my heartbeat, and

finding it increasingly difficult to quell a rising tide of panic, when a knock sounded on my front door. Tentative, yet deliberate. The timing was virtually telepathic. No, no, no, no, no. I wasn't ready. I couldn't face him. I hadn't prepared the words to make him feel sorry for me, to convince him to go away and leave me and the past alone. I didn't know why he'd come for me now and I didn't want to find out. I was afraid to let him in and afraid not to.

The knock sounded again, a little more insistent. I was frozen, unable to process any decision. I should have made a plan for this situation as soon as I saw the roses, instead of just hoping it would all somehow go away. Why hadn't I? Stupid, stupid, stupid.

I'd take physical pain over fear anytime. I'd broken my leg, falling off a wall, when I was ten. I hadn't cried because I wasn't frightened – I'd believed the ambulance would come, and it had done. Childbirth had been monumentally painful, but I'd fed off the midwives' smiling confidence and trusted that I'd get through it. All had been well. This was different. This was a living ghost, clammy and vengeful, pressing up against my home, exhaling its spectral breath against my walls and windows. I could run out the back door, but what would be the point? He'd found me.

'Caroline? It's Elaine. You've left your outside light on.'

She had lifted the letterbox and was speaking into the hall.

Oh, God. Not Mark. Not this time.

'Caroline? I just didn't want you to leave it on and go up to bed.'

'Elaine,' I said, opening the front door with a trembling hand. 'Thanks so much. I'll flick it off.'

That night, I dreamt about Mark. We were lying in bed together, slick and entwined under the sheet. I went to kiss him, but when he opened his mouth, instead of a tongue he had a darting black serpent.

This whole thing was a nightmare. I wished there was someone I could talk to, but how could I explain to anyone? I didn't know what to do. I didn't know how to stop Mark finding me, hurting me, trashing everything I had worked for years to build. Unless I could somehow evade him, and he grew tired, gave up and went away, I had a problem.

7

I had popped out of the office to pick up a packet of Imodium capsules at the pharmacy two doors down.

'I've just overheard an interesting conversation,' I told Suzanne, when I got back. 'It seems a group of girls at the high school is going on strike until they're allowed to wear trousers in cold weather.'

'Why are you telling me?'

'Sounds like a story.'

'Sounds like a good story,' Richie said, from behind his computer.

'I thought you might like to follow it up.'

'Why don't you want to do it?'

'I thought I could swap you – I'll write a couple of your Christmas-ad features and you can look into the school story.'

'Why would you do that?'

'Good grief, Suzanne, there's no need to be so suspicious. I like writing the Christmas stuff – it's easy.' And it kept me out of sight.

'OK. Where do I start?'

'Try the pharmacy – the assistant with short hair and glasses is one of the school mums, I think.'

Suzanne grabbed her coat and her notebook. As she dashed for the door, Richie looked up. 'Eh, a "Thank you, Caroline," would be in order.'

'Thanks.' She was already on her way downstairs.

I hammered out a piece on the joys of Christmas shopping in Abbott Street, pointing out that the window displays captured the spirit of the season – a stretch – and its cash registers rang merrily – whatever that might sound like. To shop in Abbott Street was to be assured of personal service, I claimed, within hearing of the resounding peal of St Gregory's church bells. Well, it was Christmas.

'I've tracked down the ringleader's mum, I reckon.' Suzanne burst back in, her eyes bright. 'She works in the hairdresser's above the vaping shop. She should be back from her lunch after two.'

'Good for you,' I said.

'Do you think Jamie would do a photo?' Jamie was in the habit of rejecting Suzanne's requests. Sometimes with justification, if they were to accompany filler pieces, or if any illustrations would be boring or repetitive, but sometimes just because she was a junior member of the team and he couldn't be bothered.

'If you get the story, it'll be a page-lead, maybe even a front, so he'll have to.'

'You think this could go on the front?'

'Providing nothing massive happens.'

I left the office at three, as I was going to the Chamber of Trade dinner later and would be expected to cover the speeches and presentations, even though I was also there as Eric Haffey's guest.

The walk between work and car wasn't far, but the exposure made me nervous. If Mark happened to be around, he could easily spot me. The fact that I didn't know how he had traced me to this town – assuming he had, assuming his presence in the department store wasn't largely coincidence – now ate at me. I might be able to use even a little insight into that to my advantage. If he hadn't much to go on, as I desperately hoped, then he might just grow frustrated and tired, clear off and leave me alone. This was the narrative I had chosen as I'd cleaned my teeth that morning, things never seeming quite so terrifying in daylight with the chirpy morning radio playing. How would I know, though, when it was safe to stop looking over my shoulder? I oscillated between moments of relative optimism and gnawing unease.

I tugged at the rear-view mirror and examined myself. The last time Mark had seen me I'd had my long black hair and a young girl's face. While I was still reasonably happy with how I looked, I was certainly different. I had lines at the sides of my eyes and a bit of puffiness underneath them. There was softening around my chin and a hint that jowls would come, one day. Was there any guarantee that, even if I walked past him in the street, Mark would recognise me?

I had recognised him.

I locked the car doors and drove home, satisfying myself all the way that I wasn't being followed.

I had a bubble bath and washed my hair, ate some oatcakes and cheese and watched the second half of an uninspiring quiz show.

Without any enthusiasm, I did my make-up, dried my hair and put on the formal dress I had bought for a press-awards dinner at which I had won a prize the previous summer. Tonight, I would be a good companion to Eric, but it would be the last time. It wasn't nice, dumping someone at Christmas, yet it would be worse to give him false expectations. I didn't want him buying me an expensive Christmas present, which I would either have to refuse or accept along with feelings of guilt. I wished I had never gone out with him in the first place, and I never would have if I had realised he had romantic intentions – it had been a civic function and I had thought he merely wanted a companion for the evening: attending such things could be awkward on your own, when everyone else was in couples. It was simply a middle-aged arrangement of convenience, and I knew other people paired up in a similar way – the last mayor, a bachelor, brought Lesley Lunt to these things and nobody thought they were romantically involved.

Eric had never tried to kiss me, other than a peck on the

cheek, much less put a hand up my skirt, yet it was clear that he wanted us to be closer. So I had to tell him, and I had to tell him tonight.

Two more Christmas cards had arrived. A partridge in a pear tree from Heather across the way, and another depicting a robed choir in the snow around a Christmas tree, from Alison, whose job Suzanne had filled when she moved to be a sub on a women's magazine.

'You look beautiful, Caroline.' Eric had got out of the taxi and come up the path to my front door, presenting me with a magnificent bouquet of flowers.

'You shouldn't have.' Oh, how I meant that. More weight heaped on my sagging conscience.

In the taxi, Eric asked whether the timing of the meal was all right for me, or if it would create problems with my blood sugar. I assured him I was used to juggling mealtime requirements, when I had to.

The Tyrrell Talbot hotel was alight with Christmas. A huge, symmetrical tree stood in the foyer and garlands adorned with hundreds of fairy lights were draped across the ceiling beams. Two leather sofas stood at either side of a real log fire and I imagined sitting there for the evening, nursing a brandy, with someone other than Eric.

'Can I take your coat?' Eric asked, and checked it in, with his, at the desk.

The function room had perhaps twenty round tables set for ten, and a decent dancefloor in front of a stage. For now, people were gathered round the bar area, men in black tie, women in full-length gowns.

'What can I get you to drink?'

'Oh, thanks, Eric. I'll have a white wine.'

While he queued for the bar, I scanned the crowd for anyone I knew.

'June! It's nice to see you.' It was June Black, of WI and Blooming Marvellous fame, who'd greeted me at the coffee morning on Friday.

'Caroline, how are you?' In an undertone, she added: 'I hate these things – at my age I feel like mutton dressed as lamb. Princess Bingo Wings. I hide what I can under a pashmina – it's the only way. Trust you to look gorgeous, though.'

'You look great, June. Don't be so hard on yourself. I don't suppose we're by any chance sitting at the same table?'

'I haven't dared to look, yet. Last year they put me beside Councillor Lunt and I still haven't recovered. Have you come on your own for work? I'm sure they'd let you sit with us ...'

'No, no. I have my notebook, but really I'm with Eric Haffey – he's just gone to the bar.'

'You and Eric? I didn't realise.'

'We're not an item, but I fear I've failed to make that perfectly clear.'

'Oh dear. It's always difficult when someone likes you and you don't really like them back. With me, it was Clive Scott. He adored me, but all I could see were his big black bushy eyebrows, which almost met in the middle – a bit too much on a nine-year-old. I wonder whatever happened to him.'

Eric appeared at my elbow with our drinks.

'I'll see you later,' June said, as I took a gulp.

The meal was first-class. To start we had Brie and walnut quesadillas with cranberry salsa. It wasn't quite the first time Eric and I had eaten together, but I noticed that, as I wolfed mine, he cut his up meticulously, as though it was all-important that he got the perfect ratio of this to that so nothing was left over at the end.

Next, we had salmon with a tarragon sauce, followed by French onion soup, and then the main course of pork with apricots.

When I declined dessert, Eric did the same.

'Please don't skip it on my account.'

'I'm not. I'm—'

'Some people think it must be awful, being diabetic, having to miss out on sweet things when everyone else is getting stuck in, but I'm well used to it, and I pick my moments to have a treat just like everybody else. What I really don't need is a heap of empty calories at the end of what's already been a fabulous meal.'

I had had two glasses of wine before we sat down and, I thought, two glasses of the red that had been poured at the table. I should probably have slowed down, although there was no doubt the alcohol was making me feel more comfortable.

Keep a clear head until you've dealt with Eric, I told myself. I also had to make a few basic notes about the post-meal presentations, though I could almost certainly have the full text of any speeches emailed to me in the morning.

A comfort break was called and I made my way to the Ladies.

Sitting in the cubicle, half listening to the idle chatter mixed with the blast of the hand-drier and the running of taps, I heard someone ask who the femme fatale was, in the silver sheath dress, sitting with Eric. Crap. That was me they were talking about, although 'femme fatale' was fanciful. Now I would have to stay shut in where I was until they'd gone or I'd embarrass all of us.

'That's the girl from the *Gazette*,' a voice replied. 'She's not as young as you'd think – she's been there for donkey's'. I always thought she'd end up reading the news on TV – she had the looks for it.'

I shivered. Why did everyone want to be famous? It struck me as the worst thing in the world – people recognising you wherever you went, thinking they knew you based on your appearance on that lit-up screen in the corner of their living room, deciding what sort of person you were because of your hair or your complexion, the clothes you wore or the tone of your voice. It wasn't the first time it had been suggested to me that I might once have had a future in broadcasting, had I wanted it, including from some of those in whose gift it might have been to offer it to me. But, obviously, it had always been out of the question.

The voices drifted away, to be replaced by new ones, and I decided it was safe for me to emerge. I would return to the function room for the speeches, but I didn't think it was appropriate to stay once the dancing started. I loved to dance, but it would give Eric the wrong signal. Instead, I would feign a headache, then sever our connection in the taxi on the way home. It had to be done.

When I returned to our table, however, I found a huddle apparently gathered around someone.

'What's up?' I asked a woman in a shocking pink frock.

'It's Eric. He's been assaulted.'

I pushed my way through the bodies and found Eric, his bow-tie askew, sitting at the table. Someone had dipped a napkin into a glass of water and was washing blood off his lips. 'What happened?'

Eric looked up at me.

'Eric, what happened?'

'I don't understand it,' he said. 'I just stepped outside for a breath of air. I went round the corner to avoid the smokers. I'd only been out there for a moment, and a man punched me.'

'Who was it?' someone asked. 'Did you recognise him?'

'I'd never seen him before in my life.'

'Did he say anything?' Another voice. 'Did he know your name?'

'He didn't say a word.'

'Was he wearing a dinner suit? Did you think he was at this event?' Questions were coming from all directions.

Eric shook his head. 'I don't think so. He was in a long, dark overcoat.'

'Have you checked for your wallet, Eric?' someone suggested.

'If he was after money, he could be on drugs.'

'He didn't take anything.'

'Then it must have been a case of mistaken identity. It's the only thing that makes sense.'

The general consensus was that this was most probably the case. The general consensus was also that Eric should speak to the manager at once and find out if there was CCTV in operation, and if the culprit could be thus identified.

'He should phone the police,' the shocking pink woman said.

A bead of sweat ran down my face.

'What do you think, Caroline? Should I report it to the police?' Eric was looking at me strangely.

Someone at the top table tapped a glass, signalling the start of the speeches.

'Sit down. I don't want a fuss,' Eric said. 'I think I was just in the wrong place at the wrong time.'

The huddle dispersed, with concerned murmurs and promises to see Eric again later. I took out my notebook and tried very hard to turn my attention to the night's official events.

'Caroline?'

I was placing my notebook back in my handbag. I hardly knew what I had written in it – I'd been on automatic pilot with the proceedings while my brain tried to process what had happened outside. 'Yes, Eric. How are you feeling now?'

'If you don't mind, I think I'd rather skip the dance. I'd prefer to go home.'

'Sure. I'm not much in the mood for dancing, either. Do you want to call a cab, or shall I?'

'I'll call. I'll call one for each of us.'

'One each? Why not share?'

The band suddenly started to play an old T. Rex song, guests surged onto the floor and I had to lean in close to Eric to hear what he was saying.

'The man who hit me – it wasn't a random attack and he didn't confuse me with someone else. He spoke to me. He said: "Tell your girlfriend I'm watching her. Tell Caroline this is from Mark."'

I gasped. It was true. Mark had been here tonight and seen us – seen me. Was he still around? Was he going to confront me? What else did he know about me, or was it just blind luck him turning up? It occurred to me that, if he was in town, he could be booked into the Tyrrell Talbot as a resident – it was the biggest hotel – and might just have chanced to observe us.

'I don't know what this is about, Caroline. And, to be perfectly honest, I don't want to. But for the modicum of interest you've shown me, it's not worth my while being a punch-bag. I would have given you everything, if you'd only let me, but you don't care for me at all – do you? You shouldn't have strung me along, when you were involved with another man.'

'I'm not involved with anyone else!'

'No?'

'No!'

'Then who's Mark?'

'I don't know.'

'I don't believe you. My mother said you'd be trouble. She didn't like it that you were a divorcee and she thought it was a funny job, writing people's business in the paper. She also told me a girl with your looks would never be faithful to someone like me.'

'Your mother has never even met me!'

'I talk to her. I have to talk to somebody.'

The band stopped playing and the dancers applauded.

'I'm leaving, now.'

'Please, Eric. Let's not end things on a sour note.'

'Why not?'

He set my coat-check ticket on the table and I watched as he made his way across the dancefloor to the exit, a couple of people stopping him to speak. I was alone.

I couldn't stay there, yet I was afraid to follow Eric out into the foyer. What if Mark was waiting? I went to the bar and bought myself another glass of wine.

'No Eric?'

It was June Black, again.

'He's gone home. Not feeling great.'

'We heard what happened. Who would hit poor Eric? Well, we're heading home, now. Are you staying on, or can we give you a lift?'

I considered my options.

'June, could I ask you for a favour? I think there's someone staying in this hotel I'd rather not bump into. Would you mind taking a look around the foyer and seeing if anyone's hanging about?'

'Male or female?'

'Male. Tall. Dark.'

'Is it the chap who punched Eric?'

'Yes.'

'Then let's not take any chances. I'll go to the desk and ask someone to let us out quietly through the fire escape – that way, we won't have to go through the foyer or the front doors at all. Joe's parked at the back, anyway. Is that the ticket for your coat? I'll pick it up along with mine.'

'Thank you. I'm so sorry to ask.'

'I'm glad you did. Men can be such a nuisance – at least, the kind who resort to fisticuffs. But what about when you get home? Will you be safe?'

'I don't think he knows where I live. I think he'd have paid me a visit there, if he did.'

We executed June's plan, and although I was shaking as we crossed the car park and, as we waited for Joe to open the car doors, nothing untoward occurred.

When we got onto the main roads, I overheard June say quietly to her husband: 'Just keep an eye on your rear-view mirror and make sure no one's following us.'

June insisted on accompanying me to the front door and waited while I turned my key in the lock. 'If this man is going to be a persistent problem, you must speak to the police,' she said.

'I know.'

I dumped Eric's flowers into a sink full of cold water, hung up my dress and fell onto my bed. But how could I sleep? Mark was getting closer.

8

Thursday had come round again – a whole week since I'd first glimpsed Mark in the department store.

After a mostly sleepless night, I got up, showered and made my sandwich for work. What else could I do? If I took a day off there'd still be the next day and the day after that. In the absence of a plan – and I didn't remotely have one – I had to keep on keeping on. I'd had to do it before, after all, putting one foot in front of the other, because what was the alternative?

As the *Gazette* was a Friday paper, Thursday was deadline day. In fact, copies would be in the shops that night. Fergus and Richie disappeared to head office to oversee the make-up process and we'd send them through any last-minute stories by email.

'You got your front,' I said to Suzanne. 'Are you pleased?'

'Texting.'

Well, excuse me for interrupting.

I did up a few bits and pieces and emailed them to Fergus, then drew a line under that week's issue. Anything else, unless it was seismic, could wait.

I buzzed Madeleine.

'Yes, Caroline?'

'Come upstairs, Mads. I've got no one to talk to.'

'You don't want to talk to me. I have only one topic – the kitchen fitters.'

'I love talking about kitchen fitters.'

Madeleine was suffering. Her home was a mess. She couldn't cook. She couldn't use her washing machine. She had to wash the dishes in the cloakroom basin. The kitchen fitters had chipped the hall paintwork and trampled the carpet. They had also eaten all the biscuits. 'And I've just found out we haven't got enough wall tiles and the line has been discontinued. What am I doing, Caroline? I had a perfectly nice kitchen. There was sod-all wrong with it. I must have a screw loose.'

'How's Jimmy coping?'

'You know Jimmy – nothing gets to him. He's up at a quarter to seven on the dot so he can have his shower and be downstairs making tea and toast for the fitters when they arrive.'

'What will you do about the tiles?'

'The shop won't take them back.'

'Put them on Gumtree?'

'I suppose. But they were perfect, Caroline – I'll never get anything else as nice.'

'Eric dumped me.'

'*What?*'

'He dumped me. At the Chamber of Trade dinner.'

'Eric dumped *you*?'

'Yes.'

'Why on earth?'

'He decided I wasn't worth the bother. Oh, and his mum wasn't keen on me, either.'

'His *mum*?'

Suzanne lifted her head from her mobile. 'What did I say? You're too picky, Caroline. Now what are you going to do?'

'I'm not going to do anything.'

'If you tried a bit harder, you might get him back.'

'I don't want him back.'

'He's no loss,' Madeleine said. 'He's only a drip. You'll meet someone better.'

'I don't want to meet someone. I'm quite happy as I am, thank you.'

'We could go out after work, for a drink. I'm afraid to go home and you never know who you might bump into.'

'Can't. I'm taking Noah and Lucas to the Christmas tree festival in St Gregory's, and later it's the carol concert with Doris and Bob.'

'I thought you were bringing the boys to the pantomime on Saturday.'

'I am.'

'Jodie and Ray have a flipping nerve, packing their kids off with you all the time.'

'They keep me company.'

'You need *adult* company, Caroline.'

'Let's change the subject. No more kitchen talk and no more criticising Caroline's life choices.'

'OK.'

'OK.'

Jodie brought Noah and Lucas to my place just before four o'clock. Noah immediately ran upstairs to use the toilet and Lucas switched on the television.

'We'll have to go in five minutes, boys,' I warned them. To Jodie I said: 'Any progress with Noah's situation?'

'The urine sample came back. He's not diabetic.'

'An infection, then?'

'No. No infection either.'

'Oh. So what does the doctor say about it?'

Jodie scowled. 'He says it's anxiety.'

'Anxiety?'

'I've asked for a second opinion. How can it be anxiety, Caroline? He's nine years old – what's he got to be anxious about? Thumb out, Lucas! Listen, do you mind if I run? I've had a big delivery at the shop and I want to get at it before Leanne does – I know exactly how I want it all displayed. Should I pick up the boys later, or ...?'

'You go. I'll drop them home – I'm guessing we'll be a couple of hours, at least.'

'Thanks, Caroline. Love you, Lucas. Be a good boy.' She blew him a kiss. 'Love you, Noah!' she called upstairs. 'Have fun!'

'Right,' I said, as Jodie's car drove away. 'You two ready to roll?'

I had come out in the practical men's parka I had bought a couple of years ago – it was big on me, but very warm, and with my fur-edged hood up and a little boy by each hand, I thought it also made a pretty effective disguise.

At the church, I gave Lucas our money to pay for the programme. He placed it in the basket and the sexton shook his hand. 'Refreshments are in the Carrack Hall.'

St Gregory's was Victorian, with traditional wooden pews, a pulpit and an altar. It smelt of polish and antiquity and, today, of fresh Christmas pine. With the light fading outside the stained-glass windows, we had come at the right time – the fairy lights glowed magically. An organist was gently playing carols.

Lucas marched up to the first tree. 'Are you allowed to touch it?'

'Better not – we don't want it toppling over. Will I tell you a bit about them from the programme, or do you just want to look?'

'Tell us about them,' Noah said.

'All right. This one is from Campbell's, the butcher's,' I read. 'Look – do you see how they've decorated it with lots of little red and white striped butchers' aprons?'

'I see them!' Lucas cried. 'Noah won't go into the butcher's shop. He has to stay in the car. He's afraid of the blood.'

'I am not,' Noah protested. 'I don't like the smell. It makes me feel sick.'

The next tree was provided by a dental surgery and was strung with disposable dental mirrors, which reflected the fairy lights nicely.

A knitting circle had dressed their tree in knitted Christmas-pudding baubles, and a craft group had decorated theirs with stuffed felt mice wearing choristers' robes and surplices.

'Can you buy those mice?' Noah asked.

'I don't think so,' I said. But I made a mental note to speak to the crafters and ask if there was any chance they could make me two for the boys.

We checked out half of the trees, then decided to have our refreshments.

Lucas piled his plate with sandwiches and tucked in, casually discarding his crusts.

Noah took a tiny, tentative bite of his ham sandwich, then set it down.

'You don't like it?' I asked.

'I thought it was butter, but it's mustard.'

'Give it here. I'll have yours and you try something else.'

Noah shuffled off to the serving table and hovered.

'So, Lucas – how's school?' I asked.

'Mrs Walsh is having a baby.'

'Oh?'

'So we're getting a new teacher.' He bit into another sandwich.

'That's exciting.'

'I'm getting Scalextric for Christmas. Do you know what Scalextric is?'

'I do. My brother had a set when we were kids. I used to play it with him, but he always won.'

'Did your brother have the Street Cruisers Race Set?'

'I don't think so. I don't think it was around then.'

'I'm getting the Street Cruisers Race Set.'

A thought occurred to me. 'Lucas, that's not what you asked Santa Claus for, when we saw him on Saturday.'

'No. I changed my mind. Can I go up and get a bun now?'

As he sped off, I spared a thought for Jodie and Ray – just when you imagined you'd got Christmas sorted, and when the toy-shop shelves were stripped bare, suddenly a new and entirely different letter to Santa appeared. Tabby had done this to us, too. One year, she had gone on and on about getting a Sugarplum Princess Barbie and, innocents that we were, we didn't start looking until December and had to chase round half the country to find a shop that wasn't sold out. Then she had announced she wanted a Sing-out Sally doll, instead. This proved even harder to source and we dreaded what would happen when Tabby woke up on Christmas morning to nothing but disappointment. She had made an entirely unreasonable late shift in her request, but still ... Then, miraculously, our local toy-shop proprietor had rung me to say he had managed to get hold of half a dozen Sing-out Sallys from Finland, and did we still want one? We were ecstatic. There was one scary moment when Tabby tore off the paper in delight and felt around for the little button to make the doll sing. What if it sang in Finnish? I suddenly thought. But it didn't.

Noah came back, smiling. 'I got a chicken one. And a meringue.'

'Good for you.'

Lucas trundled up, holding his plate in one hand, with the other steadying a collection of three cakes.

'Maybe just slow down, Lucas,' I said. 'We're in no rush and you don't want to make yourself sick.'

In the end, Lucas decided that he'd meant one of his cakes for me – he chose which one. The boys used the toilet and we resumed our tour of the trees.

'Which was your favourite?' I asked, as I drove them home.

'The teddy-bear tree,' Lucas said.

Noah said he'd liked them all.

'Well, it might not have been the fanciest one, but the food-bank tree was the one that really made me think,' I said. 'Do you know which one I'm talking about? The one with no decorations at all, and only a tin of baked beans sitting in front of it – just to remind us that some people have very little with which to celebrate Christmas, so maybe we should share a bit more of what we have.'

'Baked beans make you fart!' Lucas said, and gave a throaty cackle.

'Does Santa Claus come to poor children?' Noah asked.

'Santa comes to everybody,' Lucas said. 'He even comes to you if you're in hospital.'

'He doesn't come to everyone. Mr Parks told us in assembly that some children in other countries don't have any toys. They have to play football with a tin can and write on the ground with sticks. I don't understand why Santa comes to us and not them.'

'We'll have to save this conversation for another day,' I said, pulling into their driveway. 'Once I drop you off, I have to do a quick turnaround and pick up your grandparents – we're going to a carol concert.'

'Which grandparents?' Noah asked.

'Granny and Granddad.'

Doris and Bob were 'Granny and Granddad' to the boys, as they were to Tabby. Jodie's parents were, by their own choice, 'Nana and Pop'.

The boys unplugged their seatbelts and I pointed to my cheek, which they both kissed.

'It was nice to see you. Be good,' I said, and they scampered up the steps and rang the bell.

In a moment, the door opened, the boys streamed past Jodie and she stepped out and gave me a wave. I reversed out of the driveway and drove home.

Going to work and then visiting the tree festival had built my confidence somewhat. This was a small town, but not *that* small, I began to think. If Mark knew neither where I worked nor where I lived – and this still seemed to be the case – what were the chances, really, of him just bumping into me? It had happened at the hotel, more or less, but amid a population of fifty-three thousand there must be decent odds that our paths simply wouldn't cross again. Not many people could afford to stay in a hotel indefinitely, on the off-chance.

He certainly wouldn't be turning up at the concert – tickets for that had sold out weeks in advance. Tonight's event was a musical highlight of the year, when the combined forces of the ladies' and male-voice choirs staged an evening of festive fare in the town hall. A guest soloist always performed excerpts from Handel's *Messiah* to kick things off, and this was followed by a selection of well- and lesser-known seasonal pieces, culminating in a stunning rendition of 'The Twelve Days of Christmas', which would speed up like a helter-skelter and Heaven only knew how they managed to get the words out at the end.

Doris leant in through the front passenger door. 'Caroline, I said you could give Ronnie and Barbara a lift with us. Is that all right?'

As Ronnie and Barbara were already climbing into my rear seats, I thought it would have to be. 'Sure, Doris. Hi, Barbara. Hi, Ronnie. Can you find your belts there?'

'This is very kind of you, Caroline. Ronnie can't see to drive in the dark any more. It's a real nuisance.'

Bob sat beside me. 'Is the car going all right?'

'Yes. She had her MOT last month, and she sailed through.'

'I won't bother putting ours through again. When the certificate runs out this time, that's me done with driving.'

'Oh, Bob – why?'

'I don't trust myself any more. I'm afraid of causing an accident.'

'But you've never had so much as a bump.'

'And I never want to have. No, quit while you're ahead.'

I'd always thought Bob a good driver, if a meticulously serious one. He routinely checked his oil and water and his tyre pressure, as well as his petrol gauge, and he only put the radio on when the car was parked. Not like my dad, who drove fast and with complete confidence, his arm draped across the back of Mum's seat, Elvis on the cassette player – although look where they'd ended up.

'Have you been speaking to Tabitha lately?' Doris asked.

'We text more than we speak. She tends to fit me in when she's on the move.'

'You'll be looking forward to having her home for Christmas.'

'I can't wait.'

'Well, we look forward to seeing you both on Christmas Day. You're so good, Caroline, the way you ... you know, with the boys and Jodie.'

'Nothing else for it, Doris.'

Bob and Doris had been mortified when Ray had left me for another woman. They had promised me he would see the error of his ways and come back to me, but the divorce had dented this certainty considerably, and they could hardly boycott their son's subsequent wedding. I didn't boycott it! Jodie made Tabby a bridesmaid and I went along to support my daughter. When the boys arrived, Doris and Bob's emotional allegiances became tangled, because of course Noah and Lucas were their beautiful grandsons, so regret about me had to be modified accordingly. I sometimes believed they'd suffered more over the whole thing than I had or possibly even Tabby.

Doris and Bob were a little frightened of Jodie, I thought.

When we arrived at the town hall, the place was more than half full. We filed in and took our places in the middle of a row. I had a look at the programme, accepted a fruit jelly sweet from Barbara, admired her handbag, which was new, then turned to look behind me. Already the seats had filled up fast. A few rows back, I spotted Fergus. I hadn't known he was coming. I smiled and waved and he smiled back and raised his programme. He was tucked in tight beside his wife. I remembered that Madeleine referred to Marina, a little unkindly, as Holy Cow, because of her being so very religious, in a thin-lipped, loveless sort of way. Yet Fergus stuck with her. Who knew what really went on in other people's marriages?

I chatted to Barbara on one side of me and Bob on the other until a hush fell, the organ began and the choirs processed up the aisle – the ladies in wine-coloured robes, the men in dinner suits and bow-ties.

Doris nudged me and nodded, drawing my attention to the fact that the choirmaster was on the stage steps, shaking hands with our MP – quite a coup, having her here. If I could, I'd grab her for a quote at the end.

The choirs took their places, there was a brief lull and then everyone rose for a collective rendition of 'O Come All Ye Faithful'. It really felt like Christmas.

9

Miraculously, for the first time in a week, I woke without a crushing sense of dread. Somewhere before dawn, my terror had lifted. If Mark knew where to find me, or had key information about my life, he would have been here before now. I would stay off the streets as much as possible for the next couple of weeks, stick to the office and home, and cover up with my big parka if it was really necessary to venture out. Mark must have a life somewhere to get back to. He couldn't hang around for ever. I had a knack for believing what I wanted to believe. It had served me in the past, but it had also exposed me to some poor decision-making. Poor? Try apocalyptic. Which was this?

'You look chirpy,' Madeleine said, as I came through the ground-floor office to the stairs.

'Do I?'

But of course I did. Tonight I had my date at the High Hedges. All night.

'Any progress with the kitchen?'

'Only that when the old tiles and units were removed, the wall behind was damp. It's going to need all the plaster to be hacked off and then two new coats of sand and cement. Great, isn't it?'

'Oh, Mads, I'm sorry.'

'Me too.'

'Tell you what, let me cook for you and Jimmy tomorrow night. I could do us a big casserole.'

'That's kind of you, but Mum's invited us to stay with her and Dad for the weekend, to escape the mess.'

'Sounds like a good idea. Next week, then, come to me one evening. I can put something in the slow cooker. Just tell me when.'

'Thanks. We'll take you up on that.'

Madeleine followed me upstairs, filled the kettle in the kitchen and stood in the doorway of the editorial office with her arms folded.

'What are you looking so pleased about?' she asked Suzanne.

Suzanne was happy to reveal that one of the dailies had been on to her, wanting to pick up on her striking schoolgirls story.

'So have they asked you to write it for them?' Madeleine enquired.

'It doesn't work like that,' Suzanne said. 'They liked the article and they wanted to speak to the people I quoted and do their own thing with it.'

'So you gave them the contacts you worked for, and they gave you what? Will they pay you?'

'You don't understand. If I help them out this time, and a few more times, too, it gets me noticed.'

'Oh, does it? I remember when provincial reporters used to phone through their best stories to the dailies on publication day and get a nice little payment at the end of each month. Isn't that right, Caroline?'

'It's true,' I said. 'Your first loyalty was to your own publication, obviously, but once your paper appeared, you were free to phone in anything to the dailies' copytakers. They expected to pay you. Sometimes you helped them get pics, too.'

'Well, it's not like that any more,' Suzanne said. 'I might not get a direct payment, but I get to speak to a news editor, and if I play ball with them I'm in a good position the next time they're recruiting.'

Neither Madeleine nor I confirmed or rejected this.

'You might be happy stuck in this place, Caroline, eating scones at the Women's Institute AGM and counting the potholes on the Carrackbannon Road, but I don't plan to spend the next thirty years here.'

'The WI does bake the best scones,' I said.

'And the Carrackbannon Road is a disgrace,' Madeleine added. 'Listen, madam, Caroline has built a solid reputation as a first-class journalist with the confidence and respect of her community.'

'Yeah, yeah.'

'And she's had her fair share of stories in the dailies and in leading women's magazines. What about the award she picked up last summer for her features in the *Weekend Tribune*?'

I had started writing for the *Tribune* when Ray's career took off under Jodie's influence. I had needed validation, needed not to be the one left behind. It had been gratifying when they had asked me to submit more, the extra money had been a bonus, and even when life had settled back down and I had decided I was, in fact, still happy at the *Gazette*, it was nice to have an interesting sideline. These days, I sent them something about every four weeks, which was enough, on top of my full-time job.

'So it's *Aladdin*, tonight?' I asked Madeleine.

'Yes. A couple of proseccos first and a bag of Revels in my handbag. It'll be lovely.'

'Oh, no, it won't.'

'Don't be silly, Caroline.'

We finished at five on a Friday, but tonight I was intent on leaving a few minutes early. Just in case anyone had traced me to the newspaper office, and just in case they were waiting for me outside, ready to do anything that might get in the way of my rendezvous, I had taken precautions. That morning, instead of using the free car park a short walk from the office's front door, I had parked in Spencer Road, on the far side of the railway station. The footbridge over the tracks led directly to a narrow alleyway that ran along the back of our terrace of offices, and this was where I had scampered that morning, knocking on the door at the rear of the ad department on the ground floor to be admitted. Colleagues did this from time to time, if they had taken the train instead of their car, or simply if they had found it convenient to park on Spencer Road, for some reason, which was very doable since the station had been given a spacious new car park of its own. Arriving at the back door, or leaving by it, aroused no suspicion.

Bursting out into the cold air, I felt my eyes water, and pulled up my scarf. I ran along the alley and up the footbridge steps, almost laughing at the freedom of it. If by any remote chance Mark was watching, he would have his eye on the front door. By the time the last person filed out and locked up, I would be back in my car and on the road. It might not be an ultimate answer, but it was answer enough for tonight. I was on my way and he couldn't stop me. He could stand there in the dark, freezing, waiting, for as long as he liked. He'd missed me, this time. I was gone, driving away to meet my man.

The High Hedges wasn't the sort of place people went without a specific reason. It wasn't fabulous. It didn't have a spa or cocktails. There were no facilities for children. The people for whom it was convenient were business types who used the airport, who weren't bothered about where they sat in the restaurant and who didn't necessarily want to find themselves sharing the bar with the overflow from a wedding celebration. The inn was overpriced in all departments, but was known to provide customers with creative invoices for their employers, which enabled them to claim more on expenses than they had actually paid for their room, meals and drinks.

It wasn't exactly seedy, but it wasn't anyone's little slice of Heaven. I had never accidentally bumped into anyone I knew at the High Hedges and I never expected to, which was more or less the point.

Tonight, the Michael Bublé Christmas album was playing in the lobby. I thought I had probably got there first. I checked in at Reception, took my bag upstairs to our usual room and flopped down on the bed. I might sleep for an hour, then have a bath, make a coffee and change my clothes.

I switched on the radio for company and dozed off easily against a background of the evening news. The next thing I knew it was the theme tune of *The Archers*.

My phone buzzed on the bedside table.

Running a bit late. Book us a table for eight o'clock. And a capital *X*.

I smiled and deleted the message, rang Reception to book our table and yawned, reminding myself to make that cup of coffee.

As my bath ran, I considered my make-up in the mirror. Sometimes the steam was too much and made it all run and I had to do it again. Sometimes it was just the right amount to give me a dewy glow and I got away with leaving it alone.

I wondered how long we'd still be meeting like this. It was the most exciting thing in my life now, but could I still do it when I was sixty? Would I perhaps reach a point where I'd rather divert myself into planting bulbs or playing golf?

There had been times in my life when I'd had no sex at all,

sometimes for years, because right from the start I could only ever do it with the right person. But I'd never felt quite myself when I was celibate. I was by nature a carnal being. Perhaps this was why Eric, with his neat, organised consumption of a quesadilla starter, didn't much appeal to me – where was his animal appetite?

I unwrapped the complimentary shower cap and stepped into the soapy bubbles.

I didn't usually go downstairs alone, but the chambermaid hadn't left any wine in the mini-bar fridge and I much preferred that to spirits as an apéritif. The bar was busy, but not packed. I found three stools together and perched on the one at the end.

'A glass of Sauvignon Blanc, please.'

That would do to start with. We'd get a bottle of red with our meal.

I had brought a book with me, to pass the time, and keep others at arm's length. At least, that was the plan.

'Can I get that for you?' Looking up, I found a tall man with prominent cheekbones and longish copper hair leaning on the bar with a twenty-pound note in his hand.

The barman gave me an enquiring look.

'No. Thank you,' I said. 'I can get it myself.' I didn't want to seem touchy, so I added: 'I'm waiting for someone.'

'You might as well have a drink with me until they get here. Let me. Only alcoholics drink alone.'

I glanced over my shoulder, but there was no sign of anyone else coming. 'All right.'

His name was Cormac and it was his first time at the High Hedges. Someone in the airport had told him it was cosy, which it plainly wasn't, with staff who went the extra mile – they didn't. I commiserated and told him that, for what it was worth, the restaurant did an excellent fillet steak, with a house red they were apparently unaware was seriously under-priced.

'Thanks for that,' he said. 'So you come here a lot?'

'It has its advantages,' I said, hoping he wouldn't press me to name them.

Cormac was a sales rep for a revolutionary new washing-machine. Thus far, the manufacturer had attempted to sell direct to the public, but despite recent trends towards internet shopping, it seemed a high volume of people still wanted to buy their washers from a human being in an actual shop. Hence, Cormac was seeking to build relationships with electrical retailers.

'You must meet a lot of people,' I said, trying to think what might possibly make his job interesting.

He laughed. 'It's OK. I'm not living my dream, but it'll do for now.'

'What did you really want to do?'

'Drive Formula One cars.'

'Right. And did you ever get close?'

'I did a bit of rallying when I was younger. Nothing serious.'

What age was he now – forty-five, perhaps?

'How about you? You must work in fashion or beauty.'

Not me. But Mum had done. Josie was the senior assistant in the best women's boutique in our home town and loved it. That is, she loved the stock. Almost every week she brought home something new. I remember a stunning midnight blue long dress with a deep V-back that showed how smooth and perfect she was. And then there was the catsuit that everyone talked about. Being so petite, she often needed to have things altered, but she had a little woman she swore by who operated from a tiny place in the street behind the church. Josie wore clothes well. The truth was that she even looked great in old jeans, a T-shirt and her rubber gloves, which she always wore to do the housework, to keep her hands and nails nice.

'I'm a teacher,' I lied, because you never knew.

Cormac responded to this news with a look I didn't like and the penny dropped. He thought I was a prostitute, or the next-door thing in his mind, perhaps, a woman who picked up unknown men in hotel bars and slept with them in exchange for free drinks.

'Actually, I think I've left something in my room,' I said, reaching for my bag. I didn't want to spend another second with him.

His hand shot out and gripped mine. 'Stay and have another drink.'

It didn't sound like a request.

I glanced up, but the barman was at the other end of the counter, washing glasses, and no one else was paying us any attention. 'I think you've got the wrong idea,' I said.

'I don't think so. When I find a woman alone on a barstool, I usually have exactly the right idea.'

I tugged my hand away and he grabbed my wrist tightly. Why had I come down here? I should have settled for a cup of coffee upstairs. I was cross with myself for having accepted the drink – it would have been better to insist on paying for it myself. Now I felt like Penelope Pitstop in the grasp of the Hooded Claw, except I was in my fifties and, as well as being upset, I saw myself as ridiculous.

I felt a hand on my shoulder.

'Caroline?'

I spun round and my eyes filled and almost spilt over with relief.

'I was just keeping her company,' Cormac said.

A waiter came over. 'Your table's ready in the dining room.'

'Shall we go in?'

I lifted my glass. 'Yes, please.'

We had a rule on our nights away. No talking about work or our families. Instead, we discussed books and films – often just ones we had watched on TV – sometimes politics, about which we disagreed, food, music. We'd have a starter and a main and share a bottle of wine, before making our way upstairs.

Our intimacy was very straightforward. There was no awkwardness, never had been, and no gimmicks. It was a simple case of desire, which was all it ever took, in my experience. Tonight, everything was hot and fast – it happened that way, sometimes. We could always go back and do it slow and tender later.

We were lying on the bed, the crisp white sheet dragged up over us, when someone suddenly battered on the door.

My first thought was that the building was being evacuated – was there a fire? But no alarm had sounded.

Before I could formulate an explanation, a voice I knew well roared: 'Open this door! I know you're in there!'

I cringed in horror as panic surged through me, like a fast-acting poison. How? I had been so careful. We had both always been so careful.

We looked at each other. I dived for my clothes and hobbled into the bathroom.

The bedroom door opened and Jodie shoved her way in.

'How could you, Ray? How could you do this to me? How could you do it to the boys? We're a family! Come out of there, you slut! I'm his wife! Did he tell you he had a wife? Did he tell you he had two little boys at home?'

No, no, no, no, no.

Jodie was at the bathroom door, pushing it.

'You! Oh, my God.'

10

I didn't know what to do. I shoved the bathroom door shut and slid the bolt.

'I don't believe this!' Jodie screeched, and thumped on the door. 'You rotten bitch! Ray's *my* husband, now. Put on your clothes, you harlot, and come out here so I can scratch your eyes out.'

I was shaking so badly I could barely dress myself.

'Jodie.' Ray's voice, not the usual sleepy drawl. 'Jodie, I'm sorry.'

'Sorry? Sorry I caught you, you mean! How long has this been going on? I want some answers, Ray. I *demand* answers. I was fifty per cent sure I was imagining you were even cheating on me, but never in my wildest did I guess you were with her.

Why her? Of all people. Do you love her? Oh, my God – have you *always* loved her? Did you ever actually leave her, or has this been going on behind my back all along?'

Clothes on, I leant against the bathroom door and let my back slide down and my legs fold until I was sitting on the floor. I couldn't see their body language, but I could hear every word.

'Did you only marry me because I was pregnant with Noah?'

'Of course not. I married you because I loved you.'

'But you still loved Caroline, too. And you never stopped.'

'That's not true. When we found out about Noah, I walked away from Caroline and Tabby to be with you. That wasn't an easy thing to do, Jodie.'

'So why did you? If you still loved her?'

'Because I loved both of you. And you were having our baby. I wanted to stand by you.'

'How can you say you loved both of us? You don't get to love two people at the same time, Ray – you have to choose.'

'Don't you love both Noah and Lucas?'

'That is *not* the same and you know it. So you left Caroline but you kept on sleeping with her – is that right?'

'No. Absolutely not. For years there was nothing physical between us. When the boys were little, it was only you.'

'How can I believe a word you say?'

'It's the truth. Caroline and I have only been ... meeting, for a couple of years.'

'A couple of *years*!'

'Jodie, please keep your voice down.'

'Do not tell me to keep my voice down. Do not presume to give me any advice on how to deal with finding my husband cheating on me in a crappy hotel room with his bitch of an ex-wife.'

I swallowed hard. My relationship with Jodie had long been based in polite civility, rather than any real closeness, but I had never wished this on her. I imagined people finding out. Madeleine would say Ray had been my husband in the first place and Jodie hadn't hesitated to take him away from me, so she was in no position to judge. I didn't agree. Two wrongs didn't make a right. Whatever Jodie and Ray had done to me in the past didn't entitle me to sleep with Ray once he was married to her.

Was it true what Ray had said – that he loved both of us? I thought he probably did. Jodie was demanding and challenging and kept him on his toes, and I thought he enjoyed that. I didn't ask questions or try to push him, and perhaps there was a place in his busy life for a woman like that, too – plus the sex between us had always been great.

'What do you want me to do?' I heard Ray ask.

'Put your clothes on, for a start,' Jodie replied. 'And put that duvet back on the bed – I don't want to see your disgusting sheets.'

'Let's go home,' Ray said. 'I think we should go home.'

'You're very confident you still have a home,' Jodie snapped. 'But I don't want to spend another minute in this place, so you can come back to the house for now. Just don't read anything into that.'

'I take it you came in your car,' Ray said.

'Yes. I know yours is in the car park, but are you fit to drive or will you be over the limit?'

'I only had one glass of wine. You go on down and I'll follow you.'

'You must be joking! Leave you here with her? No chance, Ray. We'll go downstairs together and you will drive home ahead of me. You won't see Caroline again. Not ever. Not if you want to have any chance of keeping me and the boys.'

'You know I'm bound to see her – she's Tabby's mother. I can't avoid her for the rest of our lives.'

Tabby. Oh, God, Tabby. What would she say when she found out? And she was bound to. 'Please don't tell Tabby, Jodie,' I called through the door. 'Please let me do that.'

Jodie kicked the bathroom door in response. 'Why should I do anything you want?' she said. 'You're disgusting. Why shouldn't Tabby know that her mother is a filthy whore? And you can forget about ever seeing Noah and Lucas again, too. Come on, Ray – we're leaving.'

Ray raised his voice a little: 'Caroline?'

I heard a slap and Jodie said, 'Don't speak to her. Just leave her.'

The bedroom door opened and closed again, and then there was silence.

I stayed on the bathroom floor for a while, my back still against the door. I had drunk four glasses of wine to Ray's one, so I couldn't simply pack up and drive home. I supposed I could phone a cab, but then I would have to take another the next morning so I could come back and retrieve my car.

Eventually, I opened the bathroom door, crept out and lay down on the bed. Jodie wouldn't tell Tabby anything tonight – she'd be fully engaged in having things out with Ray. All I could do was lie there until morning, alone with my thoughts, then send my daughter an early text asking her not to speak to Jodie until she had spoken to me. I would promise her none of us was ill, but insist that I did need to talk to her. Then I had to hope she would forgive me.

Much as the High Hedges bedroom now reeked of disaster, I nevertheless had to drag myself out of bed on Saturday morning. I couldn't face eating anything, so boosted my blood sugar with a bottle of orange juice from the mini-bar, then stood under the shower for a long, long time. There is something terrible about crying in the shower, your tears pelted off your face and washed down the plughole with the rest of the water.

Tabby hadn't replied to my text yet. I assumed she hadn't seen it – perhaps she had spent a lovely night with her new boyfriend and was sleeping blissfully.

'I'd like to check out, please,' I told the receptionist, wondering if she was the one who had directed Jodie to our room the night before, albeit stopping short of giving her a key. For what – a bit of drama or twenty pounds, perhaps? Jodie had found our hideaway easily enough, I later learnt. She had simply tracked Ray's phone. He hadn't gone to any great lengths to dodge detection because we had put our efforts into escaping suspicion in the first place – a discreet meeting place and not a word to anyone about us, but that was all. We had thought it was enough.

Classic FM was punctuating its playlist with carols as I drove home. Christmas was ruined, that was for sure. I wouldn't be getting an invitation to share Ray and Jodie's turkey dinner now. Jodie couldn't have meant it about not letting me see the boys, though – could she? I doted on Noah and Lucas. I loved them. And they loved me. I could have been the hateful ex-wife when they were babies, twisted with bitterness, never allowing Ray and his new young wife a minute's peace. I could have phoned Jodie's parents – the famous Nana and Pop – and told them their darling daughter was no better than she should be, bedding other people's husbands, stealing other children's daddies. I could have ruined the wedding, the christenings. I could have been a menace at the school gates, bad-mouthing Jodie to the other mothers. But I didn't do any of that. I didn't want to be that person. If I could let it all go and give Ray and Jodie the space to make a new life with their babies, a good life, didn't Jodie owe me something? Didn't she owe me at least a measure of forgiveness?

There were three more cards on the mat when I got home. I didn't open them. I didn't feel they were mine – they'd been written to nice Caroline, good Caroline, who penned dutiful little pieces about the local community for the paper and was astonishingly good with her ex-husband's children. They hadn't been intended for bad Caroline, the home-wrecker.

What to do with my day? All fearful thoughts of Mark were banished by this new horror. In other circumstances, I might have gone shopping for Christmas presents, but since it looked like all the people on my list were all the people I would be banned from seeing on Christmas Day, what was the point?

There was Tabby, of course, but was I absolutely sure she'd want to spend Christmas with just me? What if she took Jodie's side and went to stay there?

I could have done with someone to talk to. My mum was more than thirty years dead, but would she have known what to say anyhow? Josie was devoted to Maxie, and he to her. They touched all the time, couldn't do enough for each other, and I don't remember them spending a single night apart. What would Mum have made of me finding a husband, losing him, then 'borrowing' him back? She and Maxie were inseparable. Their love affair was unassailable. Yes, they rowed, but never for long, and they always came back together. I don't know if they resolved their issues, or just decided that what they had was bigger than their differences. Whatever it was, it worked. I closed my eyes and swallowed as I heard the prick of the stylus landing on vinyl.

Ray's mum, Doris, was a different kind of creature altogether. She was built like an outhouse and wore a lot of thickly woven man-made fibres. She was kindness itself, but it was hard to imagine her ever having been impelled by a sexual motive. She was possibly the last person in whom I could confide my affair with Ray, never mind that she was his mum, Jodie's mother-in-law and the boys' granny.

I sighed. Maybe I'd try Madeleine.

'Hi, Mads. How's it going? Did you enjoy the pantomime?'

'Caroline? Let me just change my phone to my other ear. That's better. The panto was great. You and the boys will love it. A new chap as the dame, and he was hilarious. Just the tonic I needed.'

'So where are you? I was wondering if you'd like to come over for a while.'

'Oh, Caroline – no can do, I'm afraid. We've tracked down a really nice kitchen tile, but the only problem is it's ninety miles away, so Jimmy's driving us over, now. We should get there in about an hour, but it'll take us a while to load them up, and then we'll probably stop off for something to eat. Was it anything urgent?'

Tears leaked out of both eyes as I realised I was completely on my own and had no one to share with. I wiped them away with the back of my cuff.

'No. Nothing urgent. I'll catch you at work on Monday.'

'Sorry, Caroline – I can hardly hear you, but let's go out one night next week and we can have a proper catch-up. OK?'

'OK.'

When Tabby finally rang, just after lunch, she sounded happy and I hated to be the bearer of bad news.

'Say something,' I urged her, after I had explained.

'I really don't know what to say,' she replied. 'I don't know if you're serious about Dad, or if he's serious about you. I don't know why you'd do something so incredibly ill-judged if you *aren't* serious about each other. Do you love him?'

'Yes. But I was also willing to share him. I never encouraged him to leave Jodie. I never asked him to choose.'

'You're aware that in saying that you're subscribing to polygamy?'

'Oh, Tabby.'

'Well, you are. Of all the people you could have taken up with, why Dad? What happened to that guy Derek?'

'Eric. You sound like Suzanne – she thought I should have married him for his money. What can I say? I didn't fancy him.'

'So it was animal magnetism, with you and Dad.'

'Is that so hard to believe?'

'Well, I hope it was worth it. You've trashed our family.'

'You, Dad and I are our family – and we all like each other!'

'Jodie, Noah and Lucas are family, too, Mum. And Granny and Granddad. Even snobby old Nana and Pop. You've ruined all that.'

'Don't say that, Tab.'

'You think if I don't say it, it won't be true?'

'Maybe you could come home next weekend. You must be due some time off from the coffee shop. We should probably have a proper talk.'

'And say what? Do you want me to absolve you from your sins? Mum, it sounds to me like you've made your bed and now you'd better face the fact that you'll have to lie in it. You've brought this entirely on yourself.'

'Have I really disappointed you?'

'Yes. And I've got plans for next weekend.'

'With the new man?'

'Yes.'

'Is that all you're going to tell me?'

'It's early days. Look, I think I'll phone Jodie. I want her to know that I had no idea what was going on. I know what it's like to be cheated on and to wonder if absolutely everyone knew before you did. It's horrible. You don't know whom to trust. You might have remembered that. I need to make it clear that I never betrayed her.'

I didn't know what to say. I hated the prospect of Tabby and Jodie growing closer while Tabby held me at arm's length. But of course she wouldn't want to lose her bond with Noah and Lucas – they were her little brothers.

And because I still wanted to be part of that world, too, I blurted out: 'Jodie's GP says Noah's constant peeing is due to anxiety.'

'Oh? Poor Noah. And how has Jodie taken that?'

'She wasn't impressed.'

After a moment, Tabby said, 'I could ask Harry's mum about it.'

'Harry?'

'The guy I've been seeing. His mum's a child psychologist.'

My heart soared – then Harry would surely be a young man who cared about feelings, who wouldn't cause harm casually. I couldn't have asked for more. 'Sure. But tread carefully – I think Jodie's pretty resistant to the diagnosis.'

'Look, it's going to take a bit of time for me to process this whole affair-with-Dad thing. You've probably fucked up our family beyond repair, just to have what you wanted. It was entirely selfish and you don't appear to have given a thought to who it might hurt, which includes me.'

'Tabby ...'

'Don't ring me for a while, Mum. I'm angry and I don't want to talk to you right now.'

'But, sweetheart ...'

'You're gorgeous. You could have had anyone. What were you thinking?'

'Do you hate me?'

'No. But I don't much like you. I've got to go.' And she hung up.

I spent the next hour cleaning the house. I thought it might provide a distraction. I scoured the sink, mopped the kitchen floor and chucked out any old food that was in the fridge. I changed my bedsheets, cleaned the cold ashes out of the grate and vacuumed all the floors.

It didn't work. All I could think about was how I had wrecked my life. Tabby didn't want to talk to me, much less come home. Jodie hated me. Noah and Lucas would be bewildered and sad, and the grandparents would be horrified and might not speak to me again.

All I had wanted was to continue living my small life in peace. I had perceived a threat from Mark's sudden appearance, while completely failing to appreciate the danger I was creating all by myself or, rather, with Ray. But Jodie would forgive Ray. She would make him pay, but she would take him back. He would still end up with her and the boys and seeing lots of Tabby, all four grandparents hovering in various states of judgement, but ultimately supportive, whereas I would be shunned and condemned to solitude.

I poured myself a large glass of wine and threw myself down on the sofa.

11

Someone was in the house.

I was lying face down on the bed, fully clothed, my cheek and chin sticky with drool. I had been sleeping – for how long I didn't know. What time was it? What day was it?

I heard the sound of glass clinking on glass coming from downstairs.

Bile rose in my throat and I swallowed it.

Who was there?

Maybe it was Tabby. Perhaps she'd had second thoughts and come home to see me. I considered the wine bottles downstairs and remembered that I had been sick at least once, although I'd made it to the bathroom. But she'd know, and be appalled.

A dark, cold feeling crept over me as I remembered why I

had been drinking. It was because I had spoilt everything. I had fouled the nest, shat on my own doorstep.

But how would Tabby have got here? She would have had to take a train, and then would surely have rung me to ask for a lift from the station. My mobile might well be silently out of charge, but she could have rung the landline. I had texted her the new number, hadn't I? I had sent it to all the relevant people. I rolled onto my side and peered blearily at my bedside radio's digital clock – almost seven. But was that morning or night? It was dark outside – who knew what that meant?

Would Tabby just skulk about downstairs, though? Wouldn't she come straight upstairs to see me? Perhaps not, if I was in her seriously bad books. I rubbed my eyes with the heel of my hand. Wake up, Caroline.

What if it wasn't Tabby? Who else could have just let themselves in? Ray and Jodie had a key. Had Jodie kicked Ray out? Had he come here? Just for a night or two, or did he mean to stay? And how did I feel about that?

I tried to sit up, but the bile rose again and my head thumped.

Perhaps Jodie had come to confront me. My whole being groaned at the prospect. I wouldn't be able to do her attack justice – I would lie there inert before her, like a human punch-bag, only much less resistant, and neither of us would gain any satisfaction from the encounter.

Or perhaps Doris and Bob felt it was their duty to visit and put their oar in, if they had heard about recent developments – they had a key, too. But I didn't hear voices, so I thought whoever was downstairs had come alone.

It hurt my head to move, but I managed to stand up and limp

out onto the landing, where I stopped and listened. It sounded like my visitor was in the kitchen.

I went to the top of the stairs and, clutching the banister woozily, peered over. A long, dark overcoat was draped over the newel post.

The jolt made my head thunder with pain. Mark! Mark was downstairs! He had found me. All my head-space had been crowded out with regret and self-pity and self-loathing over me and Ray, and I had inevitably dropped my guard, with a lot of help from my friend, Monsieur Sauvignon. Now Mark was here and with him the possibility of revelations that would make Ray's and my infidelity look like a minor infringement of the terms and conditions of a crossword puzzle.

My heart was pounding, and every pulse made my poor head thump. *How* had he found me? And had he broken in? What did he actually want from me, anyway? Why exactly had he come, after all these years?

I wasn't fit for a confrontation. I wasn't entirely sober and I wasn't well.

Before I could decide what to do, my body spoke. I lurched to the bathroom and threw up into the toilet. When it was over, my legs were like jelly. I looked at myself in the mirror. *Caroline, you're a mess*, I thought, taking in my bloodshot eyes, my smudged mascara and blanched lips. Where was the mother the teenage boys would most like to fuck now?

Could I take a moment to wash my face, at least? I decided I could.

The cool running water made me feel marginally better

and I started to imagine what I would say when I went downstairs.

'We were so young,' I would point out. 'We hardly knew what right and wrong meant. We can't go on punishing ourselves for mistakes we made back then.'

I would tell him nothing good would come of living in the past – we had to look forward, not back.

'You can't go on hating me for ever,' I would say. 'You have to let go.'

But what if he wouldn't, or couldn't? What then? If he had come to punish me, it would be the easiest thing in the world for him to do.

I suddenly panicked, as I thought of the photographs of Tabby all around the house – the many pictures Ray had taken, which I loved so much. If Mark hadn't known before he came here that I had a beloved daughter, he would know it now.

Somehow, I would have to find a way to persuade him to leave us alone. I would do anything, if he would just go away again and leave us in peace.

I crept downstairs, shivering as I passed the dark overcoat.

Could I make a deal with Mark? Was there something I could offer him that would persuade him to give me back my peace in return?

I could see into the kitchen, could see a man's back at the sink.

'Why are you here?' I asked, hearing how hoarse my voice sounded. 'What do you want?'

The man turned and I gave a little gasp.

It wasn't Mark. It was Paddy Madden, with a potato in one hand and a peeler in the other.

'Caroline. Ready for some grub? This should be ready in half an hour.'

'Paddy? I thought I had burglars.'

'I rang the bell. Several times. In fact, I've called by more than once. The car was in the drive, but I couldn't get a reply. I remembered that you keep a spare key in the greenhouse, so I thought I'd let myself in just to check you were OK. You were fast asleep, so I started dinner.'

Dinner. It must be seven o'clock at night.

'What day is it?'

'Sunday.'

Good. At least I hadn't missed a day at work.

'What exactly brought you in the first place?'

'A combination of factors. Fergus told me he'd bumped into you at the glass bank and thought you donated rather a large number of wine bottles.'

'I'd been gathering them up for ages!'

'Really? Fergus didn't think so – he said there wasn't a single jam or pasta-sauce jar, so you couldn't have been saving them up for very long.'

'Bloody Fergus.'

'Bloody observant Fergus. He is a journalist, after all. So was he right?'

'I've always enjoyed a glass of wine, Paddy. You know that.'

'You've always enjoyed several.'

'I'm not an alcoholic.'

'I didn't say you were. But I've just tidied away three empty bottles and one glass – that's not the way to enjoy a drink, Caroline.'

I felt squirmy. I was acutely aware that I looked unkempt and probably smelt of sweat and vomit. 'I was having a bit of a crisis. Family stuff.'

'Ah. That explains the mysterious text from Ray. Very brief. Said Madeleine wasn't answering so could I pop round and see you were all right. Added to what Fergus had mentioned, I thought I'd call by.'

'Ray shouldn't have bothered you.'

'Oh? Why not?'

'You have enough on your plate.'

'Do I?'

'Don't you?'

'Once in a while, Caroline, it's nice to be treated like someone who might have some agency in the wider world. Let me do a bit of good, for once.'

'You do good all the time, Paddy. You're a saint, the way you look after your family. Whereas I am very much a sinner.'

Paddy turned back to the sink and resumed peeling the potatoes. 'Let me put these on to boil and then we'll see about rehydrating you,' he said.

'I don't know if I'll be able to eat anything.'

'It's cheap pink sausages, mashed potatoes and baked

beans. Food of the gods. Nobody ever said no to sausages, mash and beans.'

After a pint of water and two paracetamol, I felt a bit better and surprised myself by devouring the food Paddy had cooked. I hadn't eaten anything properly since dinner at the High Hedges on Friday, keeping my blood sugar up by dosing myself at intervals with Lucozade, dextrose tablets and the occasional digestive biscuit.

When we'd eaten, we sat on at the dining table.

'So, do you want to tell me what's happened?' Paddy asked.

'You'll go off me,' I said. 'Tabby already has.'

'Try me.'

I sighed and pushed back my chair.

'I've been having an affair with Ray. For two years. Jodie caught us in bed together.'

Paddy gave a low whistle. 'I wasn't expecting that. You're full of surprises, Caroline.'

'They have two little boys, Paddy. Two little boys whom I adore.'

'So what happens next? Does he want to get back with you or will they try to make a go of things?'

'I don't know. I can't exactly ring him, and she's forbidden him to have anything to do with me, so I'm out in the cold for now. I feel dreadful. I don't know who I am – I used to think I was an OK person, but why did I sleep with a married man for two years?'

'Not just any married man.'

'No – worse than that, a married man whose family were my family, and now I've lost them.'

'Not necessarily. Things blow over. People calm down.'

'Do you really think so?'

'I know so. When Katrina was lying in hospital, unable to move, Amy blamed me because I had bought Katrina the horse. Amy said Merlin had been too much for Kat, too spirited, and I should never have got him for her. The truth was, I'd known he was a feisty creature, but our daughter was an able horsewoman and I didn't doubt her ability to handle him. It wasn't Merlin throwing her that caused her injury, it was the fact that he then fell on top of her. Not exactly a freak accident, but a highly unusual one. Equestrian sport can be dangerous, but so can crossing the road. While Amy ranted, I just quietly got on with things and eventually she worked out her grief.'

Paddy never talked about the accident. That he was doing so now was in a selfless effort to help me.

'She forgave you.'

'More than that – she said there was nothing to forgive.'

'But what happened with me and Ray wasn't an accident. We chose to do it.'

'Even so, the storm will pass – it always does. Give it time.'

'Should I reach out or back off?'

'I'd give everybody a bit of space for a while, then maybe test the temperature of the water.'

'I've hurt everybody I love.'

'And you're paying for it. So suck it up, be penitent and, in a while, build bridges. Everyone deserves a second chance.'

I almost told him then that this was already my second chance. I almost told him about the dreadful things I'd done in the past – much, much worse than cheating with my ex-husband – and how Mark was now snapping at my shadow, closing in, possibly, to reveal all and utterly raze what Ray and I had merely fire-bombed.

But as long as there was the slightest chance that I could escape Mark's vengeance, I had to keep my secret. I swallowed my shame like I had the bile earlier.

'In other news, how is my goddaughter?' Paddy asked.

'She thinks I'm a disgrace.'

'I very much doubt that. Has she found a job yet?'

'Yes, actually. The special-education school she was working in have given her a permanent contract – it's just part-time hours, but at least she's doing what she trained for.'

'Boyfriend?'

I brightened at this. 'She's started seeing a new guy. Harry. His mum's a psychologist.'

'Oh, no – nightmare. He'll tell her all the ways you've screwed her up.'

I must have looked stricken, because Paddy held up his hands and cried, 'Joking! He'll make an able father for your grandchildren, of course.'

'I love the prospect of being a granny. I want little bodies I can squeeze and little faces I can kiss without being pushed away. I'm already looking forward to all the picture books and toddles in the park and singing 'I'm a Little Teapot'. They say you love your kids but you fall in love with your grandkids – as I fell completely in love with Tabby from the very first moment,

I can only imagine my feelings for my grandchildren will be some form of worship.'

I saw an emotion flicker across Paddy's features. 'Having grandkids – that's something else you and Amy are going to miss out on. I'm so sorry.'

'Everyone's sorry. We're all sorry. It doesn't do any good.'

'Paddy, it's very kind of you to come round, and cook, and talk, but I'm sure you must need to get home.'

'Nope. My in-laws are visiting and we irritate each other a good deal, so it's just as well that I stay out of the way. If you can put up with me for a bit longer, you'd be doing me a favour.'

'Oh! Well, then, what shall we do?'

'I think there's an *Endeavour* repeat – they're always worth another watch.'

'Would you like a glass of wine?' I asked, standing up and lifting our plates. 'Just because I don't, doesn't mean you can't.'

'Why don't we just have some tea?'

'You think I have a drink problem.'

'Do you?'

'What constitutes a problem? I don't take time off work. I keep house, shop for my groceries, see people.'

But this wasn't the first time Paddy had come to my rescue.

'You present a very good front to the world,' he said. 'But maybe you should take things a little easier. I can't imagine that drink and diabetes make very good bedfellows – what if you forget to eat, or fluff your jab? Especially when you live alone.'

I'd thought about that many times, of course – how there was no one to notice me skipping meals or to say: 'Are you sure you're just drunk and not having a hypo?' I seemed to have managed thus far on instinct or possibly luck, but how many chances could I afford to take? I didn't want to die, I definitely didn't, and I absolutely did not want Tabby to be the one to find my lifeless body, but, oh, how much better the world often looked after a few glasses.

'I'll cut down,' I offered. 'At least, I'll try.'

'You'll try to try?' Paddy said, knowing that Tabby, like Katrina, had grown up on a daily dose of *The Simpsons*.

'I mean it, I think. I need to do something.'

We washed the dishes and made the pot of tea, and then it was time for *Endeavour*, which lived up to expectations. By chance, afterwards we stumbled upon someone showing *King Creole*.

'You must need to go home,' I said.

'After this – this was his best movie, in my opinion.'

When the first ad break came, Paddy asked, 'Do you remember when Elvis died?'

'Vividly.'

'Tell me.'

'Well, my brother and I were in bed, but not yet asleep, when we heard Mum crying – really crying, and Mum wasn't usually a crier. We didn't know what to do. We had no idea what it could be. We sat on the stairs whispering and wondering. Then Dad must have heard us because he came out into the hall and brought us into the lounge, where the news was on the television. Our parents were complete Elvis Presley fanatics. They had stacks of his records, which they played all the time, and they danced right there, between the television and the front window, just whenever they felt like it.

'The next day, I remember Mum being at home with the curtains shut and the radio on, and everything the station played was Elvis music. It was like she'd lost a member of her own family.'

'At least your parents were part of some sort of pop culture – my mother and father's idea of music was the Methodist hymn book. Nothing wrong with that, of course, but hardly something you could throw shapes to.'

'When my brother and I were very young, we thought we had the coolest parents ever, because they dressed so well and had lovely hair and listened to music all the time. Then when I got into my teens I discovered U2 and The Undertones and thought Mum and Dad's taste in music was embarrassing. I later reviewed that position when they came to a school barbecue and mesmerised the entire crowd by jiving to 'Don't Be Cruel' – people asked if they were professional dancers. They never took their eyes off each other when they were dancing. I decided they had actually been cool after all. Now I reckon they were lucky, the way people who absolutely believe in God are lucky. It was a kind of faith for them and I guess it must be nice to live with that degree of certainty, without a trace of doubt.'

When the credits finally rolled, Paddy sighed and said, 'And now I really should make a move for home.'

'Do you have de-icer for your windscreen? It'll be frozen.'

'I don't think I do, actually.'

'I'll fill you a kettle and a jug.'

I watched from the front door as Paddy poured the water over his windscreen and rear window, stepping back to keep it from running onto his clothes and shoes. I remembered how, years ago, he had been a firework in the office, full of mischief and fun. Yet, even before his daughter's accident, he had also been a great friend to anyone in need – wise, discreet, not judging. I missed seeing him across the office every day.

Had there been one person in the whole world to whom I might just have risked unburdening myself about Mark, it would have been him. Standing there on my step, knowing that, if I asked him, despite the lateness of the hour, Paddy would nevertheless listen, I considered it. But in the end I just couldn't.

12

'What are you wearing tomorrow night?' Suzanne asked, warming her rear on the heater.

Madeleine had just made us all coffees.

'I haven't decided yet,' Richie said.

'Not you! I meant Caroline.'

'I haven't decided yet,' I echoed.

'Well, at least tell me if you're wearing a dress or trousers.'

'I really have no idea,' I said. 'Does it matter?'

'I need to know whether or not to dress up. What did you wear last year?'

'Not a clue. Madeleine, give Suzanne a steer here – do we usually make an effort for the work Christmas do?'

'Since somebody finally deigned to ask me, I'll tell you that

I'm taking a half-day and getting my hair done, and I'm wearing the black velvet trouser-suit I bought for going to my sister's on Boxing Day.'

'Right. So a bit dressy-uppy, then,' Suzanne said, through a mouthful of chocolate biscuit.

Madeleine turned to me. 'I was thinking about what you could get Noah and Lucas.'

I hadn't told her yet about me and Ray. I hadn't told anyone except Tabby and Paddy. Without the anaesthetic of too much wine, the weight of it now sat like a rock on my heart and lungs and it was difficult to breathe. Was this guilt, or merely sorrow? The two could be difficult to distinguish, I had found. I didn't know which was worse – the knowledge of exactly what damage I'd done with Ray or the imagined wreckage I must assume Mark still had in mind. When I pictured the boys, I wanted to cry; when I envisaged Mark coming up behind me in the street, I wanted to scream. But I did neither, hiding in the workaday, ducking behind a façade of silly chat. Keeping busy. Keeping on. It had worked for me before.

'Oh?'

'Sleeping bags. If they don't already have them. Kids love sleeping bags, for some reason.'

'Do you think?' I asked.

'Definitely. Don't ask me why. I just know that when all our lot's cousins used to come to stay, everybody wanted the sleeping bags. And the bunk beds.'

'I have bunk beds at our place for Noah and Lucas. They do love them. I don't think they have sleeping bags, though – I'll check.'

I won't, but maybe Tabby could.

'You can get them in the outdoor shop beside White's. They're not all that expensive and they'll last a lot longer than toys. The boys must be getting to the age where they'll be invited to sleepovers, so they'll want them for those, too.' Madeleine put her head on one side. 'What are Ray's boys like, Caroline? Are they more like him or her?'

I thought for a moment.

'To look at, Noah is more like Jodie, I suppose – graceful, elegant. Mousy hair, like hers, although Jodie's has *very* expensive highlights. Lucas is more of a bull, like Ray, and he got the red hair. But I don't think they resemble either of their parents in personality. Noah is very serious, thoughtful, quiet. I worry about him bottling things up. Lucas is a live wire – he grabs everything by the horns.'

'I'm never having kids,' Suzanne said.

'That's what I said, but feelings change,' Madeleine replied.

'Mine won't. I suppose I might consider it if I could have a nanny to look after it and take it away if it started whingeing.'

'You're all heart,' Richie said.

'You see, you're assuming I'm callous, but isn't it better not to have kids you don't want, rather than have them and neglect them?'

'When your biological clock starts ticking, you'll soon change your tune,' Madeleine said.

'Er, I'm thirty-three – I think if it was going to tick it would have started by now.'

'I still say when you meet the right man, you'll get broody

like everyone else,' Madeleine insisted. 'The hard face doesn't fool me, girlie.'

Suzanne gawped at her. 'What hard face?' She looked at me and Richie. 'Is that how you all think of me?'

Before we could answer, Fergus strode in.

'Right, troops – what have we got?' he asked.

'First Fifteen captain complaining that the run of severe weather means a backlog of fixtures all coming up together,' Richie said. 'It's happened before, but not this bad. Might make a back-page lead – I'll keep an eye on it. A few rumours floating around regarding January transfers, but I'll need to do a bit more digging.'

'Good. Caroline?'

'Just writing up court – it was a short one, and nothing unusual this week. Also, the food bank is in crisis. They say they're seeing a surge in clients and their stock is running critically low. They still have lots of pasta and breakfast cereals, but they particularly need tinned meat and veg, fruit juice, tea and coffee and a few other things. They're also appealing for all sizes of nappies and women's sanitary products.'

'OK. Season of goodwill – I'd like to think if we write it our local community will step up. Organise a picture and get a full shopping list of exactly what they need and all drop-off points. Anything else?'

'Snow fell on Lapland, so the twins got their wish – the charity is sending a press release and pics tomorrow.'

'Great.'

'When I get a minute, I thought I might ring round the charity shops and card shops, find out if Christmas-card sales are holding up, or if we think it's dying out. I could check stamp sales at the post office, too.'

'Yes, do that.'

'And they're running the twilight market on the plaza again, with all the artisanal food, drink and crafts – I thought we could run a preview.'

'Sounds good. Suzanne?'

'I have to speak to the proprietor of the Windmill coffee shop about their refurb for an ad feature.'

'And after that?'

'I don't have anything else yet.'

'Did you ever contact the dog pound?'

'No.'

'Well, get on to that today or it'll be too late. And it was the Mothers' Union Christmas party for the elderly at St Gregory's last night – give them a ring and find out how it went. If you're at a loose end, there's always a stack of press releases on my desk – help yourself.'

'Yes, boss.'

The food-bank people were grateful that the paper was interested.

'June Black told me you were the one to speak to,' the spokesperson said on the phone. 'She said you wouldn't let us down.'

She gave me good quotes, stating that local demand had more than quadrupled in the past year and that they were struggling to fulfil their role. 'We could really do with more volunteers,' she said. 'Especially anyone who speaks French or Portuguese, if there is anyone out there. It would be a big help. And we desperately need more stock – I can give you the list, and it's available in all our big local supermarkets, too. If it's not convenient for someone to shop for us, there's also an option to set up a direct debit and every penny of it will go on food-bank supplies.'

The picture looked bleak – more and more families on the breadline, reduced to accepting charity to feed themselves. Was there anything hopeful to report?

'Oh, absolutely!' the spokesperson said. 'We regularly have visits from people who've been clients themselves. Once they get on their feet they come and ask what they can do to help. Some volunteer and others become very generous donors.'

I wondered if I could speak to someone like that and the woman said to give her an hour and she'd see what she could do.

I'd had nothing in the fridge with which to make lunch, so I needed to nip out and buy something.

I threw on my parka and pulled up the hood before peering out the window and taking a good look up and down the street. No Mark.

Outside, the day was bitterly cold. I thought of the people dependent on food banks – what were the chances they had money for fuel to heat themselves?

'Caroline?' The voice made me jump.

'Ralph!'

'Sorry, did I startle you?'

'Maybe a bit – I must have been miles away.'

'On your lunch break?'

'Yes. What brings you out and about? I thought after this morning's sitting you'd be long gone.'

'Oh, you know, Christmas shopping.'

'Really? We're not exactly Oxford Street.'

'I'm glad I bumped into you. Have you eaten yet?'

'No.'

'In that case, could we have lunch together?'

My brain whirred. There was the fact that Ralph was another married man and a well-known resident magistrate. And then there was the matter of Mark, and me trying to stay out of sight as much as possible.

'There's something I want to talk to you about,' Ralph said. 'Please.'

I looked into his face and saw that he was pleading with me. 'OK,' I said. 'But do you mind if we just duck in here to Ramsey's instead of wandering about?'

'Are you trying to avoid someone?'

'It's a long story.'

'Ramsey's it is.'

Ralph told me he had pancreatic cancer and just months to live.

'I can't believe it,' I said, although, when I searched his face, I saw that he looked thinner, tired, ill.

'My father was dead at fifty, so I've already had fifteen years more than he did. The kids are all settled and the mortgage was cleared long ago, so it could be worse.'

'How has Judith taken it?'

'I've had a bit of treatment and she thinks I'm clear. I haven't told her it's terminal yet. I haven't told anyone.'

'You've told me.'

'Except you. That's because I have something to ask you. A proposition.' I must have looked dubious, because he quickly went on; 'I want to write a book about my life. I've seen and done a lot of interesting things and I'd like to put it down on paper. Whether or not it ever gets published isn't important – I just want to leave a record. I think I should. But when I say write it … well, I'm not a writer. It would take me for ever and it might not be any good. So I'd like you to do the actual writing, if you're willing.'

'Me?'

'You're the professional. I appreciate that you already have a full-time job, but I hope this is something you could do on the side. I could tell you my tales and you could knock some sense into them. It would mean a lot.'

'You must know much better journalists than me.'

'Don't talk yourself down. The only reason you work on a little provincial weekly is because that's what you want. You could have gone all the way to the top, if you'd decided to. I read everything you write for the *Tribune*, you know.'

'Thank you. A book, though – I've never written one, so I don't know if I've got it in me.'

'I'd provide all the material. You'd just have to weave it together. Say you'll think about it, at least.'

I ordered steak and Guinness pie because lifelong diabetes schooled you in eating sensibly if at all possible, even faced with a disintegrating family, a malicious shade, and now a dying friend. You could limp along on Lucozade for a day or two, but no longer – not if you were striving to survive. Ralph, normally an enthusiastic diner, picked at a chicken Caesar salad but managed a glass of Malbec.

'Why haven't you told Judith the truth about the cancer?'

'Because she'll want to nurse me. And I accept there'll come a time when I might need that, but I'd prefer to put it off for as long as possible. Once I say it, it's out there – there's no going back. I want us to be husband and wife, not patient and carer, while we can.'

'I can still hardly believe it.'

'I've accepted it. I'm a bit put out – I was looking forward to spending my retirement fishing – but there it is.'

We sat in silence for a moment, then Ralph said, 'I contemplated leaving her, you know, to be with you.'

'You never told me that.'

'I didn't stay with her because I loved her more, but because of all the people who would have been affected by my leaving – not least you. I didn't want to saddle you with a family I'd broken by my own hand, who would resent you or blame you as well as me. And, of course, you might not have wanted me, anyway.'

'It certainly would have been difficult. But I suppose it's flattering to know you considered it.'

'I'm not a coward, Caroline. But maybe I was a bit too pragmatic when I should have followed my heart. We'll never know.'

We ate our food and talked about books we'd read recently, and then I said I really would have to get back to work. Ralph helped me on with my coat and kissed my cheek. 'I think I'll take a walk along the towpath,' he said. 'I find it very soothing to be near water. I might ask for my ashes to be scattered into the sea. You will seriously consider writing this book with me?'

I told him I would.

I returned to the office and shrugged off my big coat. When I phoned, the charity shops reported a brisk trade in packs of Christmas cards, although it had now tailed off. The card shops told me their individual card sales were steeply down.

'I don't have figures to hand,' the man from the post office said, 'but I can tell you that young people simply don't buy stamps. It's all older folk.' He concluded that the young sent their greetings free of charge via social media.

The woman from the food bank rang back to say she had spoken to a couple from East Timor who had settled in our town: they had been directed to the food bank when their money ran out and it had been a lifeline for them until they found work. Now they were employed as cleaners in the pharmaceutical packing plant at the industrial estate, where they had set up a thriving donation point supported by the hundreds of staff.

'They work nights, but they'd pop in and see you at your

office some time tomorrow, if that suits you,' the woman said. 'Their English is far from perfect, but you'll definitely get the gist.'

'Will we finish early tomorrow since we've got the Christmas do later?' Suzanne asked.

'Fergus usually lets us go about four,' I said.

'And is there free drink all night?'

'There'll be wine on the table, and the owner usually puts something behind the bar. You shouldn't need to put your hand into your pocket.'

It was dusk as I walked to my car, having left by the fire-escape back door and gone the long way round. Just in case. Christmas carols were playing through speakers along the street and the festive-lights display on the lamp-posts had come on.

This would be Ralph's last Christmas, I supposed. He told me he had come to town because of Barden's, the little antique jeweller's on Scotch Street. He intended to buy Judith an eternity ring, and he wanted it to be something special – at least unusual, if not unique.

I remembered how Ralph had taken me fishing once, for a whole day. We had stood in the middle of the river in waders and waited and waited, silently. Neither of us caught anything, but we did share the encounter of an otter at close quarters, which was thrilling, and later a kingfisher. Nothing much happened – we progressed steadily down the river and sat on the bank for a picnic lunch. I don't think we even ended up in bed but, on reflection, that had been one of the happiest days of my life.

I tried to imagine if he had left Judith and come to me. I thought Tabby would have liked him and he would have liked her. She hadn't rung or texted me since Saturday morning. I wished she would.

Of course, if I'd been with Ralph, then I wouldn't have started seeing Ray again, and I wouldn't now be facing my daughter's disapprobation and exile from the lives of Noah and Lucas. What would Ray have made of Ralph? Would he have been jealous? Jodie, of course, would have told him his job – her position on crime and punishment largely being to lock up offenders and throw away the key. She blamed (a) bad parenting for producing bad kids, and (b) people who wanted it all handed to them on a plate. Not for Jodie suspended sentences or Open University degrees in prison. If she didn't want to hang criminals, she would happily have flogged them.

Not for the first time, it struck me how much of our lives hung on a small number of decisions. Ralph might have left Judith, but he hadn't. Ray might have given the gift-shop marking to someone else, and never have met Jodie, but he hadn't. Of course, no Ray and Jodie would also mean no Noah and Lucas, so that was unthinkable. Every day we made choices, some of which we believed small and insignificant but which would radically shape the course of our lives. And then there were other choices, ones we knew were huge, some we wished others would take away from us and decide on our behalf, decisions we would have to live with, from which we might try to run and hide, but which would return to haunt us. Oh, Mark – haven't we both suffered enough?

There was already a thin mist of ice on my car windscreen. I took the can from the pocket on the back of my seat, shook it and sprayed the glass. The can felt light – I would need to stock up on more.

I threw my bag onto the passenger seat and put on the CD player, where I had slotted in Tabby's favourite *Carols from Trinity* that morning. 'Adam Lay Ybounden'. Voices as clear as crystal. It would be nice just to go home, kick off my shoes, listen to carols, and maybe fire off a conciliatory text to Tabby.

A driver stuck in the tailback kindly waved me out of the car-park exit and into the slow flow of Canal Street. I raised my hand and mouthed thanks.

I had only moved three or four car lengths when I had to stop again for the pedestrian crossing. There was a woman pushing a buggy. The child let something fall to the ground, and a man walking behind them reached forward, picked it up and handed it to the woman. I hadn't even really been looking at them – I was more focused on the traffic lights – but the man's gait seized my attention. He was in profile, rather than face-on, but when I looked, I knew that nose, that chin.

'No,' I whimpered. For just a moment, he turned my way, touched his fingertips to my car bonnet and looked directly at my windscreen, although he seemed unable to see me. But there was no mistaking that face.

Mark.

13

I was half watching the evening news, and eating the slice of toast intended to maintain my blood-sugar level until the meal at the Arlington later without ruining my appetite, when my phone rang. The national bulletin was just giving way to the local report as the call came.

I got as far as hearing that a man was in a serious condition in hospital, but didn't catch details of the incident, as I needed to see who was getting in touch – it might be Tabby.

Picking up my phone, I was surprised to find that it was Pop – Jodie's father.

Pop was a well-known figure in our town. He had been an insurance broker for years – a very successful one, making his money before people sorted out such things for themselves online. I didn't particularly like him. He was opinionated, could be tactless and spoke to his wife, Naomi, as if she was stupid. He was boastful about his son, who worked for a merchant bank in London, but who rarely came home. And the real apple of Pop's eye was Jodie.

It was Jodie whom Pop consulted when choosing their new car – a very swish Audi – and it was she, rather than Naomi, who had selected all the cupboard fronts, surfaces and appliances when Pop decided it was time for a new kitchen.

He had funded the establishment of her gift shop – although, to be fair, Jodie had proven an able businesswoman and it looked like the shop was doing well.

So why was Pop ringing me now? Had Jodie just told him about my affair with Ray? Did he need to have his say?

I could have ignored the call, but I didn't. Maybe this was how it went – Pop would admonish me, call me names, condemn me but this might be a necessary step, and the first in the process of my rehabilitation. Which was what I wanted.

'Hello, Stanley,' I said.

'It's not Pop,' a little voice replied. 'It's me.'

My heart swelled. 'Noah?'

'Mummy wouldn't let me and Lucas ring you on her phone, but Pop said I could use his. It's a secret, though.'

'OK. Did Mummy tell you why she wouldn't let you call?'

'She said we weren't friends with you any more. I asked her why not, but she wouldn't explain.'

'It's a bit tricky, Noah. I'm afraid I did something very silly, which upset your mum, so she's very cross with me, right now. But I hope after a while she'll forgive me.'

'What did you do?'

'If I told you all about it, I think it might make Mummy even more upset. Better just wait and hope that it blows over.'

'We're going on a winter-sun holiday for Christmas. We're going to be on the beach.'

'Oh? Where are you going?'

'The Moll Deeves.'

The Maldives. Where Ray had taken Jodie for their honeymoon. That made a statement. So there was no way I would see any of them on Christmas Day.

'Who's going? You and Mummy and Dad and Lucas?'

'Yes. And Nana and Pop. And maybe Tabby.'

Tabby was going to the Maldives for Christmas with all the Rankins? It would have been Jodie's idea to invite her. Ray would never have done something so cruel.

'You must be excited.'

'I don't want to go.'

'Who doesn't want to have a fantastic beach holiday when everyone else is shivering back at home?' I was trying to sound jolly.

'Me. I like Christmas at our house. And I like Christmas at school. We're singing carols at the old people's home – we've been practising for ages. I'm supposed to be singing 'Little Drummer Boy' with Calum and now I'm going to miss it.' Noah's voice rose as he spat out, 'I hate Mummy and her stupid fucking arrangements.'

I had never heard Noah swear before. Lucas delighted in shrieking, 'Bum!' when cornered, and calling people 'Fartypants', but Noah's speech always carried an air of restraint.

'You don't hate her, Noah,' I said, sighing. 'You're just annoyed because things aren't what you expected.'

'And that's her fault,' Noah replied, a catch in his voice. 'We always have to do what she wants. I don't want to spend Christmas on the beach – I want to stay at home. Could I stay with you?'

Oh, Noah.

'There's no way your mum and dad are going to go on holiday and not bring you,' I said. 'You're their special boy. And I bet you'll have a brilliant time when you get there.'

'Dad says we can go snorkelling.'

'Well, then, that's something to look forward to.'

'I'll have to see you before we go to give you your present. I made it in Craft.'

There was zero chance Jodie would have forgiven me this side of Christmas, and that was fair enough, but I didn't want to compound Noah's misery, so I said, 'I can hardly wait. Do you know when you go away?'

'On Friday. For two weeks. Whatever you did, I'm still your friend, Caroline.'

My eyes filled with the tears that had been threatening since the call began. 'I will always be your friend, Noah – no matter what.'

'I wish you were my mummy.'

I wished I hadn't messed everything up. Just look at the pain I was causing. Would I never learn?

I heard some noise in the background and then Noah said, 'Dinner's ready. I have to go.'

'All right, sweetheart. I'm very glad Pop let you use his phone.'

'I'm sad all the time.'

Please don't say that. 'Because of me and Mummy falling out?'

'Not just that. Nana's calling us. Bye-bye, Caroline.'

'Bye, then. I love you, Noah. I love you lots.'

'I love you lots, too.'

Although I was going through the motions of eating, working, showering, dressing, my inner world was in turmoil. The pebble in my throat was now a permanent fixture. Sometimes my breath came in gasps and I was afflicted with stomach pain and diarrhoea. All of this I hid, because I did not see how I could possibly do anything else, and the additional stress of pretending that everything was hunky-dory was almost the hardest part. The enforced estrangement from the people I thought of as my family was breaking my heart, but even that paled beside the previous evening's sighting of Mark.

I had allowed myself to start imagining that he might just have gone away, when he hadn't found me quickly. Clearly I was wrong. He was close, and possibly closing, but it seemed he hadn't located where I lived yet, or where I worked. This gave me an opportunity to prepare – but prepare how?

When I had got home the day before, I had rushed round the house, still in my coat, taking down all pictures of Tabby and stashing them in drawers under beds. If he didn't know about her, he couldn't hurt her.

It occurred to me now that perhaps the Maldives holiday was a godsend – what better way to hide the fact that I had a daughter than to spend Christmas alone? And Tabby would be thousands of miles away from Mark's poison.

As I dried my hair, I resolved to text her and urge her to go with her dad and his family – it was the opportunity of a lifetime, I would say. It was my own fault that I had caused a rift and we would have plenty more Christmases together. I could lie and tell her that Madeleine had invited me to her place for Christmas dinner – if Mads found out I was going to be on my own, there was every chance she would do exactly that. I would keep it upbeat, convince my daughter that a free sunshine holiday was a great idea. I knew her passport was up to date. Would she be reluctant to leave Harry, though, when her new romance seemed to be going well? Not too reluctant, I hoped.

The cab came on time and I pulled the front door behind me, slamming it locked.

'Christmas party?' the driver asked.

'How did you guess?'

'It's all Christmas parties.'

We stopped off to pick up Madeleine. I did my best to choke down my anxieties. Showtime again for good old Caroline. 'Your hair's lovely,' I said.

'Yes, I'm very pleased with it. Trust you to look great when you probably just ran a brush through yours.'

'Excuse me! I had a shower!'

'Who else are we collecting?'

'Richie next, then Suzanne.'

'I've never been to Suzanne's place before,' Madeleine said. 'Have you?'

I hadn't.

Richie appeared on the doorstep of his canal-side apartment, wearing a dark grey suit and a black shirt.

'He's scrubbed up well,' Madeleine said.

Richie sat in the front seat and, after turning to us for a moment, spent the rest of the journey talking to the driver.

Suzanne lived in a small, white-rendered mid-terrace house in a former social-housing estate, which was now more aspirational. The driver cursed the narrowness of the street for turning, congested as it was by lots of parked cars because the houses had been built in the 1950s without driveways.

Suzanne emerged from her doorway in a long black coat.

Madeleine tutted and said, 'I can't see what she's wearing. I didn't see what you were wearing, either, Caroline.'

'Just a dress,' I said.

'Colour?'

'Red.'

'Red-red, or wine?'

'Just red.'

'You'll suit it, I'm sure – you suit everything.'

'Thank you – even if you managed to make that sound resentful rather than complimentary.'

'Sorry.' Madeleine smacked herself on the back of the hand. 'But I have to have a little snipe at slim people. It's the prerogative of the amply proportioned.'

When we arrived at the hotel, I looked all around me but couldn't see Mark. There was absolutely no reason why he would be attending a Christmas party for various local small businesses, and I still believed he had been staying at the Tyrrell Talbot when he had spotted me and set upon poor Eric. All in all, reason to try to relax just a little.

'Let's get rid of these coats,' Madeleine said. 'Then I'm ready for a drink.'

We shrugged off our outdoor garb, and Madeleine took a step back. 'You said it was a dress – but *what* a dress!' she exclaimed.

'You like it?' I had bought it in a sale at the end of the summer, because when I had tried it on it fitted me like a glove, but I had never reckoned it a showstopper. It was figure-hugging, sleeveless, with a high neck and a low, sweeping back. Maybe it was a better garment than I'd thought.

'You've got a ridiculously fine figure for a woman your age,' Madeleine said mournfully. 'You fill that dress in all the right places.'

Suzanne said nothing and we said nothing to her. She had taken off her coat to reveal an astonishingly short black skirt, sheer black tights, stilettos, and a white top with a plunging neckline. She had gone for big, spidery eyelashes and crimson lipstick, which accentuated the imbalance between her thin top lip and bulbous lower one.

Later, Madeleine would say that Suzanne was desperate to be thought sexy, but went about it in all the wrong ways. I wafted the comment away and told her it was Christmas and to leave the girl alone. There were worse crimes than wearing unflattering clothes.

The meal was about what you'd expect from a night like that, and wasn't helped by the fact that I was washing it down with water instead of wine.

'You're allowed a drink or two,' Paddy Madden whispered in my ear, as the tables were pushed back for the dancing. 'All things in moderation.'

So then, because everyone else was getting drunk and I wanted to loosen up, I had a spritzer.

'You dancing?' Fergus asked, when the band began to play a Roxy Music song.

'You asking?' I replied, with a smile.

Fergus always danced with everyone at Christmas. It was hard to tell whether he actually enjoyed it, or merely regarded it as desirable in terms of bonding with his team. He'd had a bit to drink, as had Paddy, and I fully expected that, by the end of the night, they would be in the middle of the floor with their ties around their heads.

'I wanted to be Bryan Ferry when I was sixteen,' Fergus said.

'My dad looked a bit like him.'

'No way – really?'

'M-hmm. Not that it meant anything to him – he was strictly into his fifties music.'

'I'm afraid 'The Hucklebuck' doesn't do anything for me.'

'Mum and Dad were Elvis fans.'

'Mine was the generation that reviled him – quite unfairly. I guess we needed to kick back against something. Did we miss out, do you think?'

'I still have all their old albums, but I never listen to them. Too many memories – both good and bad, now. It would wreck my head.'

'Understood. Well, that was nice. Think I can drop you off and pick up Madeleine for a spin?'

'She's adamant she won't be dancing, tonight.'

'Let's see what another couple of Gallianos can do.'

I didn't even reach my seat before Paddy grabbed my hand and whisked me back onto the floor. This time we didn't chat, just threw ourselves into the dancing.

'Where did she learn to do that?' I heard Suzanne's voice ask, but I didn't listen for an answer.

After three spritzers, I decided to go home. I wasn't going to drink to get drunk, and that was what nights like these thrived on.

A well-oiled Madeleine was putting the world to rights with Arlene from advertising, the men were leaning against a wall, chatting, and Suzanne was nowhere to be seen. I would just slip away.

In the foyer, I was digging out my phone and wondering if I would have to wait ages for a cab when Suzanne appeared at my elbow.

'You leaving? Want a lift?'

'I was heading home, yes.'

'Cab should be here any minute – I booked it half an hour ago.'

'I thought you'd be here to the death.'

'Bit of an old crowd. Plus people keep mistaking me for a waitress. I'm going on somewhere, meeting my mates.'

'Well, then, a lift would be great. Did anyone tell you we don't have to turn up for work until lunchtime tomorrow? Fergus will hold the fort by himself.'

'I heard. Fair do's.'

The car arrived, and in a few minutes I was deposited at my door.

'Thanks, Suzanne. See you tomorrow.'

'No problem. And I liked your dress, by the way. You've got style, Caroline.'

'Thanks!'

There was no sign that there had been any aggrieved visitors at my door and no messages on my landline when I checked. I kicked off my shoes, slipped out of my dress and into my dressing-gown and tried to concentrate on a late movie.

At 1 a.m., my mobile rang. Suzanne. She was probably bladdered, I guessed. Calling to be horrible, or calling to be lovely – you could never predict how it would go when some people got drunk.

'Caroline?'

'Suzanne.'

'I've just had the most amazing conversation.'

'Oh?'

She didn't sound particularly slurred.

'When I went on for a drink with the girls, I ran into this guy who was a colleague of yours, years ago. Anyway, now he's features editor on a whole stable of glossy magazines and he reckons he can put some work my way. He told me to send him three or four of my best feature articles and he'd read them, and if he likes my writing I can start pitching to him straight away. He said there's far too much being written by city slickers and jaded old-timers and he wants to encourage younger voices from the provinces, writing about what's relevant to them. I thought I might send him over the front page about the young girls who want to be allowed to wear trousers to school in winter – it's not exactly a feature, but it's something different and it was well-written, wasn't it?'

'Absolutely! That's great news!' I said, swallowing a yawn and trying to blink away the sleepiness that was starting to overpower me. 'Who was the guy? Not Colin Dobson?' Colin and I had been cub reporters together at the *Gazette* a long time ago, and I had heard recently that he'd got some big appointment. And then there was David Penrose – I had never actually worked with him, but we had done our college training together and he hadn't hung about in the provincial press for five minutes before he was off to better things.

'I've got his email address here,' Suzanne said. 'Let me fish it out and I can tell you exactly what he was called. But it's good news, isn't it, Caroline? Don't tell everyone, though – I'm going to keep it quiet until I see if I actually get anywhere. Would I have to ask Fergus about using the story about the schoolgirls, though, since it was a *Gazette* story first? I'll just be a minute. It's bloody lucky I went to the Tyrrell Talbot to meet the girls, instead of staying at the Arlington. He was called Mark something ...'

'Mark?'

'Yeah. He's staying there. He said you'd remember him for sure.'

'Was this man tall, with dark hair?'

'That's him. Good-looking guy, fifties.'

Oh, God.

'You didn't tell him anything about me ... Suzanne?'

'Not really. I just gave him your phone number. He said he'd love to catch up.'

'My mobile?'

'And your landline.'

First day of journalism school, *first* lesson – you don't give out colleagues' private numbers. But Suzanne didn't go to journalism school. And, anyway, everyone shared mobile numbers these days.

'Caroline?'

'I have to go, Suzanne.'

'Yeah. Sorry to ring so late, but I was buzzing.'

'I suppose you told him what paper you write for.'

'Yeah. Course. He was interested.'

'And you told him I worked there, too.'

'Sure. I think he might be planning to take you to lunch. Put in a good word for me – won't you?'

'Did you tell him anything about me? About Tabby?'

'No. We talked about journalism, not family.'

'And did he say anything ... unexpected, about me?'

'Like what?'

'I don't know – anything?'

'Don't think so. But he remembered you all right.'

Mark would remember me to the end of time, and I him. But, oh, how I wished we could both forget. I set the phone down and wrapped my arms around myself. He had come for me. There was no escape. But could I hold him back until after Friday, until Tabby was high in the sky, flying away?

Here it came again, the soft click as the record turned, the connection as stylus hit vinyl.

Somehow I had to.

14

I lay awake for most of the night, afraid to sleep. How well had Suzanne remembered her conversation with Mark? Could she have given him my address and then forgotten? Could she have told him I had a daughter?

Now that he had my phone numbers, he could ring me any time. My mobile would show who was calling – or, at least, that it was someone not in my contacts list – but I didn't have caller display on the landline in the kitchen.

When morning came, I had no choice but to do my jab and eat breakfast like any other day. My hand shook as I held my insulin pen.

I had spent the last hours anticipating what Mark would say if he rang, and trying to formulate my side of the conversation.

If he wanted to meet, I would agree. But I would say I was too busy with work until Friday. I hoped that would hold him at arm's length until Tabby was out of the country.

Maybe, when he saw me, we really would talk. There was always a chance that he hadn't come to ruin me, but to get some sort of catharsis, after all this time. I supposed it was possible he had moved on long ago and had sought me out now simply to draw a line under things, put the past to bed.

But I didn't really believe any of that. His punching Eric didn't speak of making peace. And the seventeen roses ...

When the kitchen phone rang shortly after 10 a.m., I immediately felt my heartbeat in my throat. Virtually no calls came to the landline, these days.

I tried to take a deep breath, be brave, focus on putting him off until the weekend, which would make me so much less vulnerable.

'Hello?'

'Caroline?'

Not his voice. Not him. A woman.

'Caroline, this is Doris.'

Doris – of course – the only member of the family who still rang me on the landline because for some reason she had it in her head that I needed to keep my mobile free for work calls at all times.

'Hi, Doris. How are you?'

'We're all right. But I'm ringing to hear about you. Ray told us what happened. He's worried about you and so are we. I rang your office, to see if we could take you out for lunch, but the man said you weren't there. Are you OK, Caroline?'

This put me in a difficult situation. I had no way of knowing whether Ray had revealed to his parents the truth about our affair and discovery, or some cover story for why I was banished from Ray and Jodie's during the normally festive season. 'Yes, I'm fine, Doris. It was the staff do, last night, so we were all given the morning off, that's all. Ray told you ...?'

'We're not taking sides, Caroline. These things are complicated and it's not always easy to say who was right and who was wrong. We still think of you as our daughter-in-law – we care about you.'

'Thank you.'

'Bob's out walking the dog, so I can say this – women have needs, Caroline. I understand that. You've had to make a life for yourself and you've done a great job of it – holding down a career, raising Tabitha, running your house and your car – but you can't do everything for yourself. Sometimes you need the heat of another body.'

Doris!

'From the day and hour Ray walked out of your marriage, Bob said: "He'll be back." He said there was unfinished business between the two of you.'

'I shouldn't have let it happen.'

'It takes two to tango.'

'I didn't hear your names mentioned in this Maldives line-up. You're not going?'

'What would we want with eating our Christmas dinner in

twenty-nine degrees? No. They invited us, but we didn't fancy it, and we didn't like the way everyone was included except you. If Stanley and Naomi want to go along with that, then that's up to them, but we said, no thank you. To be perfectly honest, we're quite happy having Christmas in our own house this year, and we're hoping you'll join us.'

'Really? That's very kind.'

I supposed it might be nice. Doris and Bob's home always felt like a real home.

'Good. That's settled. Will we have turkey, or would you like something else for a change?'

'Oh, turkey, please, Doris. It wouldn't feel like Christmas without it.'

'It might not be as fancy as what you'd get at Jodie's, but there'll be plenty of it.'

'I'm sure it will be delicious. But aren't you worried that having me over will rub Jodie up the wrong way?'

'Jodie isn't perfect. Who we invite for Christmas is our business.'

'Doris, you couldn't do me a favour?'

'What's that, Caroline?'

'Tabby's being a bit off with me, since the thing with her dad and me came out. It's completely understandable, she has every right to feel aggrieved, and I want to give her some space, but you couldn't just check for me if she's definitely decided to go on this holiday with them? Even though I was hurt, at first, about them asking her to go away at this time of year, I actually think she should join them. It would be good for Noah and Lucas to have her around if there's a bit of friction between their mum and dad. This should be one of her free mornings, if you could try her now.'

'I'll ring her straight away and call you back,' Doris said. 'Give me five minutes. And she'll come round, too, you know, Caroline, in time.'

I hung up and looked for something useful to do until Doris came back to me. I emptied the kitchen bin and the compost caddy and gave the floor a quick brush.

The landline rang again.

'Hi, Doris. What news?'

Silence.

'Hello?' I said. 'Doris?'

Nothing.

'Who is this, please?'

A cold trickle of sweat ran down between my shoulder blades.

If Mark was right there, at the other end of this line, it was the closest we had been in three decades. I'd had a marriage, a child and a career in that time, so why should I be afraid of him? Yet I was.

'Why are you doing this?' I heard my voice say, but it didn't feel like it was mine at all. Why didn't I just hang up?

The silence suddenly gave way to background noise.

'Mrs Rankin?'

'Hello?'

'Am I speaking to Mrs Rankin?'

'Yes. It's Ms, actually. But yes.'

'Your service plan for a tumble dryer is due to expire on

the thirty-first of December. For just twenty-nine ninety-nine you can renew for twelve months – that's covering you for breakdown, all parts and labour. We sent you a letter.'

My breath rushed out in a gush. I hadn't realised I'd been holding it.

'Mrs Rankin?'

'Yes, thank you. I'll think about it. Can you call me again in a few days?'

'Someone could ring you on Friday.'

'Friday. Yes, that's fine.'

I set the phone down, put my head in my hands and began to cry.

As I made my way into the office, I was coaching myself. I would ask to speak to Fergus, tell him the stalker I had mentioned had now found out where I worked, and request to work from home for a few days to stay out of his way.

Fergus would insist I inform the police, so I would nod and agree. He wouldn't know I had done nothing of the sort.

Unable to get access to me via the office, Mark would most likely ring me, now that he had my numbers. I would listen to him, indulge him in any way I could think of, and agree to meet him on Friday. And I would meet him. It was the only way to finish this.

A hand grabbed my arm and I leapt in shock.

'You're a bit jumpy! Hungover?'

It was Suzanne.

'Probably.'

We seemed to be the last to arrive – everyone else was downstairs in the ad department, with all eyes on Richie.

'And *did* you see anything?' Arlene was asking him.

'How could I?' he said. 'I was here.'

Madeleine turned at the swish of the door opening.

'Big story for one of you pair – the man attacked by the canal on Monday afternoon was none other than Ralph Nicholson, our resident magistrate. He's in hospital with head injuries. Police were conducting a house-to-house round Richie's way this morning.'

I clutched the nearest desk to steady myself. This was the report I had only partially heard on the television news the night before – I had stopped listening to check my phone.

'Who said it was Ralph?' I asked.

'The security woman from the courthouse – she was in the Candy Box when I was collecting the dailies.'

'Is he going to be all right?'

Madeleine shrugged. 'Nobody seems to know. And nobody knows what he was doing there, just walking along the canal, by himself, in the middle of the afternoon. Makes you wonder.'

'Wonder what, exactly?' I asked indignantly.

'Well, the canal's a meeting place, isn't it, for a certain type of person?'

'Madeleine, do not say another word,' I warned her.

She looked at me in pure surprise. 'What's eating you?'

'Ralph's a friend.'

'Caroline, a word in my office,' Fergus interjected.

I shot a look at Madeleine and followed him upstairs.

'Were you still seeing him?' Fergus asked, when his office door was safely closed.

'No. That all ended years ago.'

'Good. But you're still upset. Look, do you want to kill two birds with one stone? You could go to the hospital, see for yourself how Ralph is and also find out anything you can for the paper.'

'If he's in ICU I won't get anywhere near him – it'll only be family.'

'If you find that he's in ICU, that's a story in itself. If he isn't, you might get to see him.'

'I would like to talk to him, if he's well enough. I ran into him here in town on Monday – he was Christmas shopping in Barden's. He's ill, Fergus. I mean, he was already ill before he was attacked.'

'How ill?'

'As bad as it gets. But nobody knows. Not even Judith.'

Fergus wouldn't tell. 'You up to this?'

'I'm a tough old bird. You know that.'

'I know nothing of the sort.' He looked at me. 'You disappeared early last night – everything all right?'

'Just tired,' I said. 'But one more week and it's practically the holiday. I'll rest up then.'

Our owner gave us a full week off every year, from Christmas to New Year. It was one of the main reasons we all gratefully chipped in and bought him a painting by a local artist as a present.

'After you've been to the hospital, go on home,' Fergus said. 'Have a bubble bath and put your feet up.'

'OK.'

I found out from Reception where Ralph's bed was. He wasn't in ICU but was in a regular ward, where I had no trouble gaining access when I whispered to the nurse that I was family and had come a very long distance. I probably looked sufficiently fatigued for her to believe me.

She led me to a side room with its door open. Inside, I could see a woman sitting by the bedside, a young man and a young woman trying to keep a small girl from climbing onto the bed, plus another young woman fiddling with the zip on her boot.

In the bed lay a man I could so easily have fallen in love with at one time. His poor face was cut and bruised and I didn't know what other injuries might be out of sight.

It occurred to me that this was another family I could have wrecked, had I let things develop further between Ralph and me – particularly if what he had told me over lunch on Monday was true, about contemplating leaving Judith to be with me. This wife and these young people could have been set on entirely different courses by fury, resentment and loss – they could have been the victims of my choices, rather than Jodie and Tabby and the boys.

Instead, as Ralph said, 'Caroline,' in a clear voice, they all turned round and looked at me blankly.

'This is Caroline, my very good friend,' he announced. 'Since she's here, why don't you all take Jessica to the canteen and leave me to chat for half an hour.'

The woman I assumed to be Judith looked at me dubiously. 'Ralph's very weak,' she began.

'I am making an excellent recovery,' he said. 'And Caroline will only do me good.'

'You haven't had any lunch, Mum. You should eat something,' the young man said. 'Come on. Let's go. Chips, Jessica? Nice to meet you, Caroline.'

He must be Alexander, I thought – the son who had astonished Ralph by going into the Church.

The family filed out, Jessica swinging on her parents' arms and shrieking.

'My granddaughter has autism,' Ralph said, as I sat down. 'It's less commonly diagnosed in girls, apparently because they have stronger social instincts and can imitate more sociable behaviour even if it's only skin-deep.'

'I'm sorry,' I said.

'She's never going to have an easy life. And neither will Alex or Carrie.'

'Will they survive? As a couple, I mean?'

'Oh, yes, I think so. They make a good team. And they have their faith.'

'Ralph, what happened to you?'

'I was mugged – simple.'

Did he really believe that?

'I was struck from behind – quite a blow, apparently, quite a few stitches, and I fell on my face, but I'm all patched up now.'

'Did they hurt you any other way?'

'A few kicks to the ribs when I tried to get up. I quickly decided it was wiser to stay down.'

This was my fault. Mark must have seen us together and followed Ralph to the canal. 'Did you get a good look at them?'

'Unfortunately not. I fell when I was hit and covered my head when I was on the ground. I've told the police I'm pretty sure it was a man, pretty sure it was one chap on his own. Er, is this concern for my welfare or are you news-gathering?'

'We won't print anything you don't approve. Did they say anything?' Don't answer. Please don't tell me the man who beat and kicked you warned you off and told you this was because of me.

'Not a word. Just reached in, took my wallet and left me lying on the canal bank.'

'He took your wallet?'

'I understand it's quite a common feature of a mugging. Almost obligatory.'

Then it hadn't been Mark at all! Mark had no reason to steal from Ralph – not if he could afford to stay at the Tyrrell Talbot. It really had been a mugging – a targeted rather than a vindictive attack on a well-dressed man, walking alone, who looked like he might carry a fair bit of cash. Oh, wonderful!

'Is there anything I can do?'

'Not a thing. It's good to see you, though. Good to know you care. Thank you for coming.'

'I was frightened. I didn't know how badly you were hurt.'

'Ever since I found out I was dying, I've felt strangely indestructible – it's the most peculiar thing. What can life throw at me now? Colours are more vibrant. Music is sweeter. I look at you sitting there and I wish you would close the door and climb into bed with me. Throw caution to the wind – isn't that the most wonderful expression? *Throw* caution *to the wind!*'

'A little bit of me will die with you, you know, Ralph.'

'Thank you, Caroline. I will cherish that little bit, in my grave.'

We talked about fishing – all the places he would take his rod when his injuries mended. He told me about his orchard at home, and how he hoped to see the apple blossom one last time, if not the harvest.

Driving home, I felt utterly relieved that this latest horror, at least, was not down to Mark, not down to me.

I pulled into my driveway, looked up and down the street and saw no one.

There were more cards on the hall mat, and a fat brown Jiffy bag without a name or address. Turning it over, I discovered that it wasn't even sealed. What was it?

I tipped it up and coaxed out the contents. As it emerged, my hands began to tremble. A man's leather wallet. I opened it and saw the driving licence facing me through its film-fronted pocket. It was Ralph's.

15

I suppose I had known Mark would track me down eventually. What was clear, now, was that he was taking some sort of pleasure in toying with me. He could have made a direct approach when he spotted me at the Chamber of Trade Christmas dinner dance, but he had preferred to get at me then through poor, unfortunate Eric, and now via Ralph, who didn't deserve in a million years what he'd got on the canal towpath.

I had been incandescent when I found the wallet the day before. How dare Mark! How dare he hurt someone dear to me! And to take a trophy and then present me with it! He was sick.

He hadn't always been. Once, I had thought the sun rose and

set with him. I would have done anything for him – *did* do, and he for me. But we should never have gone where we went. One thing just led to another, though, and the rush of passion must have drowned those little voices in our heads that had to have been, even then, telling us to stop.

No one ever knew what we did, except the two of us. No one ever found out. I had long stopped thinking that anyone ever would until two weeks before, when I caught that first glimpse of him in the department store.

Where had he been all those years? Had he told anyone our secret? And the same gnawing question: why had he come for me now?

Tabby wasn't going to the Maldives. When Doris finally reached her, apparently Tabby gave her granny a bit of an earful – she was flat out at school, not just with her part-time speech and language hours, but helping out in her time off with bus trips to the pantomime and the cinema and with big messy play sessions for the little ones and a Christmas disco for the senior students. It was meant to be a special time of year and the staff were determined to give the kids all the fun possible. When she wasn't in school, she was needed in the coffee shop, where business was booming. What had made anyone think she could just take off to the sun for two weeks? I felt ashamed – it seemed I still thought of Tabby as a girl, with the freedom of a student to grasp any juicy opportunity that came along, when in fact she was a working woman with serious commitments and responsibilities.

The one good thing was that she was way too busy to come home.

Mark had found me. He knew where I worked, he knew where I lived, he had my phone numbers. He had been watching me, too, so who knew what else he was aware of? Whether I was in the office or on the street or in my home, I was waiting for the hammer to fall. I was a fly trapped in a spider's web, my torn wings glued to the threads, knowing the spider was coming to devour me, and it was torment. But he didn't seem to have a clue about Tabby and I meant to keep it that way.

I was sitting on the sofa, nursing a sad little soup in a cup when I heard a car pull up outside. This could be it.

The doorbell rang.

The doorbell? I think I'd half expected Mark to smash his way in with an axe. The doorbell seemed rather ... polite. But why not?

I hesitated. Once I opened the door, there would be no going back. All the poisonous past would come flowing in. I knew Mark wanted to hurt me, but I didn't know how badly. Was I in physical danger, or was it just my reputation he wanted to destroy? I could have rung the police – could have rung them anytime; *should* have called them after Eric, after Ralph – but I still held out some selfish hope that I might talk Mark round, persuade him to spare me, trade on the fact that we had loved each other once. If I reported him, I'd blow my chance to do any of that. Everything would come out, if he decided it would.

I crept into the hall. The doorbell rang again.

'Who is it?' I said, hearing how weak and ineffectual my voice sounded.

'Caroline? Let me in. It's me – Madeleine.'

Madeleine?

'Hurry up – it's Baltic out here.'

I opened the door.

'Well, come on! Are you going to let me in?'

I stood back. 'Of course. What are you waiting for?'

Madeleine held out her glass. 'Any more of that wine?'

We had been sitting in my lounge for half an hour and I still didn't know why she had come. 'Aren't you driving?'

'I was getting to that. Caroline, can I stay here tonight?'

'Stay here? Why?'

'Jimmy and I have had a bit of a ding-dong.'

What could I do? She was my friend – she was entitled to turn to me. But what if Mark chose tonight to show up? I'd have to listen to Madeleine, show willing, then gently but firmly talk her into going home. And as quickly as possible. 'I see. Well, you know there's always a bed for you here, if you need it. But is that really the best course of action? Wouldn't it make more sense to talk to Jimmy than to me?'

'A night apart will do us both good,' Madeleine said. 'Do I have to go to the fridge myself?'

I took her glass, filled it, brought it back.

'You not having any?'

'I'm trying to cut back.' I needed to stay sharp. 'So what's the row about, or shouldn't I ask?'

'Jimmy's got his knickers in a twist over the cost of this new kitchen.'

'OK. It is a pretty big job. But why now? Why not before the two of you decided to go ahead with it?'

Madeleine made a wincing face. 'I didn't exactly tell Jimmy the whole story.'

'What do you mean?'

'I sort of let him think we had a bond maturing that would cover the cost of things.'

'Madeleine ...?'

'But really I took out a new credit card in his name and used that to pay for everything.'

'Madeleine!'

'I know. A statement came from the credit-card company. I accidentally left it sitting about and Jimmy found it. Anyway, I thought he'd roll his eyes, huff a bit and then laugh about it. Bloody Madeleine – spending more money.'

'But he didn't?'

'He was furious, Caroline. He really flew off the handle.'

'You don't mean ...'

'Oh, he didn't hit me or anything. Jimmy would never! But I've pushed him too far. He said what's the point anyway of the new kitchen? In six months I'll be bored with it and asking for a new bathroom, or a sunroom, and how do I think we're supposed to keep paying for all these projects?'

'And is he right?'

'I didn't think I was that bad. But maybe I am.'

My phone rang. I let it ring. 'So how have you left things?'

'He said we should sell the house, clear all our debts and buy a smaller place.'

'And what did you make of that?'

'It's a bit drastic – isn't it?'

'You don't have to tell me, if you don't want to, but it would help me to answer that if I knew how much debt you were in.'

'I've lost count.'

'Ballpark figure.' Hurry up, Madeleine – I need you out of here.

My phone rang again. 'Sorry,' I said. 'Let me just check who it is.' If it was Mark I didn't know what I was going to do.

Jodie. The missed call was from her, too. Ringing to have another go, no doubt. I could do without that.

'Anything important?' Madeleine asked.

'Definitely not important.'

'Are you in pain, Caroline? The way you're holding yourself ...'

'Stomach cramps. Must be something I ate. Let me just pop to the loo.'

Five minutes later I was back on the sofa, stomach still churning, with Madeleine telling me about her mortgage and the extra twenty K they'd borrowed against the house to do the roof. 'It cost twenty thousand to replace your roof?'

'Fifteen. The old one was asbestos, so it was pricey to remove and dispose of. But I wanted enough for a summerhouse, too, and the trip to Malta.'

'OK, so not counting the mortgages?'

'I don't know exactly. Fifty thousand?'

'Fifty thousand pounds on top of your mortgage? You must be paying out a fortune every month. Does that include the new kitchen?'

'Not really.'

'Madeleine, it either does or it doesn't.'

'Oh, all right – it doesn't. The kitchen's on top. The figure has just sort of crept up, little by little, over the years.'

'And Jimmy never said anything before?'

'I do all the household admin – I do the *Gazette* stuff at work, so I'm good at it, and Jimmy has always been happy to let me.'

'So he didn't know.'

'Well, that's what he's saying – but a blind man could work out that what the two of us were earning wouldn't cover what we were spending, so he must have realised on some level. I don't understand why he's acting so shocked all of a sudden.'

'But he knows the full extent of the debts now?'

'Pretty much.'

'Madeleine?'

'I've booked a little holiday, for after Christmas, for when the kitchen's all done and dusted. I didn't think it was the right moment to tell him.'

'OK. So Jimmy wants to downsize in order to clean the slate and start again, but you don't fancy it. What alternative do you propose?'

For once, Madeleine seemed lost for words.

'Would you prefer just to keep on doing what you're doing? It must be a hell of a burden to carry.'

Madeleine looked at me and I thought she might be about to cry.

'Jimmy said ... he said if I don't wise up and agree to sell the house, then he's leaving.'

'Oh, Madeleine.'

'He means it, Caroline. Jimmy Wilson is not a man given to making rash statements. He's had enough.'

A bit of a ding-dong, indeed!

'Then why on earth are you here? Why aren't you at home saving your marriage?' You need to go home, Madeleine, and I need you out of here.

'I don't know. Because I want him to worry about me, maybe – worry where I am and if I'm OK.'

The tears came then, and what could I do? I put my arms around her and held her tight. She cried and cried.

Afterwards, I persuaded her to ring Jimmy and at least let him know where she was and that she was all right. Then, pretty well convinced that Mark would arrive any minute, but at a loss to see how I could eject Madeleine, I defrosted a tub of chilli from the freezer and thought what a poor dish it was for the condemned woman's last meal.

'Who's that who keeps ringing you?' Madeleine asked, when my phone went again.

I picked it up. 'Jodie.'

'Aren't you going to answer it?'

'I don't much feel like talking to her.'

'Because I've spoiled your mood – brought you down.'

'No. Don't you ever just choose not to pick up?'

'I'm too afraid of missing something interesting.'

'This won't be interesting – trust me.'

'Please yourself.' Madeleine sighed and readjusted herself on the sofa. 'Your Christmas cards look well. This is a nice room, Caroline – have I ever told you that?'

'Mmm.'

'You're a much more content person than I am. I'm constantly looking for the next thing I can buy or do or change – if it isn't my hair it's a holiday, and if it isn't a holiday it's something about the house. It's like an itch. You don't seem to suffer from that chronic restlessness.'

'I thought I had everything I wanted, until very recently.'

'What does that mean?'

'Oh, just that things sometimes aren't as good as they seem.'

My phone rang again.

I glanced at it, wondering why Jodie had decided to become so persistent tonight.

But it wasn't Jodie, it was Pop – or, at least, it was Pop's phone.

Noah?

'Actually, I will take this, Madeleine,' I said.

'No problem. I'll wash up our dishes.'

'Hello?'

It wasn't Pop, and it wasn't Noah, either. It was Jodie, and she sounded hysterical.

'Slow down, Jodie. Please,' I said. I hadn't managed to make out much of what she was saying, but she wasn't angry – she was frightened.

I felt all of the colour drain from my face and neck as I pieced together the fragments of her sob-racked speech. Ray was away at a photo-shoot and she couldn't reach him. She was at the hospital and could I come, come now, right away. He had taken paracetamol. She didn't know how much. Nana and Pop had just arrived but she needed me. Noah needed me.

'My little boy!' she gasped. 'Caroline, they think he might die!'

'I'm coming, Jodie,' I told her. 'I'm coming.'

Madeleine told me to go, go – she'd stay at my place at least until I got back.

I tore out into the dark, chill night, jumped into the car and sped away. The roads were quiet and the distance not far but it was all taking too long. I needed to get there, needed to find out properly what was happening. I needed to be there for Jodie and her parents and Lucas – Lucas! Where was he in all this? – but especially I needed to be there for Noah.

Why had Noah taken paracetamol? By accident? On purpose? Jodie didn't subscribe to medicating problems – she believed in exercise, drinking water, eating properly and pulling yourself together. It was hard to believe she'd had much of a stash even of painkillers.

I arrived at the hospital. The car park was dark and largely empty. The day clinics had closed long ago and it was past visiting time. I took my ticket from the machine and clamped it between my teeth, rolled up my window and swung the car into a bay. Then I grabbed my bag and ran.

'Caroline!'

As I approached the revolving door for the second time in two days, a familiar voice called my name.

'Ralph.'

He was standing some way from the doors, under a section

of overhanging roof with the other vapers, all puffing away in their dressing-gowns.

'I wish you hadn't witnessed this.' He held up his e-cigarette guiltily. 'I wasn't expecting you again, so soon.'

'Sorry, Ralph – I'm not here for you, this time. My ex-husband's little boy has been rushed in, I think – the facts are a bit hazy.'

'Then you must go. Don't let me keep you. What age is he?'

'Nine!' I was pushing my way into the door as I called over my shoulder.

'Kids are resilient!' Ralph called back. 'Let me know if he's all right.'

The foyer was almost deserted and there was no one staffing the reception desk. I looked around frantically for someone to get help or direct me.

'She's just nipped to the loo,' a cleaner who was brushing the coffee-dock floor called. 'She won't be a minute.'

I didn't have a minute. This was too much. Hurry up, hurry up!

When an overweight woman in a red tunic and a lanyard appeared and squeezed nonchalantly in behind the desk, I mumbled and bumbled my way through a ragged explanation.

'Visiting's over,' she said.

'I'm not here for visiting,' I replied, trying to keep my voice calm, although I felt like reaching behind the Perspex screen and shaking out of her the information I needed. 'I'm here because the family asked me. This little boy is very sick and, at the very least, they need me to look after his younger brother, who is probably with them all now in extremely unsuitable circumstances.'

'Has the child been admitted?' the woman asked, sounding bored with me already, and tapping at her keyboard.

'I presume so.'

'Which ward?'

'I don't know – that's what I'm asking you.'

'Do you know the name of the consultant?'

'No. I don't know anything. I've just had a frantic phone call from his mother, who is somewhere in this hospital and going out of her mind with worry. As am I.'

'What's the child's surname?'

'Rankin. I'm Rankin, too.' I dug into my handbag for my purse. 'I can show you my driving licence, if that helps.'

She clicked again on her keyboard, eyes on her monitor. She didn't look at me. 'That won't be necessary. Imelda?' As she called, the cleaner from before trotted over.

'Yes, Davina. What can I do for you?'

'I need you to show this lady to the right place.'

I followed Imelda through a maze of corridors and was grateful for her guidance – I would never have found this from mere instructions, the way I felt.

'This is you now,' she said gently, smiled and melted away.

A few feet ahead of me in the corridor I could see an ashen Pop sitting on a hospital chair. Then I saw Jodie, standing, in a posture so alien from her usual confident dancer's stance that

I hadn't even recognised her at first. She was being comforted by Naomi, the only one of the three who looked strong.

Before I could register another thing, a shape tumbled off the chair next to Pop's, bowled up the corridor towards me, and a little mousy head thudded against my tummy just as a pair of arms flew round my waist and gripped me tightly.

'Noah?' I gasped. 'But I thought ...'

I looked from the small, slight figure attached to me and up at Naomi. She shook her head. Then she pointed to the door of the ward beside us where her grandson must be lying in a bed and, if Jodie was right, fighting for his life, and she mouthed, 'Lucas.'

16

*L*ucas? It was *Lucas* who'd taken the paracetamol?

I gathered that he had drunk some of a bottle of children's medicine – no one knew how much – and had been put straight onto a drip to try to mitigate the toxic effect on his liver. But now wasn't the time for lengthy explanations. Much as I wanted to see Lucas, to squeeze his little hand and kiss his forehead, to sit by his bed and will him to be all right, that wasn't my place. My role was to support Jodie, Stanley and Naomi, in particular by taking Noah home and staying with him.

'I'll take good care of him,' I told a grey-faced Jodie, who had just stepped away from Lucas's bedside to take a breath. Her teeth were chattering.

Noah stood stiffly, his duffel coat over his pyjamas, as each of the adults hugged him tightly. Pop could hardly let him go.

Doris and Bob had been alerted and would keep trying Ray, who had gone to Bruges that morning for work.

'We didn't want to ask them to take Noah, with Bob's angina,' Naomi explained.

Someone would ring me if there were any developments.

We drove across town, where the Christmas decorations lit up the dark, and I wondered if any of us would be celebrating this year or whether we were plunging into an everlasting night.

I checked my rear-view mirror relentlessly, just in case Mark was following, and satisfied myself that he was not. Not that I imagined he would harm Noah, but this was most definitely not the time for a scene.

Jodie and Ray's house was in a small, modern development of large properties in the town's most exclusive suburb. I parked in the wide driveway and unlocked the front door with the key Naomi had given me. Jodie hadn't set the alarm.

'Let's get your coat off,' I told Noah, opening the cloaks cupboard. 'Would you like something to eat?'

'No, thank you.'

'Well, I'm going to have a cup of tea – would you like a cup of tea? Or some warm milk?'

Noah nodded.

'Warm milk?'

'Yes, please.'

The house wasn't cold, but I still felt shivery. I sent Noah for his dressing-gown and quickly texted Madeleine. I had to remain at Jodie's, I told her, but she was to make herself at home at my place and stay as long as she liked. I apologised if supplies of bread and milk were running low.

When Noah didn't return, I went looking for him and found him standing on the landing outside the boys' bedroom door. 'What's up?' I asked.

'I don't want to go in there.'

'Oh?'

'I don't want to see Lucas's empty bed.'

'That's all right,' I said. 'I'll fetch your dressing-gown. You stay there.'

'But where am I going to sleep if I can't go in there?' Noah asked, his voice little more than a whimper.

'How about if I sleep in Lucas's bed, tonight, to look after it for him?' I said. 'I could read to you until you fall asleep.'

'But not just yet,' Noah said.

'No. Not until you're ready.'

Jodie's kitchen was huge, shiny and very clean. The island was nearly as big as my whole kitchen. I persuaded Noah to have a bowl of cereal like me and we ate them at the long refectory table. This wasn't even the main dining table, which stood in its own room, sat twelve, and was dressed with fine china, cut glass and seasonal blooms when we all came together for Christmas dinner.

'We forgot to light the Advent candle, tonight,' Noah suddenly remembered. 'Can we light it now?'

I hunted in the many kitchen cupboards for matches, found them eventually, lit the candle and placed it between us on the table.

'It's better if we switch off the lights,' Noah said.

'Go on, then.'

The candle burnt slowly and it felt like a vigil.

'When the number fifteen burns down, we have to blow it out,' Noah explained. 'Sometimes we forget and then we have to skip a day.'

'Would you like a story?' I asked.

'After the candle.'

So we sat and waited, and when the fifteen had burnt through we went into the lounge where we lit the fairy lights on the tree and read a chapter of *The House at Pooh Corner*, which I'd given Noah one birthday. It made us both laugh to hear little Piglet fantasising about what bold things he'd say to the heffalump when it landed in his trap.

'And now I think it really is time for bed,' I said. 'Ready to clean your teeth?'

'All right. I know where to find you a toothbrush. They're in the drawer under the wash-hand basin.'

'Great! Thanks.'

When Noah got into bed, he folded his hands beneath his cheek and gave a long sigh.

'Try not to worry,' I said, stroking the mousy hair off his forehead and knowing what unsatisfactory advice that was.

'I think it was my fault,' Noah murmured.

'What was?'

'Lucas. I think he took the medicine because of me. I called him a baby.' A tear leaked out of Noah's right eye, trickled down the side of his nose and fell onto the carpet.

'Oh, Noah. We don't know why Lucas took the medicine,' I said. 'You know what a joker he is – he might have thought it was a bit of a prank. Or he might have had a headache or a sore tooth and thought he was doing the right thing.'

'I love him. I don't want him to die.'

'I know.' I pulled up a corner of sheet and wiped his eyes. 'Would you like another story?'

'Could you just talk to me?'

'Sure.'

'Tell me again about when you were a little girl. Tell me about you and your brother.' He wanted to hear tales of a happy childhood, naturally. Anecdotes that would make him feel secure.

'All right. When I was a little girl, I had a big brother. He was a year older than me and everybody called him Wee Maxie.'

'Why did they call him that?'

'Because our surname was Maxwell, and people called my dad Maxie for short, or sometimes Big Maxie, because he was tall – so his son became *Wee* Maxie.'

'Tell me the bit about the baker's son.'

'We knew other boys who had nicknames that related to their fathers – one boy at school was known as Wee Bap, because his dad worked in a bakery.'

Noah gave a little titter. 'And tell me about how Wee Maxie took your stuff.'

I sat down on the floor and leant my back against Lucas's rumpled bed. 'It used to drive me mad, when Wee Maxie took things that belonged to me. I wouldn't have minded sharing, but he always broke everything. I loved drawing and colouring, and I took extremely good care of my felt tips – that's markers, to you.'

'Mummy doesn't let us have markers, in case the ink gets on the furniture. We're only allowed coloured pencils.'

'My mum was house-proud, too. Lots of mummies are. Anyway, I used to keep them in a pink fluffy pencil case, but Wee Maxie would come along when I was doing something else ...'

'What were you doing?'

'Oh, I was probably out on my bike with my friends.'

'What were they called?'

'There was Alison. And Deirdre. And Julie. And Dawn.'

Noah yawned, and I made a mental note to come up with more lists, if it would help him get to sleep.

'So Wee Maxie would come along when I wasn't there and take my felt tips, but he left all the tops off them, and by the time I discovered what he'd done, they'd dried up. Useless. I was so cross.'

'What else did he take?'

'I've told you this before.'

'Tell me again.'

'My roller skates. My mum and dad bought me roller skates for my seventh birthday. They weren't like the roller boots that you see now – they were flat grey metal and they had a key that went underneath that you could turn to make them bigger or smaller, depending on the size of your feet.'

'And what did Wee Maxie do?'

'He decided to take my roller skates for a spin himself, but his feet were bigger, so he had to extend them. He did it too roughly and he broke them.'

'What did you say?'

'I can't remember exactly, but I'm sure it wasn't very nice.'

'Did you say, "I hate you"?'

'It's quite possible. And sometimes I did feel like I hated him. But not for long, because really I loved him and he knew that.'

'Did you go to after-school, when you were a little girl?'

'No, I didn't. My mum only worked in the mornings and on Saturdays, when I was very young. After school she was at home with us.'

'With you and Wee Maxie.'

'That's right.'

'Lucas doesn't like after-school.'

'Oh? Why's that?'

'Roberta put mustard on his tongue because he said a bad word.'

She did *what*? 'Who's Roberta?'

'She's in charge.'

Was she, indeed? Watch this space.

'And she told him that God could see him even when he was doing a poo.'

'Noah, did Lucas tell Mummy and Daddy about Roberta?'

'I don't know. I don't think so. But he didn't want to go there any more.' Noah yawned again, and this time he rolled onto his stomach and I knew he was falling asleep. He'd had a long and eventful day.

'Night-night, Noah,' I whispered, and when he didn't

answer I thought it was safe to step out onto the landing and make a couple of calls. I'd have to let Tabby know what was happening – she had a right to be informed and she would be furious if I didn't contact her. And I would ring Fergus and tell him I couldn't work the next day. I wasn't in the habit of phoning in sick and in these circumstances I was sure he would understand.

Fergus was as sympathetic as I'd known he would be. He told me to take as long as I needed, and asked if there was anything he could do. I thanked him, said I'd keep him updated and that I thought it was in the hands of the doctors and nurses now.

Try as I might, I couldn't reach Tabby. If she was sulking with me, she couldn't have picked a worse time. All I could do was keep on ringing at intervals.

I would have loved a glass of wine from the well-stocked cooler in the kitchen, but I wasn't willing to let Noah wake up and find Lucas's bed empty as he had feared, so I took off my shoes, jeans and cardigan and lay down under Lucas's duvet.

Noah's special requests for stories from my childhood had got me thinking, and now distant images ran across the insides of my eyelids. I could hazily remember a time when we were very young: Wee Maxie and I had shared a bedroom, like Noah and Lucas did now – two parallel beds pushed against the walls and between them on the floor a tufted rug that Mum had made from a kit. I remembered long summer nights when it had been too light and too warm to sleep and my brother had invented expansive narrative games we could act out without leaving our beds, and the Christmas morning I had told Madeleine about when I had woken in the dark to discover a pram for my baby doll, and lots of plastic bangles and strings of bead necklaces, while Wee Maxie got a cowboy outfit and a magic set. Later Wee Maxie moved into the small single bedroom, where he was the first to exchange our warm woollen blankets for a trendy duvet – or 'continental quilt', as it was known to us back then. And I got to keep our old room to myself, with Josie papering my walls with the wonderful pussycat wallpaper.

We had been such an ordinary family in many ways. We ate very traditional meals of meat, potatoes and vegetables, we had a half-decent car, bicycles for the kids, and a holiday every summer, if only to a mobile home at the seaside, rather than Spain. And yet there was something extraordinary at play there, too. Mum really was a stunner, with her long, lacquered hair and her smoky eyes, and Dad could have been a film star with his looks.

But even at that, even though they were individually beautiful, it was as a couple that they became truly mesmerising.

'How did you know Dad was the one?' I asked Mum, when I was about fourteen and starting to wonder about boys.

'Because he was,' she said.

At the funeral, I overheard a story about them. Once upon a time, Mr Arnott from the end of our row had made a pass at Mum. She turned him down. Everyone thought Big Maxie would kill Mr Arnott. But he didn't lay a finger on him. He took him to the Bridge Inn and bought him whiskey all night and told him he was sorry for him, because if Josie Jackson had turned Big Maxie down when he had asked her, he would have lost the will to live.

Nothing could ever have split them up, and nothing ever did. They died as they had lived. Not that there was much comfort to be had when it happened, but what little there was, Wee Maxie and I had taken it from that.

I'm not sure of the exact chronology of everything that occurred after that. Jodie stayed at the hospital overnight and the next day, and Ray went there straight from the airport. Stanley and Naomi and Doris and Bob flitted between the ward and Ray and Jodie's house, and I stuck close to Noah.

It was Naomi, taking a break in the conservatory, who filled me in on what had happened. Lucas had gone to bed at seven thirty on Thursday night and Noah half an hour later. Jodie had been downstairs, looking through catalogues for the shop, when at around half past nine she felt something caught between her teeth and went up to the en-suite for dental floss. Looking in the cupboard above the basin, she noticed that the bottle of children's paracetamol was facing back to front. She knew that was wrong, for a start. She took it out and looked at it. It was empty. Meticulous Jodie knew she would never have replaced an empty medicine bottle in the cupboard, much less with the label facing behind.

Jodie had run to the boys' bedroom, thrown the light on and shaken them. Noah had objected; Lucas had smelt like the strawberry paracetamol. She asked him what he had done but he wouldn't talk to her.

She called 999.

'They asked her at the hospital how much paracetamol she thought Lucas had taken, but Jodie really didn't know – it was a long time since she'd needed to use it. All she could tell them was that if the bottle had run low, she would have bought another, which she hadn't. It could have been nearly full. They wanted to know if he could have taken anything else – anti-depressants, for example, but she told them there was nothing else. They had no need of anything.'

Bloods had been taken in Accident and Emergency to check Lucas's paracetamol levels, liver function and other things Naomi couldn't remember, and Lucas had been put on a drip to counter the seemingly all-important toxicity to his liver and moved to the children's high-dependency unit, with the possibility of transferring him to the Children's Hospital thirty-five miles away if his condition deteriorated.

'If he goes into liver failure, that's it,' Naomi said. 'The only hope left would be a transplant, the doctor said, although, as a six-year-old child, he'd be at the top of the list.'

'What are the chances of finding a donor organ in time?' I asked.

'The doctor said "vanishingly small".'

Naomi added that, although it hadn't been explicitly put, everyone at the hospital seemed to doubt that a seven-year-old boy could have conquered a child-proof lid, but she and I knew Lucas to be preternaturally strong, as well as dogged when he decided upon something. Look how easily he had opened the supposedly child-proof gate and almost let the animals out at the Santa farmyard nativity.

The hospital had been obliged to inform Social Services, who had sent someone to talk to Jodie and Ray. She had asked a lot of questions. In other circumstances, Jodie would have railed at that. Naomi said she had been as meek as a kitten.

The waiting was unbearable. The hands on the clock moved lethargically from one tiny increment to the next. I did my best to feed the grandparents when they turned up and shield Noah.

Had Lucas willingly taken an overdose? Was he that unhappy? He was such a fun-loving child, or so I had thought. I remembered Noah's remarks about after-school – who knew how lonely or frightened a seven-year-old boy could be if the wrong person said the wrong things? Or had it been some sort of prank or trick gone wrong?

I wished I could see him, talk to him.

'Does God ever make a mistake?' Noah asked me, perched on a high stool at the breakfast bar, solemnly eating a bowl of tomato soup.

To my shame, I pretended not to hear the question.

Madeleine came round with a large cottage pie – from the deli, rather than homemade, as she was still without a kitchen, but kind nevertheless – and a jigsaw for Noah. I set it up at the kitchen table for him and brought her into the snug to talk away from the grandparents.

'Did anyone call at the house?' I asked her.

'Not while I was there. Were you expecting someone?'

I shrugged and lied: 'Not especially.'

'Poor Lucas. I suppose all you can do is wait,' Madeleine said.

'That's about it. It's awful.'

'I know. I'm so sorry, Caroline. What must Ray and Jodie be going through? Our three have always sailed through life – the most illness they've ever had is chicken-pox. You take it for granted until something like this happens.'

'But how are things with you? Have you sorted out matters with Jimmy?'

'Yes. We're moving house.'

'That was a quick decision!'

'Quick, yes, difficult, no. Sitting round at your place, imagining what it would be like to be in Jodie's shoes, I thought I'd never cope without Jimmy. A nice house is all very well, but not much fun on your own and very little comfort if trouble comes your way. Look at this place – it's lavish, but right now Jodie and Ray would trade it in for a caravan if someone could guarantee them that Lucas would get the all-clear. Jimmy's the best thing that ever happened to me, Caroline. I forgot to keep appreciating that. I rang him and he came and got me – I didn't even miss a night in my own bed.'

'So what happens now?'

'We're going to finish off the kitchen, enjoy Christmas, then ask the estate agent to put it on the market in the new year. It's a good house, and it's in good nick – I think it'll sell easily enough if we put it on at the right price.'

'I'm sure it will. Any thoughts on where you'll go?'

'Somewhere close to work, so I can walk or catch a bus – that way we can downsize to one car.'

'You're really putting things in order.'

'And do you know what? It feels great. It's a relief, Caroline. You were right when you said all that debt was a burden, and now we're setting it down at last.' Madeleine craned her neck to look out the side window. 'A taxi's just rolled up in the driveway. Maybe it's Jodie. Oh, please let it be good news.'

But it wasn't Jodie. Out of the back seat climbed a stocky sandy-haired figure wearing a long green coat and carrying a large bag.

I jumped up. 'It's Tabby!'

17

Tabby first bounced into the world weighing nearly nine pounds, with a shock of red-gold hair and bright blue eyes.

I had loved being pregnant. There had been a bit of sickness at the start, reducing to low-level nausea for a couple of months. I could smell the butchery counter, with faint disgust, the minute I set foot in a supermarket, and I went off coffee. But I adored my bump and liked the lustre of my hair and the way I never felt cold.

Ray took it in his stride. While I bought baby magazines and read every line – what size was it now? A walnut? A plum? And were water births safe? Or home births? – Ray took the view that women had been having babies since the dawn of time and the whole thing was pretty wonderful, but didn't require a great deal of thought.

The labour was fast and intense. We had opted in the end for a hospital birth, gone there at four in the morning and Tabby was born in time for breakfast. I would have liked more pain relief, and Ray thought if he insisted that I would get it, but I knew from the midwives' demeanour that it wasn't happening and that it was just me, them and the gas-and-air. Which was pretty good, I have to say.

She howled, when she was born. I was glad to hear her. It meant she was breathing.

Ray held her first, wrapped up and mewling, but settling in his arms.

'Let me see her,' I had to tell him.

He sat on the bed and gave her to me. 'Not bad, for a first attempt,' he said, and kissed me.

Doris and Bob came round to our place while Tabby and I were still in hospital, and took delivery of the cot, the car-seat and all the other bits I'd been wary of having in the house before she had safely arrived. Bob assembled the cot and Doris washed all the sheets and blankets in non-bio detergent and dried them.

I had to send out for bigger Babygros – the new-born ones I had packed in my hospital bag didn't fit. My favourite was a soft yellow one that, along with her fluffy hair, made my baby look like a duckling.

Tabby was a bit chunky from the start, although everyone seemed to regard this as a plus point – a sign that she was robust, invulnerable. Feeding her was exhausting, and I seemed to have to eat constantly to keep up with her, but she thrived – the health visitor was very pleased with her weight gain. 'And you so petite,' she observed.

There were a lot of practical considerations – the bathing, the nappy changes, the never-ending laundry, and all while my body still ached – but they were, in honesty, a bit of a blur. The clarity came with the epiphany of motherhood itself – an almost sacred appreciation of a world seen anew in all its magnificence, a place of humbling beauty fit for my golden child, and simultaneously an animal, feral feeling that I would respond savagely to any threat whatsoever to this infant of mine.

We bought a pram, of course we did, from the nursery shop on the main street, even though really I felt a gilded carriage would have better fitted the bill. We chose navy blue, vaguely thinking ahead to when we would have more children and avoiding anything too overtly 'girly'.

Tabby and I got the best of Ray, I thought, when he worked just contracted hours at the *Gazette* and was happy with his wages being paid every month. Yes, he often had to cover evening markings, but there were two freelancers to pick up most of the weekend sport, so our Saturdays and Sundays were generally family time. The trip to the winter wonderland aside, I knew that Noah and Lucas saw precious little of their father. Running his own picture agency, managing a team of photographers as well as taking pictures himself, was way more than a full-time job. Jodie might have transformed his career and with it his income, but at a price.

We all spoilt the young Tabby. I probably let her have too

many sweet treats because I didn't want her growing up feeling I had deprived her as a result of my own diabetic discipline. I bought her more clothes than strictly necessary, because she liked dressing up, and Ray took her to the toy shop every time she was bored. We let her sit up later than we should, because we enjoyed her when she was happy and didn't want to make her sad. Doris and Bob loved having her to stay at their place, where she had her own bedroom, which Bob had papered lovingly in pink stripy wallpaper. Doris made her chips in a terrifying open pan and Bob took her on walks with Shane to buy chocolate and crisps.

Consequently, Tabby emerged from the chrysalis of infancy as a somewhat selfish, demanding, unreasonable and grumpy little butterfly. To the world, she was probably a little madam. To me, she was still my amazing, beloved child – challenging, yes, but that simply proved she was assertive, her own person.

Doris and Bob were with me – they adored her. Ray had been known to call her 'a pain in the arse' when she was being sulky, but never where she could hear him.

When she started school, Tabby didn't make friends easily. I suspected she was inclined to be bossy and expect her playmates to fall into line. When she did seem to get closer to someone, it never lasted long, and even though I thought it might well be her own fault, I fretted constantly and lost sleep worrying about her being lonely.

Ray said school would soon sort her out, rub off her sharp corners. But time passed and not much changed. The first birthday party invitation came, and I was so enormously grateful for Tabby being included that I bought a ridiculously expensive present. It did not come from any generosity of spirit – I only wanted the other kids to notice it, and know that this was what resulted when you hung out with Tabby, and decide that she was someone worth having around.

I have loved Tabby with all my heart from the moment I first set eyes on her, and I will love her for ever. I have always known that I would do anything for her – to protect her, to please her, to elevate her in any way I could. I could never bear to lose her.

When Tabby joined high school, she went from demanding to sullen. She became preoccupied with her appearance, hating her fair eyelashes and brows, her hair, her freckles. Hating, it seemed, herself.

It was a terrible time. I gave her all the money she asked for to spend on cosmetics that might give her an emotional boost. She had a clothes fund that I'm sure far exceeded anything spent by her peers. She was rude to me and snappy, and when she confided in me at all it was to tell me bitterly that the boys she knew all thought she was ugly and barked at her when she went past.

And then there was that stupid juvenile list of the most fuckable mothers, which just about put the tin hat on things.

Little did I know that an even worse blow was about to strike Tabby and me – just as she was in her adolescent doldrums, Ray announced that he was leaving. And not merely going to a new lover, but they were imminently to have a new child, too.

I should have been crushed for my own sake, but there wasn't room for my sorrow, because Tabby's grief was so great. She blamed me, which was shocking, because at first I didn't understand – I wasn't the one walking out, so what had I done wrong? But, of course, mine was the love that was utterly, utterly assured – I was the only one she could risk kicking out at because she knew I would take it and stick around.

Life was horrible for a while. It was difficult and lonely. I was very glad of the routine of my job, and of Madeleine, who listened patiently, and of Paddy Madden, who had a teenage daughter of his own, whom he adored although she was a handful.

Then salvation came in the form of the improbably named Hendrew Wainscott – christened after his two grandfathers, Henry and Andrew – a new arrival in school. Hendrew was a bit of an outsider, too, and he was gay, so fancying or not fancying Tabby wasn't an issue and he certainly wasn't going to put me on any adolescent lust list. I don't know who took who under whose wing, but soon Hendrew was round at our place every weekend, and Tabby had someone to go for a walk with, or into town, or to the cinema or bowling.

Things grew from there. Somehow, between them, they began to attract more people and in a matter of months Tabby had a 'crowd' for the first time in her life – girls and boys.

Then Noah arrived, and Tabby was enchanted by him. She really took to being a big sister. Jodie, to be fair, did not exclude her. Tabby and Hendrew often called round to Ray and Jodie's place when Ray was working, and watched Noah so Jodie could lie down or have a bath.

Hendrew and Tabby stuck together throughout the rest of their school years. They were both prone to crushes –

sometimes on the same guy – encouraged each other over the slightest spark of reciprocated interest and commiserated with each other when it was clear nothing was happening.

Hendrew was an attractive-looking boy, I thought. He had a long, fine-boned face, dark hair in a cut that suited him, and a simple but stylish way of dressing. He was the only 'out' teenager either Tabby or I knew, though, so his options were limited.

I credited Hendrew with rehabilitating Tabby's and my relationship. I didn't know quite what he'd said or done, but she stopped using me as an emotional dumping ground and started hugging me, thanking me, including me. Not excessively, but enough. It made all the difference and I would always be grateful to Hendrew for that. He made Tabby into an objectively nicer person, and set her on the road to become the still-vulnerable but lovely young woman she was today.

I wasn't surprised when Hendrew decided to study interior design, or when Tabby expressed an interest in finding a speech and language course near him, so they could continue to support one another.

They both started off in halls of residence, and in the first week there, Hendrew met Dawson Carling on a bus returning from Lidl and fell instantly in love. This time, the feeling was mutual. Hendrew and Dawson started courting and Dawson became Tabby's new additional best friend. In second and third years, the three shared a two-bedroom flat and, after graduation, they agreed they wanted to continue living together. Hendrew and Dawson found work first, and Tabby took the coffee-shop job while she looked for something within commuting distance that matched her degree. Dawson travelled a lot with work, and even though Tabby loved them both, I suspected she enjoyed often having Hendrew to herself.

Their current flat was a lot nicer than the one they had shared at uni. This one was in a Victorian terrace and located on the ground floor, which gave me the comfort of imagining Tabby could escape easily if ever there was a fire. Hendrew and Dawson had the larger front bedroom with the bay window, but Tabby's room at the rear of the building was perfectly nice, with a big sash window that overlooked the little garden. There was an open-plan living-dining-cooking area that felt homely, even if the kitchen was well past its sell-by date, and a bleak but immaculately clean shower room.

Hendrew, with his design skills, had done what he could with a dated rented property, but he regretted things he couldn't change, or which would have been unjustifiably expensive when none of them actually owned the place – like the positions of radiators, which dictated, to a large extent, where the furniture could go, and harsh strip lights where everyone would have preferred something more atmospheric.

Ray had offered to help Tabby with a deposit, if she wanted to buy a place of her own. 'I know they all get on, but the guys are bound to want their own space eventually,' he said.

I didn't like to think of Tabby living all alone, coming home to an empty place, with the breakfast dishes just where she had left them and no one to talk to or cook dinner for. I knew it was exactly what I did myself, but I was made of different stuff from my daughter.

Maybe if this new guy turned out to be special, though ... It wouldn't take much for my imagination to sprint away, covering love, marriage, Tabby carried across the threshold of a new home, a baby in a high chair, then another, a toddler's hand in each of hers as they all splashed in puddles – 'We are a grandmother.' No wonder Tabby was careful what she told me – I wanted it all for her, I wanted it now, and it was too much.

Ray and I had never conceived again after Tabby. It just didn't happen. We didn't fuss about it, and we didn't ask why. I was so thrilled with my one child, I didn't really mind – Tabby was enough for me. Tabby was always enough.

And then what happened, happened, with Ray and Jodie, and suddenly there were Noah and Lucas and, completely unexpectedly and somewhat bizarrely, they became my special boys, too. Noah's earliest memory, he loved to recount, was the day Lucas came home from hospital. Nana and Pop had been looking after him, and Ray had fetched Jodie in his then car. Noah had run to the front door to meet them and Ray, who was opening the door for Jodie, was trundling her new wheelie case, which Noah hadn't seen before.

'I thought Lucas was in the case!' Noah would repeat gleefully, going on to explain that the case actually held his mum's nighties and toothbrush, and that Jodie followed with the infant Lucas in his car seat.

Noah couldn't remember a time pre-Lucas. It was

unthinkable that he might have to learn to live without him in the future.

Everyone hugged Tabby and she hugged everyone.

'Do you want to see our Christmas tree?' Noah asked her.

'Yes, please,' she said, taking his hand.

She was wearing her work trousers, tunic and lanyard under her coat. 'I've got jeans and a jumper in my bag, but I thought it might do no harm to flaunt my "professions allied to medicine" angle if we go to the hospital.' She coughed a dry tickly cough. 'As a speech therapist, I should know better than to try to conduct a three-hour conversation in a nightclub,' she croaked.

She'd been out with Harry again, I deduced, with a smile. With a new relationship, you wanted to talk all the time. 'Do you want a glass of water?' I asked.

She nodded, and added, 'Any chance of a sticky sweet?'

I had fruit pastilles in my coat pocket. I usually had something of that sort about me – they looked less peculiar than the dextrose tablets if I needed a little sugar boost on the move.

Madeleine brought the water, I brought the pastilles, and Noah sat on Tabby's knee and played with her ponytail.

'So, fill me in on Lucas,' she said, and put her ear-buds into Noah's ears while Naomi told the story over again. 'If nobody has any objections, I'd like to pop over to the hospital and try to see him – even if it's just for a few minutes.'

'I was hoping to go myself,' I said, 'if you don't mind staying here with Nana and Pop and Granny and Granddad, Noah.'

'I don't mind. As long as you come back. Will I make Lucas a card?'

'Tabby and I will have to go now, to catch evening visiting, but why don't you make one while we're away and Lucas can have it tomorrow?'

'What should I draw on it?'

'What does Lucas like?' Tabby asked.

'Doughnuts. And dinosaurs.'

'There you are, then,' she said.

In the car on the way to the hospital, Tabby said, 'Jodie must be desperate if she's letting you back into the fold after what you did. I'm here because of Noah and Lucas, and we'll have to do what's necessary, but I'm furious with you.'

'I know. I deserve it.'

'Is it really over, this time, between you and Dad?'

'It really, truly is, Tabby. I promise.'

'OK. We can't deal with it in the middle of all this – that doesn't mean I forgive you. Has Jodie stayed with Lucas the whole time?'

'Yep.'

'Then she'll be exhausted. If she really doesn't want to leave the hospital, I could ask the staff if there's anywhere she could take a shower.'

'But she hasn't got any clean clothes to change into. We could bring some in the morning.'

'Let's at least try to persuade her and Dad to take a walk to the canteen, have something to eat, read a newspaper. It's too intense, just sitting at Lucas's bedside without a break.'

'Agreed. How did you hear about Lucas anyway? I rang and rang, but I couldn't get any answer.'

'I didn't want to talk to you – that's on you, not me, but it was rotten timing for a fall-out. Dad eventually got me.'

'So it was just me you were angry with? Dad gets off scot-free?' I could have bitten my tongue. 'I shouldn't have said that, Tabby. I'm sorry.'

'I can't talk to you about it. I need to focus on the boys.'

The car park was much busier than it had been the night before and we had to drive around to find a space.

When I told Tabby that Lucas was in the children's high-dependency unit she knew exactly where to go – she had done a placement in the hospital when she was training and had got to know the layout well.

Jodie sat on one side of Lucas's bed and Ray on the other. Lucas lay between them, sleeping.

We exchanged greetings and Tabby asked if there was any news. Ray nodded his head to one side and we stepped into the corridor to hear what he had to say.

'Dr Barnes, the senior registrar, said the toxicology report was back and it looks like the paracetamol was the only thing Lucas had taken,' Ray murmured softly. 'Of course, Jodie was pretty mad at that, as that was what she'd told them all along.'

Tabby nodded.

'He said they're in regular phone contact with the top woman at the Children's Hospital, so Lucas is getting the benefit of the most expert advice without having to move him,' Ray continued. 'They're still doing bloods – it's all about his liver, now. It seems it's just a waiting game.'

'But for how long?' I asked. 'When can they tell you more?'

'Dr Barnes says if he can make it through to this time tomorrow without his liver failing, we'll be in a more hopeful position.'

If? If Lucas could make it until tomorrow? Even though I'd known in theory how serious Lucas's situation was, that 'if' hit me in the gut.

We went and looked at the peaceful little bundle in the bed. I wondered how much he had picked up about the trouble he was in. Was he frightened to find himself here? Did he have any idea that he might be dying? Dying at seven years old – it was unbearable. Tabby calmly made her suggestion about a trip to the canteen, particularly since Lucas was sleeping.

'We should take them up on it, Jodie.' Ray looked across at his wife. 'We need to eat some time.'

'What if he wakes up?'

'If Lucas wakes up, we'll tell him you've gone to have tea downstairs and you'll be back soon,' Tabby said firmly. 'We'll keep him chatting.'

Reluctantly, Jodie let Ray lead her away.

Lucas continued to sleep, his red hair damp and sticky on his forehead.

'Do we know whether this was an accident?' Tabby asked.

'No one's said anything to me. I don't know if anybody's

tried talking to Lucas about it yet. You heard Naomi say Social Services have been round, whatever that means.'

'They have to. When a child gets access to a paracetamol overdose in the home, then it has to be looked into. And they won't just take Lucas's word for what happened, or even Jodie's – it's a child-protection issue so they'll have to investigate. Even assuming Lucas recovers, he won't be going home until the safeguarding people are completely happy that it's a safe environment and that Jodie and Ray are trustworthy.'

Tabby's cough started up again and I passed her the packet of fruit pastilles. 'Keep them.'

'Thanks.'

'So, how have you been? How's work? How's Harry?'

'School's been super-busy. We went to see *Beauty and the Beast* at the town hall.'

'And did your kids enjoy that?'

'Some of them got really into it – a few went up on stage for the interactive audience thing before the big finale. It was a bit over the heads of the younger ones, but they got their fun from going out on the bus and having crisps and chocolate, so I guess there was something for everyone. We had our Christmas craft fair, too. In fact, I bought you something.'

Tabby delved into her capacious bag and fished out a large painted pebble. 'I thought you could use it as a paperweight.'

I held it in my hand, so relieved that she was talking to me, so grateful she was allowing me to be in her presence. 'Thank you. I love it. Was it really painted by one of the students?'

'She used a stencil but, yeah, it's all her own work. Turn it over – look, there's her signature – Katy.'

'Your school sounds like a wonderful place.'

'It is. Look, Mum. I think Lucas is waking up. Lucas?'

Thank you, thank you, for still calling me 'Mum'.

'Hi, little brother!'

'Hi, Tabby.' His small limbs went rigid as he gave a long stretch. 'I'm in hospital.'

'I know.'

Lucas was very quiet and we resisted the urge to try to coax him to talk. I was sure Tabby wondered as much as I did why on earth he had decided to drink from a bottle of paracetamol, but she didn't broach the subject and I thought it might be ethically or even legally wrong to try to prompt a revelation in the absence of his parents or perhaps a social worker.

Instead, I chatted about Christmas, and how Noah and I had kept the Advent candle up to date and how there were only nine more sleeps until Santa came.

'There's a tree just round the corner from here – you can get up and see it when you're feeling better,' Tabby said.

Just then, a woman in a navy trench coat approached us. 'Sorry to interrupt,' she said. 'I was looking for Mr or Mrs Rankin. I'm Adele Nelson. I'm from the safeguarding team.'

'They've just gone to grab something in the canteen,' Tabby said. 'We're expecting them back any minute, though. Pull up a chair.'

Lucas looked at the woman warily. I knew how he felt – suddenly I was afraid to open my mouth in case I said the wrong thing. Luckily, Tabby had no such anxieties.

'I'm Lucas's sister – well, half-sister. Tabitha Rankin. This is my mum, Caroline. If you want any background, ask away.'

But before Adele Nelson could respond, Jodie and Ray reappeared.

'What's going on?' Jodie asked. 'I thought we'd answered all your questions.'

A nurse approached. 'I just want to check this drip,' she said. 'Carry on. Don't mind me.'

'There was one thing I need to do,' Adele said. From her shoulder-bag she produced a bottle of children's paracetamol. She slid it from its outer box.

'Lucas. Could you do something for me? Could you open this bottle, please?'

She handed it to Lucas, who took it, looked at Jodie, looked at Tabby.

No one moved.

Lucas looked at the bottle in his hands. He pressed down on the lid, twisted and pulled – see, he knew exactly what to do!

But the lid wouldn't come off.

Lucas tried again – he pressed down, twisted and pulled. 'I can't,' he said. 'It's too stiff.'

'Thank you, Lucas,' Adele said. 'That's all I needed to know.'

18

Jodie looked at Adele. 'What do you mean? Do you think *I* gave Lucas the medicine? Do you think I poisoned my own child?'

'Hang on a minute,' Tabby said, delving into her bag. She pulled out a jar of daily multi-vitamins, the ones I bought for her because I worried. 'Try that one, Lucas.'

Lucas took the jar, pressed, turned the lid and screwed it off with ease.

'Fancy that,' the nurse said.

'That's not the same,' Adele said. 'That jar's bigger – it's easier.'

'I would have said its being bigger made it more difficult, when you've only got little hands,' Tabby replied. 'But just to be sure...'

She drew a cough-mixture bottle from her bag. It was of similar size to the paracetamol bottle. 'Try this one, Lukie.'

Lucas took the bottle, pressed, twisted and removed the lid in a blink.

'I think the difference is the fact that the lid has been opened before,' Tabby said. 'I find those child-proof tops almost impossible on a brand new container, but they get easier after that first time.'

Later, Jodie said, from that minute on, she sensed a change in attitude to her on the ward. 'Thank God Tabby came when she did,' she whispered to me, when Adele left. 'I knew that social worker didn't believe me.'

'How long are you able to stay?' I asked Tabby, as we drove back to Jodie and Ray's.

'I'll have to catch a train back tomorrow evening.'

'Hopefully we'll have better news about Lucas by then.'

'Mum, would you mind if I crashed at their place instead of going home? I think I should spend the time with Noah.'

Would I *mind*? I'd been trying to think of a way to engineer it ever since Tabby stepped out of the taxi – Mark didn't know about Ray and Jodie's place or about Tabby, as far as I could tell. As long as she hung out with them and avoided home there was no reason she couldn't spend the weekend without incident and then be on her way. But it wouldn't do to sound *too* enthusiastic.

'If that's what you really want. Actually, it's a good idea. Noah needs cheering up.'

'I've got my change of clothes, and Jodie keeps the guest room well supplied.'

'Then that's sorted. When did you last eat, though? I imagine the grandparents will have had Madeleine's cottage pie by now.'

'I had a sandwich on the train.'

'That's not much – and it was hours ago.'

'I could go halves on an Indian.'

'Shall we phone it through from Jodie's and let them deliver? At least we get to wait in comfort.'

'Yeah.'

This was better. This was not the shutting-me-out Tabby I had feared. Did it mean that, beneath her disappointment in me, she still cared for me, loved me, trusted me?

'And you can tell me about Harry.' I closed my eyes. Don't reject me – I'm doing my best.

'I can tell you *a bit*. I'm not doing the full Q&As.'

'Understood.'

In the end, we shared a lamb rogan josh and a butter chicken, pilau rice and naan. I hadn't thought I felt hungry, but the food and the relief that Tabby seemed to be softening towards me gave me an appetite, and between us we ate the lot. I would have to do a few extra units of insulin to avoid a hike in my blood sugar, but that was fine.

Having slotted our plates and cutlery into the dishwasher, Tabby poured herself another tall glass of water from the bottle in the fridge, and we returned to the lounge, where Noah was slumbering under a fleece blanket on the sofa. We plonked ourselves down on the other.

'So. Harry,' Tabby said at last.

I tried not to look as eager for news as I felt.

'He's intelligent. Interesting. Patient.'

Patient? What did that mean? Why would he need to be patient with Tabby?

'Does Lennie like him? And Hendrew and Dawson?'

'Harry hasn't been to the flat – he can't. He's allergic to cats.'

'Oh, no!'

'I know – there's always something, isn't there? I'm not sure what to do about it. I do love little Lennie.'

'Couldn't Harry take an anti-histamine or something?'

'Not sure. He said if Lennie jumped up on him he'd be wheezing in minutes. Even if I put Lennie in a different room, just being around the throws and cushions where he sleeps could be enough to set Harry off.'

'But you like him. You think there's potential.'

Tabby allowed herself a little smile. 'I can't remember ever finding a guy so incredibly easy to talk to. At first, I was a bit worried we'd run out of things to say, but that doesn't seem to be the case.'

'Well, that's a good start.'

'It gets better.'

'Oh?'

'For possibly the first time ever, I have a feeling that he likes me even more than I like him. You never thought you'd hear me say that, did you?'

It wasn't Tabby's norm – that much was true. She had always

been the more loving than beloved, which had saddened and frustrated me and made me want to beat her few boyfriends about the head.

'I think it's since I got my permanent contract at work,' she continued. 'It's given me confidence, Mum. School know me by now, and they've decided I'm up to the job. It's such a boost.'

At last, Tabby was finding a little self-belief. And of course that would make her feel more attractive, which in turn would make her more attractive to others. Less needy, if we were being honest. Perhaps it had been coming for a while, though. Within the family – among all of the grandparents in particular – Tabby had been awarded a certain status since doing her degree. She was the first to have gone to university, about which everyone had got very excited.

'Assuming we're still seeing each other at Christmas, I thought I might bring him to meet you.'

If she'd been planning that, then for all that I had disappointed and infuriated her by seeing Ray, she hadn't completely hated me. This was my reward, surely, for the days, months and years I had absorbed her anger and abuse when she'd been a child, and kept on adoring her. 'I'd love that. You'll have to tell me what to buy him for a present.'

'I'm a bit anxious about the whole gift-giving thing, actually – it seems a bit soon to be spending serious money on each other, but I can't hand him a Lynx shower set. Maybe something like a Paul Smith shirt.'

'And have the two of you ...?'

'Mum!'

'I just need to know whether to make up the spare room!'

'For your information, I'm not in any rush. I'm enjoying being courted, for once.'

I was satisfied. Tabby was seeing someone, taking it carefully and feeling buoyant about the way the relationship was going. She was even bringing him home in a matter of days. It was all I could ask for, and I was determined to have dealt with the Mark situation before the young couple came to see me.

'So, any gossip about town?' Tabby asked.

'I bumped into Emma Christie at a coffee morning. She's getting married.'

'Yes, I saw it on Facebook,' Tabby replied. 'To Stefan Moorhead. Good luck to them. Did I tell you, his was the first willie I ever touched?'

'No!'

'Yep. In the utility room at Tory Rutherford's sixteenth birthday party, behind the clothes airer. He said if I felt him he'd go out with me. So I did, and he told me I was a slapper and pissed off.'

'Oh, Tabby!'

'I was so desperate for him to like me. You must remember. But don't worry – I'm not that girl any more.'

'Of course you're not. And, anyway, mistakes people make in their teenage years shouldn't be held against them. Nobody knows anything in their teens and all should be forgiven or, better still, forgotten.' Are you listening, Mark? 'Maybe Emma will invite you to the wedding.'

'Doubt it – I see her posts on Facebook, but we haven't really stayed in touch.'

'I don't think I have much else to report. The paper's full of Christmas stuff, of course, but not much hard news.'

'And how are my godparents? Paddy still working from home?'

'Mainly, yes. He came round for a while the other night – we watched TV. I think sometimes he just needs to get out of the house.'

'Don't seduce him, Mum. Seriously, not Paddy.'

'You make me sound like some sort of temptress! I'm a middle-aged mum who's getting a double chin.'

'Your chin is perfectly fine, and you know you're still beautiful. And if you're mad enough to have a fling with Dad then I'm really not sure what you're capable of – but not Paddy, Mum. They've all been through enough.'

'Paddy and I are just two old friends. If anything were ever going to happen, it would have been a very long time ago. And it didn't.'

'The thought never crossed your mind?'

'Never.' Not really. Not seriously.

'When I come home for Christmas, I'll pop round and see Katrina. You should go home now and get some sleep – you look tired, Mum. You've had an intense couple of days.'

Tabby didn't know the half of it.

'Shall we put Noah to bed first?' I asked, and explained about him fearing to sleep alone in the room he'd shared with Lucas.

'No problem. You sit in with him while I take off my face and do my teeth, and I can crash in Lucas's bed.' I managed to carry Noah to the bedroom without waking him, and, minutes later, Tabby crept in to join us.

Minutes later, Tabby crept back into the bedroom in red tartan pyjamas, devoid of make-up. Despite our conversation about how she had grown into a confident woman, with those blonde lashes and scrubbed cheeks she still looked to me very much like my little girl.

I drove home through the dark night, thinking again about Lucas, praying to a God I couldn't fathom and didn't really believe in that he would pull through. Maybe if he lived, I'd believe, but I doubted it.

There were no strange vehicles in the street or unexpected items on the hall mat – just more cards, which I opened, glanced at and set in a pile. Tomorrow, if there was better news from the hospital, I would do something about putting up my decorations. I should try to buy the boys' pyjamas, too. If I bought Lucas his, he'd have to live.

Tabby had been right – I was exhausted and slept deeply until my alarm went off, heralding Sunday morning and prompting me to have my jab and breakfast.

At around ten, still in my dressing-gown, contemplating the ironing, I got a call from Tabby to say that Ray had been in touch. The latest blood results were back and the consultant had indicated that Lucas's family could now be, quote, 'cautiously optimistic' about his recovery.

'That's brilliant!' I cried.

'I know. Look, Nana and Pop have gone to the ward to let Jodie and Ray come home for a few hours, and Granny and Granddad are here making a roast lunch. Why don't you take a day to yourself, Mum, and just chill? Watch an old movie or something.'

'I should probably write my Christmas cards – they should have been posted long ago.'

'Sod the Christmas cards – you need to think of yourself. Everyone agrees you look knackered.'

'Thanks!'

'Take it in the spirit it's intended. You'll be back to work tomorrow, I guess, so rest up today.'

'OK. I might put up a few decs, though, to celebrate Lucas's news.'

'All right. I'll let you know if there are any further developments.'

'Do, Tabby. And it was great to see you. Can't wait to have you home for Christmas. Give my love to Hendrew and Dawson.'

Cautiously optimistic – that had to mean Lucas was out of danger. It was practically permission to expect a full recovery. Rightly or wrongly, that was how I meant to interpret it anyway.

The news filled me with energy. The holidays were nearly here, and I was way behind with my preparations. I would get showered and dressed, bring out the step-ladders and put up the strings for the Christmas cards. If I had an early lunch, I could drive over to the garden centre and choose a tree. Then I might put some carols on the CD player, start addressing envelopes and Christmas could begin. Lucas was going to be all right, so festivities were back on. Fuck Mark. Tabby was out of the way and that was the main thing. He wasn't going to run my life – I wouldn't let him.

I strolled along the pebbled walkway admiring the green, glossy Christmas trees but anticipating the arduous task of getting one into the back of the car and dealing with it at home. There was no sign of the nice man who had helped me in the past.

'If I buy a little root-ball one and bring it indoors, will it keep its needles for a couple of weeks?' I asked the assistant.

'Give it plenty of water every day, don't put it near a radiator and it should be all right,' he said.

I decided I would take one, not because I believed him, but because I wanted to believe him.

Then I spotted a display of bird tables – that might be a nice thing to get for Tabby, to put outside her bedroom window at the flat. So I bought one of those, too, and some garden bird seeds and fat-balls, before worrying that perhaps what I had done was create a feathered buffet table for Lennie.

Back home, I lugged in a small solid plastic table I sometimes used on the patio and set it in the hall. It would give my little tree some height. If Tabby had been there, she'd have clambered into the attic and passed the boxes of decorations down to me.

As it was, I had to climb up, heave myself onto the ledge of the hatch and root around for what I wanted before staggering back down the steps, one box at a time.

Christmas decorating isn't something one should do alone, but I was already getting excited about Tabby coming home for the holidays and I wanted the place to feel lovely to her because I really did miss her and hoped that, when the right time came – and it might be coming soon, if this Harry thing worked out – she would want to return, not actually to live with me, of course, but perhaps nearby.

'Tomorrow Shall Be My Dancing Day' was playing jauntily as I dressed my little tree in its ancient strands of tinsel and coloured baubles. There was the teddy one Doris had given us that said 'Baby's First Christmas' – would I be buying a similar one for Tabby one day soon?

I had been grateful when the fairy lights I had spread out on the rug lit up first time, and now they were draped on the spiny branches – one set was enough for a tree this size.

Tree done, I assembled the garland for the mantelpiece. It had started with a plain green base, and we had added tiny white lights and various accoutrements over the years – a sprig of plastic berried holly, a bunch of frosted purple grapes, a silver bell, a golden pear. The effect was surprisingly not of a heap of random afterthoughts but a full and sumptuous affair.

As I was standing back admiring the garland, Elaine's face appeared at the front window. She was smiling and waving. I grinned back and indicated that I was going to the front door to meet her.

'Hi, Caroline. How are you?'

'Good, thanks. Just about finished decorating the house.'

'I'm doing the rounds, inviting everyone over for Christmas-morning drinks. Are you available?'

'I'd love to come.'

If Lucas could drink poison and survive, then I could, too. Mark was toxic, all right, and his attacks on Eric and Ralph showed that he could be vicious. But how clever was he, actually? I had been mulling this over and decided I would out-think him, talk him round or wheedle – do whatever it took to get rid of him while keeping my nice, small life intact. His behaviour of recent days was warped, but it was a warped form of love – wasn't it? And that love was something I could use to defeat him.

'And what about Tabby?'

'Count Tabby in, too, Elaine. I know she'd love to see you. Can we bring anything?'

'Just bring yourselves.'

That was what she said every year.

'We'll look forward to it. How's Gareth?'

'Flat out. The Beavers are off visiting Santa in his forest lodge and there were too many of them for one coach, so Gareth's driving some of them in the mini-bus.'

'I hope they have fun!'

'Yes. Me, too. So we'll see you both about ten-ish on Christmas morning?'

'We'll be there.'

'Oh, and before I forget, Gareth said there was a guy here looking for you yesterday – I think you must have been out.

Gareth asked him if he could give you a message, but he said it didn't matter, he'd come back. Gareth said he was driving a big dark saloon car, if that's any help.'

I wasn't shocked. Not any more. Ever since finding Ralph's wallet on my hall mat I had known Mark had tracked me down and it was a matter of when, rather than if, he turned up.

'I'd better get going,' Elaine said. 'They're showing *Mary Poppins* on ITV at five o'clock and I really want to see it again.'

She set off for the next house and I noticed, creeping towards us up the avenue, a long dark saloon car. Elaine turned and gave me the thumbs-up, as if to say, 'Oh, great – here's your friend back, now.'

The car pulled up by the kerb and I felt my breathing quicken. Slowly, the driver's door opened and a figure in a long black coat stepped out. He was as imposingly tall as I remembered, and as he strode up the driveway he carried the same limp as before.

I heard the gentle revolution of the turntable, then the stylus dropping softly onto vinyl.

In a moment, he was right in front of me, but not exactly towering over me, because I was standing on the step.

'Caroline.'

'Mark.'

19

I stepped back from the doorway. 'Are you coming in?'

Mark advanced. I closed the front door behind him and he followed me into the lounge.

'Sit down,' I said, conscious of the tremor in my voice and adrenalin rushing, gushing, flooding me. All my courage of the past twenty-four hours flapped and flew away, like startled birds. 'Should I make coffee? It'll only be instant – I'm out of pods.'

How banal, those first words after whole decades.

Mark shrugged. 'Instant's fine.'

Part of me wanted to escape to the kitchen, to breathe, to put space between us. Another part wanted just to stand there and look at him, take him in, observe the face I had once adored, a body I had yearned for, acknowledge the changes the years had worked. Did he feel the same? This was the first time in over thirty years that we had seen each other face to face, the first time we had heard each other speak.

'Do you want something to eat? A scone? Or I could make a sandwich.'

'No, thanks. But you go ahead, if you need the carbs.'

I didn't think I'd be able to swallow a thing, and I felt grateful that I had no reason to think my blood sugar would be running low.

In the kitchen, I filled the kettle and tried to compose myself. Whatever game Mark was playing, he was here now, and I had an opportunity to influence what he did next. All I wanted was to persuade him to go away and leave me alone. Could I do that?

'Milk?' I had put my head round the doorway and found Mark still on his feet, with his back to me, looking at the surroundings. I didn't think it was obvious that the portraits of Tabby were missing – especially with the cards and decorations adorning the place.

'Just a dash, please. Your cards are nice – you seem to have a lot of friends, Caroline. People obviously hold you in high regard.'

Was that just something to say or did it imply a veiled threat about what I stood to lose?

I carried the coffees through with trembling hands and we both sat down.

Mark looked as handsome as I remembered him – dark, clean-shaven, and with that emphatic chin. Under the long coat he wore a textured black shirt, open at the neck, and charcoal jeans.

Back when I was in school, girls had adored him, limp and all. For a while, he'd dated Sara Withers, who was pretty but shy, and Ursula Elliott, who was the first mixed-heritage girl in our school, and stunning. He had been seeing Olivia McKinney, queen of the sixth form, when things first happened between the two of us, but he broke matters off with her the very next day. He didn't tell her why.

It had been August, and the month had started off blazing hot, with hose-pipe bans, sunburn for the unfortunate, and the tarmac melting on the roads. Dad had a fortnight's holiday from the warehouse and Mum had the same time off from the boutique, but they weren't going away until the following week, so they lazed about the little back garden on sunloungers getting tanned. They drank gallons of tea in the mornings and read the papers, and Mum had just discovered Campari, which she tippled in the afternoons, while Dad had cans of Carling Black Label, which he cooled in the sink, because we only had a little fridge.

Mum still came indoors every day to cook a traditional dinner, her apron over shorts and a bikini top. For that week, watching Mum and Dad, playing my albums in my bedroom with the curtains shut against the sun, linking arms with my friends as we strolled through the public gardens with our Immac-ed legs and our strawberry lip gloss, I had no idea what was about to happen. I didn't know this was my last time with them and the seismic quake of loss that was coming. I had absolutely no inkling of how I was about to become entangled with Mark. *Absolutely no inkling?* Was that really possible? Didn't a girl always know? Well, I didn't. Cross my heart. I didn't believe he saw it coming, either. Not until later. Not until the record started turning, the stylus touched down softly and Mark, strong and tender, took me in his arms that first time. He hadn't danced since the pitchfork incident, but this was a slow one, and he could manage that, very well indeed.

Back then, Mark was a stickler for doing the right thing. He didn't mess girls about. And he was chivalrous. He let Olivia McKinney tell everyone she was the one who had dumped him. Surely all that goodness couldn't have completely disappeared – surely I could appeal to something of the old, decent, honourable Mark.

'Your coffee OK?'

'Coffee's fine.' He lifted the mug to his lips, and I noted with horror that it was a Mothers' Day one Tabby had given me years ago. The lettering was faded by hundreds of cycles in the dishwasher, but I would swipe it away at the first opportunity, nevertheless. 'You've cut your hair.'

I tugged at a few strands at the nape of my neck. 'Lower maintenance.'

Mark nodded knowingly. 'But you haven't let yourself go. I knew you wouldn't.'

He rose from his seat and looked out the front window. 'So this is where you ended up – a middle-class cul-de-sac in a little provincial town. It's nice enough, I suppose.'

It was better than nice, it was wonderful. It was everything I wanted.

'How did you find me?'

Mark turned and looked at me. This must be strange for him, too, I thought, seeing me close up for the first time with the flecks of grey hair and the fine lines. I didn't usually give them much thought – I had never been particularly vain about growing older. I put it down to what happened to Mum. When I had reached the age she had been when she died, it had unnerved me. When I exceeded it, I had been struck by the fact that I had no road map for going forward, as a woman. Mum hadn't been around to show me the way. I had tried to imagine her older. She would still have been striking, I felt sure. As time went by, I had felt grateful for the years I was enjoying that had been denied to her.

Mark took a long breath, raised his eyebrows and set down his mug. 'Luck, initially. I was getting some dental work done. Picked up an old magazine in the waiting room and flicked through it for something to do. Imagine my surprise when I saw Caroline Maxwell smiling from ear to ear holding aloft a shiny award for journalism. Well done, by the way – sorry, I should have started off by congratulating you.'

The awards dinner for my *Weekend Tribune* prize the previous summer – of course people had taken photos. I vaguely remembered being lined up and snapped, but to be honest, I had had rather a lot to drink with the meal. It never occurred to me to ask where the pictures might appear.

'I took the magazine with me. The caption gave the town where you lived. I went home, had a think, and decided to look you up. It wasn't completely straightforward tracking you down – you still used your maiden name professionally, but I couldn't get any joy with that from Directory Enquiries so I guessed you must have married. I could hardly believe it when you turned up at my hotel for some dinner-dance, but you managed to give me the slip. I struggled to get a lead after that – it never occurred to me that a big-shot, prize-winning magazine journalist would still be a reporter on the local weekly rag, so it was pure good fortune that I ran into that slutty girl from your paper, and she led me straight to you.'

Slutty? That wasn't a 'Mark' word ... not the old Mark.

'You didn't have to hurt Eric, or Ralph – he ended up in hospital, you know. I'm not involved with either of them – not romantically. And even if I had been, what business would it have been of yours?'

'I didn't have to hurt them, but I wanted to. That is, I wanted to hurt you, Caroline.'

'But why?'

'You know why.'

'Mark, all that was *thirty years* ago! More! I'm not the same person I was back then and I'm sure you aren't, either.'

'Aren't you? I am. I haven't forgotten a single thing, so why should I let you?'

I sighed. 'Have you really come all this way from wherever you live now just to dredge that up again? What's the point? It's in the past – let's leave it there.'

'I can't.'

I snatched up both our mugs, strode to the kitchen and dumped our remaining coffee into the sink. With my hand wrapped tightly round the Mothers' Day one, I quickly shoved them into the dishwasher.

Mark followed me.

'What happened back then broke me,' he said. He was standing right behind me. I leant on the counter.

Without turning, I said, 'It broke me, too. I thought my life was over when you walked out. I had no one to turn to and it took me years to rebuild myself.'

'But you did it. You're happy now – admit it.'

'What's wrong with being happy?' I swung round to face him. 'I paid for what we did. I didn't forgive myself for years and years, but eventually I decided enough was enough. I thought I deserved a second chance.'

'So you married some guy called Rankin. Who was he, anyway?'

'Someone I worked with.'

'Did you love him?'

'Of course I loved him.'

'Was it Love with a capital L, though? Like it was for us?'

'It was different.'

'How?'

'It didn't hurt.'

'Where is he now?'

'He met someone else.'

'Oh? Younger?'

'Yes.'

'He must have been mad.'

'You left me, too!'

'Not for someone else! I would never have.'

'So what now?'

'What do you mean?'

'Why have you come looking for me? What do you want?'

Mark looked at me as if the answer was obvious and I was particularly dim for not understanding. 'I want you to suffer.'

While I had spent three decades building a whole new life for myself and burying the bones of the past, Mark, though he looked affluent, groomed and vital, had apparently been less successful. We returned to the lounge and sat on opposite ends of the sofa, not speaking.

The brittle silence was broken by the doorbell suddenly chiming.

'Ignore it,' I said.

'Good luck with that,' Mark replied. 'You haven't pulled the curtains – whoever it is only has to look in the window and see you sitting there.'

'I'll get rid of them,' I said, and went to the door.

It was Madeleine. 'Caroline! Sorry to interrupt your Sunday evening but I was walking home after a few glasses of wine at Arlene's and I suddenly needed to use the loo. I thought, There's no way I'm going to get home without wetting myself, but if I make a slight detour I could probably hold out until Caroline's. How glad was I to see your light on from the end of the avenue.'

Madeleine was proposing to come inside? Shit. Could I shuffle her upstairs to the bathroom without her noticing Mark?

'Well? Are you going to let me in? I'm not joking, Caroline – I'm bursting, here.'

Just as I was saying, 'Come on, then,' and bundling her past me, a low, distinctly male cough came from the lounge. I had pulled the inner door over, but hadn't shut it tightly. As if in slow motion, Madeleine gave me a searching, eager look and went to nudge the door open with her toe. I had to stop her. I needed to think lightning fast, cause a diversion, curtail Madeleine, somehow. I opened my mouth, but no sound came. Thoughts clawed for meaning, like kittens about to be drowned, but my strategic functioning choked and stalled and the kittens were plunged into the bucket, where they thrashed, then stopped. So this was it. This was how it happened. The moment had arrived: the collision of my past life and my present. And I was helpless. I was mute and I was rooted to the spot. Powerless. Facing my doom. Not ready. Not ready at all. We both looked into the room, where a tall figure stood in front of the fireplace, looking back.

Madeleine's face broke into a huge smile. 'Well! I don't have to ask who you are! You're like two peas in a pod! It's my great pleasure to find you here, Mark! I'm Madeleine, and I can't tell you how wonderful it is finally to meet Caroline's big brother.'

20

It was Monday evening. I had arranged to swap places with Jodie and Ray at the hospital, and sit with Lucas while they went home for something to eat and to spend some time with Noah.

I went straight to the supermarket from the office to buy myself a sandwich, and some of the honey kefir that Lucas liked.

As I was perusing sandwiches in the chiller cabinet, fancying granary bread, but preferring the fillings in the white ones, I sensed someone hovering behind me.

'Sorry. I'm taking ages. Am I in your way ...?' I began. But as I turned, I saw that it was Eric Haffey, carrying a wire basket in one hand and a bouquet of the supermarket's flowers in the other.

'Hello, Caroline,' he said, with a thin smile.

'Eric – hi,' I replied. This was the first time I had bumped into him since the night Mark had punched him at the dinner-dance. Eric had said some harsh things then, too.

Not much wanting to look at him, I found myself instead studying the contents of his basket – Butter Puffs, a jar of Gale's lemon curd and a box of Mr Kipling Almond Slices.

'For Mum,' he said, raising the basket slightly. 'A few treats, as I'm going out tonight.'

I searched for a suitable response.

'A date,' Eric added, a note of triumph in his voice, and tipped the flowers slightly towards me.

'Oh!' I said. 'Great!'

I remembered the flowers Eric had brought me, during our brief association – they had been expensive, hand-tied arrangements from the florist's, not something hastily grabbed in front of the self-service checkouts. It hadn't taken him long to start looking for a prospective new partner, but it seemed that, this time, he had resolved to minimise his investment.

'You might know her. Eileen Gadd. She's on the Blooming Marvellous committee.'

I remembered her. I had been covering their AGM for the *Gazette* and June Black and some others had been promoting a bold new planting initiative. Eileen, a dreary person who wore clothes that were a generation too old for her, was presenting all sorts of potential pitfalls.

'Oh, come on, Eileen!' an exasperated June had finally exclaimed, and there was a moment's silence as everyone processed where they had heard that expression before. Everyone tittered, except Eileen, who had possibly never watched *Top of the Pops*, and who had only looked bewildered.

'I think I know who you mean,' I said. 'By the way, did you get your kitten?'

'I decided against it. Mum thought it would scratch the upholstery.'

Eric lingered, although I didn't think there was anything more to say.

'So ...' Eric said.

'I'd better press on,' I told him. 'I'm visiting a young friend who's in hospital.'

Eric took the hint and backed away, and I returned to the chiller. I didn't tell him to have a lovely time. I didn't even say goodbye. I had decided that I didn't particularly like Eric and I couldn't see any good reason to fake it.

'Thanks for coming,' Ray drawled, when I arrived on Lucas's ward. 'We've barely seen Noah for days, and we really should ...'

'No problem,' I said. 'Glad to do it. Hi, Lucas.'

'Hello,' Lucas said, lying flat on his back in the bed with his arms aloft, continuing an intricate pattern he was working out on his fingertips and thumbs.

Ray and Jodie kissed him goodbye, told him they would see him in the morning, then hurried off for home.

'Did you bring me anything?' Lucas asked, still doing the thing with his hands, and not looking at me.

'Nothing very exciting,' I said. 'But I did pick you up some of your kefir – you'll have to drink it soon, though. We don't have a fridge to put it in.'

'OK.'

This was still a very subdued Lucas – a million miles away from the mischievous imp with whom I was used to engaging. No cheeky smile, no throaty cackle.

'How's the hospital food?'

'Nice.'

'What did you have tonight?'

'Chips. And sausages.'

'Any pudding?'

'Ice cream.'

'Lucky you! You won't want to go home!'

Lucas lowered his hands, but kept his eyes on the ceiling.

Something told me not to say another word, not to try to jolly him or chat about trivial things, but just to let him be.

Wordlessly, I took out my sandwich and began to eat. Lucas didn't react. When I had finished, I stood and placed my empty wrappings in the foot-operated flip-top bin in the corner of the ward, then took a slug from my water bottle.

I sat down and avoided catching Lucas's eye. Naomi had informed me on the phone that, despite Lucas successfully opening Tabby's cough bottle in front of an audience, Social Services were far from finished with the case. As Tabby had predicted, bringing Lucas home was no simple matter. Jodie, now confident of Lucas's survival, had railed at the social worker and demanded to know when Lucas would be discharged from hospital. When the ward staff had tried to explain that they must liaise with the safeguarding team, Jodie had accused them of ganging up against her.

It would work itself out, I supposed. Eventually, even if it took some investigation, Jodie and Ray would be declared fit people to look after the boys. They would be told to keep medication securely locked up in future, probably, but no one who spent time with them could consider them capable of actively harming Lucas or Noah.

The same nurse I'd seen the other night came along. 'Mum and Dad gone home for a while?' she asked.

'Lucas has a brother, Noah, they wanted to check in on,' I offered. 'It's been a tough time for him, too, with all this going on.'

'Maybe Noah will be able to come and see you tomorrow,' the nurse suggested, pausing by the bed. 'You could show him what Santa brought you.'

My ears pricked up.

'Has Santa been to see you?' I asked Lucas.

He nodded, and I looked at the nurse, who winked and said, 'Show us what you got, Lucas.' Lucas reached across to his bedside locker and gripped a cute blue plush puppy with a pink tongue.

'He's fab!' I said, although it was clearly a much inferior product to the expensive cuddly toys Jodie stocked in her gift shop. 'Have you given him a name, yet?'

'I couldn't think of anything.'

'Well, what's blue?' I prompted.

'Stilton,' the nurse said.

'Stilton?' Lucas asked, with just the first slight hint of interest.

'It's a type of cheese,' the nurse explained.

'Stilton,' Lucas repeated, and, holding the puppy by its back, trotted it across the bedcover. 'Stilton, sit!' He made it sit.

'The Rotary Club organises it, every year,' the nurse murmured to me. 'The presents are only small, but they cheer the kids up.'

She took Lucas's temperature and his pulse, and asked him if he wanted to sit up a bit or lie flat.

'Lie flat.'

As soon as she'd gone, he loosened his grip on the fabric puppy and resumed staring at the ceiling. 'When I die, I don't want to go to Heaven,' he said, in an even tone.

'Oh?' I replied softly. 'Why not?'

'Because I don't want to go anywhere when I die. I just want everything to be over.'

'Is that why you took the medicine? Because you wanted everything to be over?'

'I thought it would make me sleepy, just put me to sleep and I'd never wake up. Mummy always said that's what happens if you help yourself to medicine without her giving it to you. A little bit is good for you, but a lot is poison. It puts you to sleep and it kills you. But it didn't.'

'Why did you want that, Lucas? Were you very unhappy?'

'Yes.'

'What was making you so unhappy?'

'Everything.'

'Like what? Tell me.'

'Just everything. Don't you know what everything means?'

I wasn't sure how to respond.

'I just wanted to stay at home, but I never get to stay at home – I have to go to school and stupid after-school and French club and gymnastics and drama and Kumon maths and I'm so tired. And Mummy says I'm too old to suck my thumb, but I can't help it. I wish I had died. Now what am I going to do?' Lucas's face crumpled, then, into a twist of pink and tears.

'Oh, Lucas,' I said, and scooped his little body into my arms.

'I don't want to go places all the time with people I don't even know!' he wailed. 'I just need to stay at home and I just need to suck my thumb! But I'm not allowed.'

Having sat with Lucas until he had had supper of toast and the kefir and fallen asleep – for the night, I hoped – I returned to my car in the hospital car park and, yawning, set off for home.

Madeleine had been thrilled to find Mark at my place, the previous night. Over the years, having let slip that I had a brother, I had casually encouraged her to believe he lived in Dubai, with his wife, Amina, working as an electrical engineer. I'd told Tabby the same story and deliberately kept things vague – he was a distant uncle in a faraway land. He wasn't part of our lives. Madeleine had coaxed me to do more to nurture the relationship and believed it was a mixture of sadness and laziness at my end that explained the sparse correspondence between us. All fabrication, on my part – I'd had no idea what had become of Mark. And, of course, Madeleine knew nothing of the dark history we shared.

Having taken the pressure off her bladder in my bathroom, she had trotted back downstairs full of enthusiasm, and showed no sign of making a prompt exit.

'So, Mark, are you planning to stay for Christmas?' she'd asked.

'Things are still a bit up in the air.' He gave me a look. 'So you've been friends with Caroline for a long time?'

Madeleine launched into an explanation of how we had met at the *Gazette*, when the then editor, Lewis, had brought her in to shadow the office manager who was nearing retirement, and recruited me straight from training college to start as a cub reporter.

'Caroline arrived on Day One wearing a trench coat like the ones they wore on *News at Ten*, and I immediately decided she must think a lot of herself, especially as she was so pretty. But first impressions can be misleading, and I soon got to know her and discovered she was one of the nicest people you could ever meet – no big head, despite her looks, and totally down to earth.'

'And are you still with the *Gazette*, Madeleine?'

How could Mark be so composed? I was dying, here, far out on the end of the plank, not knowing if or when he would throw me overboard.

'Oh, yes – I think I'm there for the duration, now.'

'You must have seen some changes.'

'Big-time. When I started, the storeroom was still full of the editorial department's old typewriters, and the reporters were getting to grips with these clunky great Amstrad computers.

This was even before we changed over to Apple Macs and had to learn to use a mouse. Advertising was a lot easier to come by, back then – pre-Gumtree and eBay, people brought in their little classified ads, written out in biro on a piece of paper, selling everything from Irish setter puppies to three-piece suites. It didn't cost them much, but it all added up for us, and readers bought the paper as much to read those ads as anything else. Do you remember, Caroline?'

I nodded.

'Of course our circulation was very healthy, in those days,' Madeleine continued, 'so retailers were keen to get a show – there were times we actually had different traders fighting over a spot on the front page or page three. Not so now – they all have their own Facebook pages and do it themselves. They don't need us.'

'Do you think newspapers will ever make a comeback?' Mark asked. 'Maybe people will grow disenchanted with social media and things will go full circle.'

Stop this. Stop this right now. Stop pretending to be interested in Madeleine and newspapers and everything else you don't give a shit about. Please go home, Madeleine. My world is imploding and I don't want you watching.

Madeleine shook her head sadly.

'I can't see it. Our readers are almost all older – the new generation coming through get their news on their phones. My kids text me all the time to tell me what's going on long before I see it even on the TV news – and television can react a lot faster to developments than print can.'

I had to stop her there. Madeleine starting to talk about her kids came dangerously close to her mentioning that I had a daughter.

'I suppose it's time we let you go home,' I began, turning to her, 'since we've got work in the morning.'

Madeleine looked stricken. 'Forgive me! You two must have so much catching up to do and here I am, barging into the middle of it. I was just so excited to see you both together at last. Typical Madeleine, I'm afraid, Mark – I get carried away.' She shrugged on her coat and gathered up her handbag. 'I'd ask you both over to supper one night, but Caroline knows I'm in the middle of a big kitchen refurb – another example of me being altogether too enthusiastic and losing the run of myself.'

Mark and Madeleine assured each other of the pleasure of having met, before I was finally able to close the front door behind her and lean my head, momentarily, on the glass.

'She seems nice,' Mark said.

'She is,' I replied. 'Look, I'm going to have to eat something now, or I'll go low. Are you planning on hanging about or what?'

'Do you want me to leave?'

Yes! I wanted him to disappear and never come back. But since he showed no signs of doing that of his own volition, I was going to have to figure out how to make it happen. 'I don't know what I want.'

'You used to know.'

'I'm going to make a toasted sandwich. It's just as easy to make two.'

Mark followed me to the kitchen again and leant against the

larder as I took out bread – I had enough, this time – and went to the fridge for ham and cheese.

'Are you a grater or a slicer?' he asked. 'Mum was always a grater.'

'Whatever's convenient,' I said.

'Nice sandwich press,' Mark observed, and it was on the tip of my tongue to boast that, yes, it was a present from Tabby, when I caught myself, bit back the impulse and settled for just buttering the bread.

'Proper butter, like we always had,' Mark said. 'Everyone else was eating Flora polyunsaturated spread in the little plastic tubs, but not the Maxwells – we didn't trust it. Do you still count all your carbs, for your diabetes, or do you just wing it?'

'It's not quite so strict any more, but I still have to be more thoughtful than other people about what I eat. It'll always be a balancing act of insulin and carbohydrate – when you inject, I can't see how it could ever be any different.'

'When we were kids, I used to feel so glad it had happened to you and not me – I liked my Curly Wurlys too much – but then I was beset by guilt for feeling that way.'

'Poor you.'

I placed the sandwiches in the toaster, pressed down hard and locked. They sizzled. The food smell curdled with my knocking anxiety and I thought I might retch. How did I imagine I was going to eat anything?

'I see they've levelled Granny and Granddad's farmhouse and built a monstrous bungalow,' Mark said. 'When did that happen?'

'I don't know. I only saw it for the first time the other day.'

'When you went to visit the grave?'

'Yes. You'd been there, too, I saw. A nice way to unnerve me, when I was marking my parents' deaths.'

'The roses, you mean. Seventeen red roses, just like I gave you the first time we ... well, you know – because you were seventeen years old.'

'Why do that?' I asked crossly. 'Why not just lay a holly wreath like a normal person?'

'But you and I aren't normal people, are we? What we did wasn't normal.'

'So we're going to talk about it, are we? Is that why you're here, Mark, to talk about what we did?'

'I can live with what we did,' Mark said, and I instantly registered that his tone had changed to one of menace. 'That doesn't keep me awake at night, doesn't make my skin crawl or want to throw up – though it might shock Madeleine and the nosy guy next door and all your other Christmas-card friends. It's what *you* did, Caroline, that I can never forgive. That's why I'm here and that's why I'm going to make you pay.'

'Your sandwich is ready.'

'Keep it. I don't think I could eat anything you've touched.'

'Mark, please.'

'I'll call you tomorrow and tell you what happens next. Make sure you answer.'

Mark swept out of the kitchen and I raced to follow him. 'What do you mean *what happens next*? What are you going to do?'

But he was already leaving by the front door.

'You'll find out tomorrow.'

Once again, as I had learnt to do when Mark first left me, and again when Ray went, I had got up the next morning, showered and gone to work. Keeping on keeping on was what I did. I had spent an anxious day with my phone on my desk, but it hadn't rung there and it hadn't rung at the supermarket or the hospital, either. When I pulled into my driveway at ten minutes to ten and still hadn't heard anything, I sat in the darkness and checked for a missed call – there was nothing.

I went inside, poured myself a glass of wine and sat on the sofa, with my phone on the arm – sat there until the clock showed midnight. 'Tomorrow' had come and gone and Mark had not rung me. Why not?

21

It was Tuesday morning, four days before Christmas. I hadn't seen or heard anything of Mark since Sunday evening and it was making me extremely nervous.

'Right, troops,' Fergus said. 'I know you're all tired at this stage, but if we can manage one last push and get this week's paper filled, we've got a holiday to look forward to.'

'Will we finish early on Friday, boss?' Suzanne asked. 'It's Christmas Eve.'

'If we can manage it, I'd like us to finish on Thursday,' Fergus said. 'And there's no reason we can't.'

'Happy days.'

'So. What have we got? Caroline?'

'We've received annual figures from the council about recycling – they're way below target, and I suspect they're trying to sneak them out while everybody's busy thinking about Christmas.'

'OK. Will you speak to the local Green Party rep?'

'I'm waiting for him to call me back.'

'Good. Anything else?'

'I thought I'd do a short piece about the amenity centre opening hours over the holidays – that always seems to catch people out.'

'Find out what the latest story is with dumping wrapping paper and cards, too – what can go in the green bin and what can't.'

'I thought I might speak to a few shopkeepers and someone from the Chamber of Trade to hear what business has been like this December,' I said, tapping my pen against the edge of the desk. 'Is internet shopping hitting them as hard as ever, or harder, or is there any sign of the high streets rallying? That's all I have right now, but I'll do a bit of ringing round, see what else I can turn up.'

'Good. We still need something for the front. Jamie's at Riverside Primary School for the nativity production this morning, so there's our pic, but we need a hard news story, too.'

Riverside Primary was Noah and Lucas's school.

'Suzanne? Got anything that could do a front?'

'Sorry, boss.'

'Well, see what you can dig up, both of you. Actually, Caroline, do you fancy going along to that nativity show and doing a piece? Maybe get a few cute quotes from the kids? That kind of thing's your forte.'

'Sure.'

While Fergus discussed the sports pages with Richie, I rang the school and found out that the play started at ten thirty and they would reserve me a front-row seat. I just had time to grab a quick coffee and then I went.

The road near Riverside Primary School was parked up, bumper to bumper. I had to doubleback and find a space in a nearby housing development, making sure not to block anyone's driveway – the residents probably hated days like these.

It was already twenty past ten, and I forced two Imodium capsules past the throat pebble, slung my bag over my shoulder and sprinted so I wouldn't be late.

Anne McAvoy, the principal, spotted me by the assembly-hall doors and came to greet me. 'Caroline – thanks for coming,' she said, over the hubbub of a packed hall. 'Please don't judge us too harshly – we've had a wave of chicken-pox in school and there's had to be a good deal of last-minute reassigning of roles.'

'I'm not here to find fault, Anne. I love a nativity, so this is a treat.'

'Oh, good. Come with me – your seat's just up here.'

'Any chance of a quick word with some of the children, when you wrap up – if that would be OK?'

'Of course.'

'You know we only print kids' first names, now – it's a sign of the times.'

'Yes – and we send out a consent form to parents at the start of the year, to ensure they're happy for their children to be photographed – one of our tick-boxes mentions engaging with the press, so that's sorted. If you don't mind me asking, what's the latest on Lucas? I haven't heard from Jodie for a couple of days.'

'He's out of danger, but I'm not sure when he'll come home from hospital.'

'I thought he must be getting better, or this is the last place you'd want to be.'

A tall child in school uniform and a Santa hat appeared at the principal's shoulder.

'Yes, Sienna?'

'Mrs Mackle sent me to tell you everything is ready for you to start.'

'Thank you.'

Anne looked at me. 'Cross your fingers for us.'

'Stop worrying – everyone's on your side. And nativity audiences love the odd blooper.'

I sat down and watched as the swing doors on either side of the stage opened, and dozens of children, dressed as angels and shepherds, filed in and sat down. Anne crossed to the 'wings', where she exchanged a few words with another teacher. Then she took to the stage, microphone in hand, and addressed the audience. 'Good morning, boys and girls,' she began.

'Good mor-ning, Miss-us Mac-Ah-voy,' they chanted.

The parents tittered and Anne smiled, rolling her eyes.

'And good morning to all our guests. We thank you for coming and we hope you enjoy this morning's nativity production. For those of you who don't have to rush off, mince pies and tea and coffee will be available from the hatch at the back of the hall after the performance. And now, Riverside Primary School proudly presents *The First Christmas*.'

She stepped down, the overhead lighting was turned off and the audience applauded before a small girl in a blue robe and a small boy with a tea-towel on his head and a brown beard on elastic limped across the stage to the singing of the angels and shepherds – a song I hadn't heard before but which was a variation on the theme of the long, dusty road to Bethlehem.

The swing-door to the left side opened a crack, as if someone was peeping through. It opened a little wider, and I saw a small figure in stripy robes and another beard on elastic, this child carrying an over-sized set of keys. Noah.

In a moment, he was up on stage.

'I'm sorry, my young friends – there is no room in my inn, and I'm afraid it's the same story all over the city. The best I can offer you is our stable – at least it's warm and dry.'

Mary, Joseph and the little girl beside Noah looked at him expectantly. Oh dear – had he dried?

'*My wife ...*' someone whispered loudly from the front of the stage.

Noah frowned.

'*My wife will bring ...*' the whisperer tried again.

But Noah wasn't co-operating. He remained stubbornly silent.

Afterwards, I learnt that the line had been, 'My wife will bring you blankets.'

'Noah Rankin – what was the matter with you?' I overheard a teacher ask him in the corridor, not unkindly, but clearly puzzled.

Noah didn't respond.

'Noah, answer an adult when they ask you a question,' another teacher, or possibly a classroom assistant, said sharply, making my hackles rise.

Noah mumbled something – he was still wearing his beard.

'What was that?' his interrogator demanded.

'I said, "She's not my wife"!' Noah snapped. 'I don't have a wife. I'll never have a wife.'

'Don't take that tone with me, Noah.'

I watched, wondering whether my intervention might only make things worse for Noah, but as I did so he drained of colour and slid onto the floor.

'Noah?' Now I dashed forward.

The sharp-voiced adult grabbed a passing child.

'Fetch Angela or Mrs Robinson. Quickly.' To me, she added, 'They're both first-aiders.'

We laid Noah flat and I put my coat under his head. In a moment, he opened his eyes.

'What happened, Noah? Do you think you're going to be sick?' I asked him.

'I have a very, very, very sore ear,' he murmured.

'Since when? When did it start hurting?' I asked.

'Last night.'

'And did you tell anyone?'

'No.'

Angela arrived.

'What happened?' she asked.

'Noah Rankin just collapsed in a heap,' the no-longer-cross-voiced one told her. 'He says he has a really sore ear.'

'Noah, could I have a little look at your chest, for a minute?' Angela said. 'You don't have to take anything off, just pull up your jumper and let me undo your shirt buttons.'

'OK.'

When Angela pulled up his clothes, Noah was sporting a chest and tummy *covered* with bright red spots.

'Chicken-pox,' Angela pronounced. 'A few of the kids have mentioned it starting with earache or a headache. Poor you, Noah. He'll have to go home.'

School had to speak to Jodie or Ray, but I waited while they did so, and it was agreed that, as they were waiting to see Lucas's consultant at the hospital, I would drive Noah home, where Nana and Pop would meet us and sit with him.

'Your ear must have been very sore,' I said in the car. 'It made you faint. Why didn't you tell anyone?'

'Because I was frightened.'

'Frightened of what?'

'Of the medicine. What if I took too much and got poisoned like Lucas?'

Oh, Noah.

'Is your ear still sore?'

'It's getting better.'

'Would you trust me to give you just a little bit of painkiller, if I read the bottle and measured it very carefully? I could get Nana to check it, to be doubly sure.'

'No, thanks.'

'OK.'

'I suppose I won't be able to go carol-singing to the old people, now.'

'No. I suppose not.'

'Have you ever had chicken-pox?'

'Yes. When I was about your age.'

'What happened?'

'Not much. Mine started with a very sore place on my forehead, then a lump behind my ear, and the spots appeared. Once the spots came, I started to feel better. But they did get extremely itchy after a few days.'

'Did you scratch them?'

'I tried not to. If you scratch them, they tend to leave a mark.'

'What kind of mark?'

'A tiny white scar.'

'For ever?'

'I think so.'

'I'll try not to scratch mine.'

'Noah, can I ask you something?'

'Ask me what?'

'Do you enjoy going to all your clubs and activities, or does it make you feel a bit tired?'

'Very tired.'

'OK.'

'That's not what I thought you were going to ask me.'

'Oh? What did you think I was going to ask you?'

'About not saying my lines and never wanting to have a wife.'

'If you don't want to marry, that's your choice, Noah. Although I'm sure a lot of people who end up married didn't think they would, when they were kids.'

'I didn't say I didn't want to get married.'

A blue-lit ambulance suddenly appeared in my rear-view mirror and we had to pull up with two wheels on the pavement to let it through.

'I'm hungry,' Noah said, as we dismounted the kerb and edged back onto the road. 'My lunch box is still on the trolley in school. Can we get a drive-thru at McDonald's?'

'Sure,' I said. 'Do you want to continue what we were talking about before?'

'No, thanks. Can I get a Happy Meal? And a chocolate milkshake?'

'Course.'

Back at the office, I wrote up my nativity piece, got hold of the Green Party guy for a reaction to the recycling figures, put through the amenity site opening hours and got a mixed response from traders on their Christmas business.

I kept my phone beside me, checking it obsessively even though it hadn't rung – there was nothing from Mark.

When we locked up for the evening, I rang Jodie – I had avoided calling Ray throughout the whole Lucas crisis, because ... well, because.

'We've just got back from the hospital. Doris and Bob are sitting with Lucas, and Mum has cooked dinner for the rest of us,' she reported.

'In that case, if you're home for the evening, there's something I need to talk to you both about,' I said.

'If this is about you and Ray, I really don't have what it takes to deal with it right now, Caroline,' Jodie replied. 'My child is still stuck in hospital, and—'

'It's not that. It's about Lucas,' I told her. 'He talked to me a little bit last night, and I need to share it with you.'

'What is it? Just tell me,' Jodie demanded.

'It's nothing to panic about. Let me come round.'

'Mum said we should be ready to eat at seven. Give us until eight, when Noah's in bed.'

'See you then.'

Jodie was adamant. 'Lucas loves his activities,' she insisted. 'We hear him singing his little French songs to himself in bed at night – don't we, Ray? And he's made loads of friends at after-school.'

'I'm not saying there aren't good things about his clubs and lessons,' I said, trying to sound reasonable, but desperate to get her to listen. 'But does he really need *all* of them?'

'So you think he'd be better off lazing about playing video games?' Jodie said.

'It doesn't have to be either/or,' I tried, looking at Ray for support.

'Maybe it is a bit too much for him, Jodie,' Ray conceded. 'If Lucas has told Caroline that's what's making him unhappy ...'

Jodie glared at me. 'Why did he say this to you, anyway? What did you say to him?'

I spared her the bit about Lucas indicating that he hoped there was no Heaven, and that, once dead, he could literally rest in peace. But for his sake I had to get through to her.

Fortunately, Nana and Pop were in the snug, where they could overhear. They came into the room quietly. Stanley spoke first. 'Jodie, I think you should listen to Caroline. Your mum and I are very proud of you and how you're bringing up the boys. They have everything a child could wish for – a lovely home, a big safe car, a mother and father who love them, holidays, toys, you name it. But their feet never touch the ground. They're always off doing something – French and maths and after-school. It's all rush, rush, rush, busy, busy, busy.'

Jodie's eyes filled with tears. 'Mum? Is this what you think, too?'

Naomi nodded, then came forward, sat on the arm of Jodie's chair and placed her hand over her daughter's. 'I do.'

'Right! Well, that's that, then. Things will have to change. I'll give up the shop and stay at home to look after the boys. I won't have a life, and Noah and Lucas won't have anything to put on their CVs, but if that's what everyone has decided, then that's how it's going to be.'

'Now you're being silly,' Naomi said. 'I will look after Noah and Lucas after school. I've always wanted to. I can collect them, bring them here and they can have a snack and play with their toys. They'll be fine with their nana, and I can still bring them to one or two clubs, if you want. You can relax and enjoy building up your business. When you come home from work, the dinner will be ready and the boys will still have plenty of energy for spending time with you.'

Jodie looked at Naomi. 'Are you serious?'

'I'm always serious, Jodie. Have you ever heard me tell a joke?'

'I think it's a great idea,' Ray drawled. 'But five days a week is a job – you'd have to let us pay you.'

'Don't insult me,' Naomi said, but nicely.

'Look, I'd better go and leave you to it,' I said. To Jodie, I added, 'Lucas only told me because I happened to be there at the time – he could just as easily have said it to any of us.'

'Just a minute, Caroline, before you go,' Pop interjected.

'Yes?'

'Naomi and I appreciate your concern for Noah and Lucas and, as regards the after-school business, we don't disagree with you. We have come to think of you almost like a second daughter, and Tabby like our grandchild. We never said it to you, and perhaps we should have, but we always knew that the way Jodie got together with Ray was wrong—'

'Dad!'

'Let me finish, Jodie. Ray was your husband, Caroline, and the whole thing sat very badly with us. But things change. Ray and Jodie and the boys are a family now. You've got your own back on Jodie, and the slate is wiped clean. But that has to be an end to it. Naomi and I kept our feelings to ourselves with Lucas so ill, but now I can say this: if you ever, ever climb into bed with Raymond again, if you ever, ever meet him behind Jodie's back, I will destroy you. You can take that as a promise.'

A month ago, his speech would have rattled me, chilled me. Tonight, with Mark after me, less so. *Get in line, Stanley*, I thought darkly.

Naomi followed me to the front door. I put my hand on the door-knob, and she placed hers over it. 'Stanley might get you sacked, if you keep carrying on with Ray,' she murmured in my ear. 'He knows people. But I would bide my time, Caroline. I would walk into your house and I would kill you in your sleep and I would walk out again. Jodie is my beloved child, and I actually would. Now, I hope we'll see you and Tabby for lunch on Christmas Day. We'll eat at one so we're cleared up in time for the Queen.'

I had just slammed the car door shut on myself when my mobile rang. Mark. It must be. Announcing my fate at last. But when I looked, it wasn't. It was Fergus. 'Hi,' I said. 'What's up?'

'Sorry to bother you after hours,' he said. 'I'd deal with this myself, but I'm at a big family dinner with Marina's folks.'

'Deal with what?'

'A story's breaking. I got a tip that police have found a car crashed down an embankment at Willow Hill. Driver still in the vehicle, but deceased. My caller reckons the car's been there for a couple of days, but it's only just been discovered. Probably the black ice that was on the roads on Sunday night. No details of the driver's identity yet, but some poor family is going to have an empty place at the table this Christmas. The emergency services are at the scene now – think you could go and take a look? Bring Suzanne with you, if she's up for it.'

For a moment, I couldn't say anything. The pieces fitted. It explained why what had sounded like an urgent threat from Mark had then seemed to evaporate inexplicably.

'Caroline? Are you still there?'

'Is that all you know?' I could hear my voice shaking. 'Does your contact say if the driver was male or female?'

'Sorry, no word on that, yet.'

'What about the car?'

'My tip is that it's a large, dark vehicle. But that's the sort of thing I need you to check. There's every likelihood a name will be released before we go to press, but you know there are little details you'll pick up by being on the ground as things unfold.'

'Yes. OK. I'll go and see what I can find out. Have you called Jamie, or do you want me to?'

'I'll ring him now. You try Suzanne. And don't worry about being in the office first thing – eleven o'clock will do since you'll have been working tonight.'

I took a long, slow breath, then nearly jumped out of my skin when someone rapped on the car window. I rolled it down. 'Ray! You startled me.'

'Sorry. Everything OK? Car all right? I wondered why you hadn't driven away.'

'Everything's fine. Fergus called about a story.'

'At this time? Don't you ever quit?'

'It's fine. I'll check it out, but I won't have to write anything until tomorrow. I'd better go.'

'Glad you're OK.'

Was I OK? I really wasn't sure. The person in the crashed car could be anyone. But Mark had sounded so definite that he would ring me on Monday, and he hadn't, and hadn't rung today, either. Was it possible that my problems were over? But if this was how it ended, I'd lost my brother in shocking circumstances. Mark's body could have been lying undiscovered at the side of a field in the chill December air for forty-eight hours. I had loved him once as much as I feared him now. It might not be him. It might be. How did I really feel?

22

I picked up Suzanne at her house and we set off for Willow Hill.

'Do we know if it's just the one stiff, or were there passengers?' she asked me.

'Fergus only mentioned a driver, but I guess it's up to us to find out the details,' I said.

When we arrived on the scene, two police cars were in attendance, plus a fire tender.

Michael from the *Chronicle* was already there, speaking to Martin Lynch, a police inspector I'd known since he was a constable.

'We should get in there,' Suzanne said.

'Give them a moment,' I told her. 'Martin won't tell Michael anything he won't share with us, too. I want to see if we can get a look at the vehicle.'

Approaching the embankment, I couldn't feel the ground beneath my feet. Was I about to see Mark's car?

In the event, there was nothing to see – nothing that made the situation any clearer anyhow. The car appeared to have skidded off the road, plunged down the embankment and turned over. What we were looking at was, essentially, the underside of the car, so any chance I had of identifying it as Mark's was non-existent. I couldn't tell the colour, much less the make or model – not that I was sure what Mark's was anyhow. It might have been a Volvo, might have been a Lexus, might have been something else.

'Caroline – how are you?' It was Michael, at my shoulder. 'Shitty time for a road accident – there always seems to be one just before Christmas. Why is that?'

'What's Martin saying?'

'Body's still in the car. Male. No passengers. The car's a hired one, but they're not releasing any further details yet.'

'Hired from where? Do you know?'

'The new franchise at the airport, apparently. So I guess that means our man isn't local – or doesn't live locally now, anyhow. Someone back home to his family for Christmas maybe.'

I shivered.

'It's freezing,' Michael said. 'You letting Suzanne have this one?'

I followed his gaze and saw Suzanne talking to Martin, her notebook poised. 'Why not?'

Michael went off to interview the leading fire-fighter and I took a breath. As I pulled my coat tighter around me, I felt the vibration of my phone ringing in my bag. I dug urgently to retrieve it – was it Mark at last? Did I want it to be, or would I prefer he was the man lying at the bottom of the embankment?

Peering at the screen, I saw that it wasn't him – it was Dawson, Hendrew's partner. 'Dawson. Hello.'

'Hi, Caroline. How are things?'

'Fine, fine. Everyone OK your end?' I tried to sound casual, but the only reason I had answered was in case he was getting in touch to inform me that Tabby was unwell or had had an accident. I liked Dawson, but I didn't need one of his chatty calls while I was standing out in the December night at the possible death scene of my brother.

'There's no drama, or anything like that,' Dawson said. 'Tabby's great. She's relieved that Lucas is getting better, obviously, and she's out with the famous Harry.'

In that case, I would try to curtail things. 'I'm actually a bit busy, at the minute, Dawson. I'm out on a story – could I call you back?'

'Sorry, Caroline! Yes, of course, ring me later. But could you make it tonight, if poss? I'm tied up with work all day tomorrow and then Hendy and I are going away.'

'OK. Give me an hour. Was it anything in particular?'

'Oh, vaguely.'

'I'll call you when I get back to the house.'

I went and sat in my car while Suzanne spoke to the leading fire-fighter, and then to Jamie, who had turned up.

'They're not saying much,' she complained, as she dropped heavily into the passenger seat beside me.

'Don't worry – you've got plenty of time to learn more. Tomorrow morning, I'd suggest you come back and knock on a few doors – ask the local residents about that stretch of road. Had they been worried about it? Should there have been a barrier along the top of the embankment? Are there any hidden hazards that catch motorists out, if they're not familiar with the surface? You could find out whether the gritter lorry comes this way, too – and, if it doesn't, has anybody been saying it should?'

I heard myself rattling out the things I would do if it were my story, because I'd covered similar incidents so many times before, but it was automatic: my inner thoughts were circling deep down inside me, like a funnel cloud threatening to become a tornado.

Back home, I put up my latest delivery of Christmas cards, flopped down on the sofa and tried to gather my thoughts. Tomorrow morning I was confident we would have a name for the dead driver. The jigsaw pieces fitted with it being Mark – a car of a similar size to the one he had driven to my house, and also the fact it had been hired at the airport, plus the sudden lack of contact from him when his promise to ring me had seemed so certain.

There was nothing I could do but wait. It wouldn't be for long. Even if the victim's name was withheld officially for a while, Martin Lynch would tell me off the record.

I didn't feel much like ringing Dawson, but I had said I would, and that was what I did, what I had learnt to do, however shocked or sick or tired I had felt – keep on keeping on. I loved Dawson, but he could be an awful old woman, and it quickly became clear that this was precisely why he was ringing.

'Caroline! Thanks for returning my call. So – looking forward to the holidays? Did Tabby tell you Hendy and I are jetting off to Lanzarote the day after tomorrow? We both had time off, and suddenly decided to have Christmas in the sun this year. I don't know which is better – Christmas on the beach or coming back and being the only ones to have a real tan in January.'

'No, I hadn't heard. Good for you.'

'It was all very last-minute. We'll send your present with Tabby, though – hope you like it.'

'Oh, Dawson – I haven't even got yours yet. Things have been a bit tricky around here lately. It will be there when you get back from your holiday. Promise.'

'Don't be silly, Caroline – we don't give presents to get presents. Hendy and I love choosing things for you because you suit everything. We're in Tabby's good books because Hendy found these amazing beanbags for her to give Noah and Lucas – a dinosaur one for Lucas, obviously, and a bear one for Noah. You don't think Noah's too old for bears? Tabby really likes both of them.'

'I'm sure the boys will be delighted.'

'How did you think Tabby was, when you saw her?'

'Concerned about Lucas, mainly. Otherwise, pretty good – why do you ask?'

'Is she bringing this Harry person to meet you over Christmas, by any chance?'

'*This Harry person* – you don't sound impressed, Dawson. Why not? What's up with him?'

'Oh, nothing, probably. It's just that we're used to knowing everything Tabby gets up to, and she hasn't introduced us to Harry yet. There's this business with his allergies – but still ... Although I did just happen to look out the front window when he came to collect her last night.'

'Oh?' Dawson was lovely, but incorrigibly nosy.

Dawson didn't say anything.

'Dawson? What was it?'

'Caroline, I'm the very last person to pass judgement on anyone else's relationships ...'

This was completely untrue – Dawson had an opinion on everything and everybody. 'But ...?' I prompted.

'Hendy told me to mind my own, but you know anything I say to you is coming from a good place.'

'Go on.'

'Well, I don't have to tell you that Tabby's not exactly over-burdened with self-esteem, Caroline.'

I waited.

'So if someone singled her out for attention, she might feel flattered, but ...'

'Spit it out, Dawson.'

I could practically feel him pursing his lips and anticipated his, frankly, prim sensibility to be at work.

'He's older, Caroline. Harry is an older man.'

'Is that all?' I hadn't twigged it from Tabby's admittedly limited accounts, but like mother, like daughter, I was thinking, remembering how exceptionally well I had got on with Ralph Nicholson and how attractive I had found his pewter hair, his repertoire of apposite Shakespeare quotations and his knowledge of the female body. 'When you say "older", I take it you mean there's a bit of an age gap and not that he's on a Zimmer.'

'No! He'd still qualify as hot totty, and he was taking her ice-skating. And Hendy insists that, though Tabby might be vulnerable, she won't fall for any old sweet-talk – but what do you think, Caroline?'

'I appreciate you telling me, Dawson. And I do know it comes from a place of love. But I don't necessarily think it's a cause for concern. Maybe someone with a bit of experience is exactly what Tabby needs – he might appreciate her qualities better than a younger guy.'

'That's what Hendy said.'

'I haven't heard any mention of him having any kids – although it wouldn't be the end of the world if he did – Tabby has tonnes of experience. And she is bringing him to see me in the holidays, so it's not like he's running shy of meeting her family.'

'That makes me feel a lot better, Caroline. I'm sorry if you think I was being a terrible fusspot.'

'Of course, if I don't like him, you have my permission to kill him,' I replied. 'I'll help you destroy the evidence.'

'Naturally. Mother knows best. Not including my mother, obviously.'

Dawson's mother was still trying to set him up with girls from her church.

'Dawson, I've got to go – I've got another call coming in. Have a great time in Lanzarote and give my love to Hendrew.'

'Go, Caroline! And thanks for the chat.'

'Hello?'

'Caroline? It's Martin Lynch. I've got a name for our dead friend.'

23

One of the staff from Santino's had helped Madeleine carry coffees and pastries for everyone round to the office. They were on the house – a Christmas thank-you for all the trade we'd given them through the year. 'Fergus – cappuccino,' Madeleine said. 'Richie – green tea. Caroline – flat white. Suzanne – where's Suzanne?'

'On the phone,' Richie said. 'She'll be down in a minute.'

Madeleine gave the ad staff their drinks. 'Help yourself to sweet treats – they've given us more than enough.'

'So, how's the kitchen coming on?' Richie asked Madeleine. 'Will it be done in time for Christmas?'

'It had better be!' Madeleine said, lifting a raspberry ruffle square. 'They say today should finish it, but the whole place is going to need a thorough scrub before we can actually use it. Jimmy's twin nieces have just got home from uni, so I said if they'd come round tomorrow and give me a whole day's cleaning I'd pay them well. There's no way I could manage it all on my own with just forty-eight hours to Christmas Eve, and the girls will do a good job – plus they're glad of the money.'

'Win-win,' Richie said, putting his palm up to decline when Madeleine offered him a pastry.

'It'll be great to be able to use the washing machine again and do my own laundry,' Madeleine said. 'It's no fun trying to wash your smalls in other people's houses.'

A red-faced man pushed open the front door and stepped inside. 'I want to speak to the editor,' he said.

'How can we help you?' Madeleine enquired, setting down her paper cup.

'Are you the editor?'

'I'm the editor,' Fergus said.

'I want to complain.'

'About us or to us?' Fergus asked.

'What do you mean? Are you trying to make a fool of me?'

'Not at all, Mr ...'

'Ogle.'

'Mr Ogle. I'm Fergus Hanson. I merely want to know if you're complaining about something that has appeared in the *Gazette*, or wish us to help with your complaint about someone or something else.'

'I want to complain about the potholes on the Carrackbannon Road. They're a disgrace.'

They were, and they opened up every year – fissures and

indentations in the surface filled with water, the water froze, expanded and suddenly you had craters.

Fergus looked at me, part-hopeful, part-apologetic.

'Let me grab my notebook,' I said.

The dead man in the crashed car was Stephen Austin Cooper, forty-eight, single, no kids, visiting from Rockport, Massachusetts, with the intention of spending Christmas with relatives he was meeting for the first time. They'd wondered why he was so late.

'"Rockport is a seaside town in Essex County, located approximately forty miles north-east of Boston, at the tip of the Cape Ann peninsula,"' Suzanne had read aloud from a web search earlier. 'Population just under seven thousand. Wouldn't call that a town – more like a village. What sea would that be? The Pacific?'

'Atlantic,' I told her. 'Poor guy – coming all that way to end up like that.'

When Martin had given me the name on the phone the night before, I had scarcely known how to feel. A man was still dead, and that was terrible, but he was a stranger, which meant that Mark, and all the power he held over me, was still out there.

Suzanne wrote her story – yes, the locals thought there should be a barrier along the edge of the embankment, or the road widened along the other side, where there was only a flat field, which would make the job perfectly straightforward. Brian Donaldson, whose field it was, would let them have the land. No, the gritter lorry didn't service that road.

'Speak to Brian Donaldson and get his confirmation that he'd give up a strip to widen the road, if invited,' Fergus told her. 'And see if the police will give you a statement welcoming that.'

'Will it go on the front?' Suzanne asked.

'Very likely,' Fergus said.

I wrote my piece about the nativity play and sharpened up a press release about a few new recreational classes starting in January at the further education college – upholstery, holiday Spanish, getting the best from your digital camera.

My phone was never out of my sight, but still Mark didn't contact me. Every time the thing rang, I jumped, even though part of me wanted it to be him telling me what was happening. I needed to know what was coming next.

Although the town was bustling with shoppers, most of our usual go-to places for stories – the schools, youth organisations, social groups and committees – were winding down or already on recess for the season, so news was thin on the ground. I scratched about and got a whisper of a planning application for a drive-thru restaurant, a residential home under threat of closure and the appointment of a new choir-master at the Church of the Ascension in one of our larger villages. This kept me gainfully employed for the rest of the day.

Just as I was packing up, Tabby texted to say the coffee shop was closing at 4 p.m. on Christmas Eve, and could I pick her up at the flat at five, as she couldn't manage Lennie, with all the presents and other luggage, on the train. I texted her back to say I'd assumed that was what we'd be doing, and wondered how the hell to get Mark off my back before then. Just two days before Tabby came home – time was running out.

I stopped at the garage shop and picked up an individual quiche Lorraine and a tub of coleslaw for dinner – not very inspiring, but it was hard to summon up a huge amount of enthusiasm with no one else to cook for.

Councillor Lesley Lunt was peering at packets of sliced ham. I dodged out of the way, hoping to avoid her. Too late.

'Hello, Caroline. How are you? All ready for Christmas? I'm sure it's a busy time for the *Gazette*, as it is for me – so many functions, and people are terribly disappointed if you can't make it. Still, we do our best to get round as many as possible, don't we?'

I was saved the bother of deciding whether to agree or disagree as Councillor Lunt carried on regardless. 'That was a dreadful business up at Willow Hill, with the American gentleman. What was he doing away up there, do you think? The BBC didn't offer any explanation on the lunchtime news.'

I knew, because Suzanne had brilliantly dug out the story, that he'd been there visiting a shebeen a couple of miles further up the hill – but that would be revealed, under her byline, in this week's paper, and not before. I would make sure she sold it to the dailies, too, and didn't give it away to them this time.

'Well, have a nice Christmas, Caroline. Sonia, my daughter, is celebrating with her in-laws, this year, so it will just be Eddie and me. I'll be doing the Christmas dinners for the elderly, of course, as always, and then we'll have our meal in the evening. I must look at the *Radio Times* and see if they're showing a film. Christmas is the only time I see television – I'm always out. Of course there's not much worth watching, these days, is there? I loved *Morecambe and Wise*. And *The Two Ronnies*. Family entertainment.'

More cards on the mat, a supermarket special-offers leaflet and a flyer about loans. I slapped them onto the side table and took my groceries to the kitchen.

Ding-dong. The doorbell. I'd only just got in. Had someone been watching? Waiting for me?

My fists were balled tightly as I returned to the front door. I released them, stretched out my fingers. If it was Mark, I would talk to him, reason with him – we were adults now, no longer teenage kids.

But when I opened the door, it wasn't Mark. It was a woman. Petite. With long black hair that looked dyed, but expensively so. She looked like Mum. No, cut her hair and she looked like me.

'Caroline?'

'Yes.'

'You don't know me. I'm Sylvia Maxwell. Mark's wife. Can I come in?'

24

'Would you like a glass of wine? I'm having one. Sit down, please.'

'No wine, thanks.'

Sylvia perched on the edge of my sofa, her thick woollen coat bundling up at the shoulders. She folded her legs to one side and crossed them at the ankles, like a debutante, though I thought she was probably forty.

I went to the kitchen, chose one of the balloon wine glasses and poured a large measure of Chardonnay. I placed one hand against the larder door, drank half of what I'd poured and topped it up before returning to the lounge.

'He didn't tell you he was married, did he?' Sylvia said, sounding like she already knew the answer.

I shook my head.

'But he has seen you,' she added.

'Mark came here on Sunday evening. He stayed awhile, lobbed a grenade or two, then buggered off. He said he'd ring me on Monday, and he sounded like he meant it, but I haven't seen or heard of him since. Has he been with you?'

'I haven't seen Mark for weeks. That's why I came. To find him. And to find you.'

'Have the two of you broken up?'

'He hasn't said so. But he was very upset.'

'He made that clear. Did you know we hadn't set eyes on each other in over thirty years? The last time I saw Mark I was eighteen years old and he was nineteen. We didn't part on good terms, and I have absolutely no idea why he's suddenly reappeared.'

'I might be able to help you with that.'

I looked at the small figure on my sofa. She was pretty, made-up like a little doll, and she looked fragile. I didn't want to hurt her, but I did want to find out what she knew about my brother's intentions. 'I'd be grateful for anything you can tell me.'

And so Sylvia explained how she had met Mark ten years earlier, when she was waitressing in Greece. She and a friend were classroom assistants who had gone for a holiday in Crete and had got themselves jobs in a beach-side taverna, which would enable them to stay for the whole summer. When September loomed, the friend had returned to the UK as planned, but Sylvia had met Mark by then and decided to stay.

'I wasn't a kid – I was thirty-one – but I really fell for him. And he seemed infatuated by me.'

'What was he doing there?'

'Mark owned Aphrodite's nightclub in Matala, the holiday village where all the hippies used to come in the sixties. He was already very successful in the hospitality industry – he had bars in Newcastle and Dundee, too, and he'd put money into a couple of places on Ibiza, but he had business managers who ran them. He was hands-on in Greece, though.'

'I didn't know about any of that.'

'He was very impressive. The nightclub was a goldmine, and Mark lived in a beautiful villa about a mile beyond all the tourist development, with a pool, a housekeeper and a gardener. He told me he'd been waiting for me to come for years, and now I was finally there. It was intense, but it was exciting, too.'

'So you both lived there, from that time?'

'I moved in with him and, after a few weeks, he took me to dinner in the taverna where we had first met and proposed to me. It felt like something from a film. I didn't question any of it – I said yes.'

Sylvia looked at her hands, at my Christmas cards, at the television switched off in the corner – anywhere but at me.

'It all sounds idyllic. If you don't mind me asking, what went wrong?'

'Mark had made it clear from the start that he wanted us to have a family. As he was already in his forties, he didn't want to wait. I agreed. It was what I had always wanted, too, and, as I said, I was already past thirty. Everyone told us we would have beautiful children, and we imagined bringing them up in the sunshine and fresh air, taking them to the beach in the mornings, feeding them on fresh food from the market. Because Mark had Maria to look after the villa, I didn't have to do any chores, but we were both clear that we'd raise our children ourselves – no daycare or nannies. It was how we both wanted it.

'Mark wanted them to learn Greek as well as English, and he said we could spend time on Ibiza so they could learn Spanish, too. He had everything mapped out – when the children were small, we'd live a simple life on Crete. When they got older, we'd move to the UK for them to get their education, and return to Greece for our summers. Once they got to uni, we'd retreat to Crete full-time again, knowing they'd want to bring their friends to stay in the villa, maybe with the opportunity of work in Mark's businesses, if they fancied it.'

She was starting to sound hoarse.

'Sure you don't want a glass of wine?'

'Could I have some water?' Sylvia drank the whole glass, and set the empty tumbler on the coffee table. 'We stopped using contraception, but it was over a year before I conceived. We'd started worrying a bit, but when the doctor confirmed the pregnancy, we were over the moon.'

'So you have a child.'

'I miscarried. At thirteen weeks.'

'I'm sorry.'

'I was in pieces, but Mark was fantastic. He let me mourn, then booked us a holiday in Switzerland to try to brighten us up so we could try again. We struggled even longer to conceive this time – eighteen months – celebrated again when the pregnancy was confirmed, miscarried again.'

Sylvia looked directly at me. 'How many times do you think a person can put themselves through that? Month after month when you hope, and pray, and then you bleed, and there's nothing. And then, when you finally test positive, and know your baby is inside you, you can't keep them.'

'I don't know.'

'We suffered six miscarriages, two unsuccessful rounds of IVF and I had decided I couldn't do it any more. It was time to accept that it was just going to be Mark and me. But Mark wasn't ready to give up. He persuaded me to try one last round of IVF. He practically begged me. After all he'd done for me, the life he'd given me, I said I would.'

I thought I knew what was coming.

'Failed. Again.'

'So you're saying he's mad with grief,' I said. 'You must be, too.'

'I'd been accepting slowly, for years, that this was my fate, Caroline. I don't think the same was true of Mark. And then, just as we were confronted by our childless future, by complete chance he saw that photograph taken at the awards dinner. He went into himself – he wouldn't talk to me. He spent hours in his study and, eventually, when he was out, I went in there, wondering if perhaps he was keeping a journal, thinking it might tell me what to do. Instead, I discovered he'd hired a private detective.'

'A detective?'

'To track you down, find out about you and relay everything back to him. He was jealous that you were happy and he wasn't. In fact, he was enraged.'

'But Mark found me himself. He saw me at a hotel in town, and then he spoke to someone from work. He pretended to be an old pal and she unwittingly helped him get to me.'

Sylvia shook her head. 'No, Caroline – you're wrong. Mark has known where you live for some time. How do you think I got your address? If he's tried to make it seem like anything else, he'll have his reasons.

'Mark hates you, Caroline. I don't know why, but he does. You don't have to tell me what this is all about – I don't care. I still love him. I need to find him. But I think you're in danger. I'm not going to pretend I'm looking out for you, because I'm not. It's Mark I'm worried about – I'm afraid of him going too far.'

'What does he mean to do to me?'

Sylvia stared at her long, pink nails, then looked up into my face. 'He wants to torture you, like he's been tortured.'

25

Sylvia went back to her room at the Premier Inn and I stood in front of the empty fireplace, wondering what to make of it all. I fetched myself another large glass of wine, drank it, craved more, but persuaded myself not to pour it. A slow, warm slide into oblivion was very, very tempting – but what if Mark came back? It might not happen tonight, but it might. From what Sylvia had said, he hadn't finished with me yet. I needed to keep my wits about me.

I could see why the Greek locals had told them they would have beautiful children – they must have made a handsome couple. How heartbreaking, then, that all that gorgeous DNA would cease with just the two of them.

Mark, a successful businessman. He'd been training to become an electrician, after school – Big Maxie had urged him to get a trade, because there was good money to be made and you would never be out of work. I suspected Dad wished he himself had done an apprenticeship, so he could have been his own boss, instead of taking orders from men for whom he didn't have much respect at the warehouse.

I put water on the little root-ball tree, washed up my few dirty dishes, checked my watch multiple times. When was it safe to go to bed? When could I draw a line under the day and stop worrying until tomorrow?

Around eleven, I made myself some porridge in the microwave and, at midnight, I decided I wasn't going to hear from Mark that night, and went upstairs.

Mostly, I had been preoccupied by Sylvia's story about the difficulty in conceiving, the shared elation of pregnancy, and the lonely hell of miscarriage. It was only as I lay there in the dark that one particular implication of her account of Mark hiring a private detective occurred to me: when, precisely, had the detective made his enquiries? Had he done it all by web searches and long-distance digging, or had he come here and observed me? And what about Mark? How long had he been watching?

As I lay there, the pebble re-formed in my throat. When was the last time Tabby had been home? Could the detective have seen her? Could Mark? Did he know I was a mother?

I pulled out my phone. Sylvia had left me her number. She could tell me if Mark knew about Tabby, surely. But then again, if he didn't know, I would have given it away to Sylvia, who could simply inform him.

What to do? I needed to find out if Mark knew I had a daughter. Could I trust Sylvia? Would she help me to protect Tabby? She owed us nothing. Yet she had come to warn me, so perhaps, if only to prevent Mark from getting himself in trouble ...

I rang her number. It went straight to voicemail. Damn!

I called Sylvia's number every hour from one in the morning until 8 a.m., when she finally picked up.

'Sylvia? It's Caroline. You have to tell me, does Mark know I have a daughter?'

'I told you last night – it was the awards ceremony photograph that set him off. The one of you and Tabby. He was so upset that you had a child when he couldn't.'

The awards dinner. I had brought Tabby as my plus-one, for a big, shiny night out in our fancy frocks and, I suppose, to impress her. If I had drunk a bit less I might have had a clearer memory of who had been in the pictures that had been taken. She must have been lined up beside me, and her details included in the caption.

If Mark wanted to hurt me, really hurt me, I had always known that the number-one route would be via Tabby. I had to ring her, warn her, get her out of Mark's reach.

'Sylvia, I've got to go,' I muttered, and immediately called Tabby's number.

It rang and rang and eventually rang out. Where was she? Why wasn't she answering?

I tried Hendrew's number, but his mobile was switched off, and I suddenly remembered that Dawson had told me on the phone that the pair of them were flying to Lanzarote – they might well be in the air already.

With a ghastly bleak feeling, I recalled my conversation with Dawson on the telephone two nights before – *He's older, Caroline. Harry is an older man.* He had called him 'hot totty', and Tabby herself had described him as 'a looker'.

Not this. Please, not this.

Mark – what the hell have you done?

26

I phoned Fergus and told him I couldn't make it into work. 'Something's come up.'

'No worries – the paper's pretty much filled already. But I was planning on taking everyone for an end-of-term drink at Ramsey's after lunch – think you can make it?'

'I doubt it.'

'OK, then. Never mind. Well, merry Christmas, Caroline. Have a good one.'

'You too.'

I put petrol in my car with a shaking hand. The fumes by the pump made me feel nauseous.

'Caroline!'

I looked round and saw Harold Kirkpatrick filling the tank of the brand new Fiesta.

'First time we've put petrol in her!' Harold called. 'Have to keep reminding myself she's not diesel. We enjoyed seeing the piece in the paper – we sent a copy to our son in Canada.'

I waved back. When all this was over, if it was ever over, would I have to move to another country to escape the revelations? Would everyone here know the things I'd done? Would Tabby agree to a new start? But how could she leave the boys? How could I? Was there any possible way of getting to the other side of this without Tabby learning the truth?

With her favourite *Carols from Trinity* playing innocently, as if this were just another Christmas, I drove as hard as I dared up the motorway.

When I got to the flat, Lennie was sitting in Hendrew and Dawson's bedroom window, looking out. Seeing me, he cried, and pawed the glass. I jabbed the doorbell, but had the sinking feeling it was ringing in an empty home.

Come on, Tabby – answer, I willed her. I rang three times, but there was no response.

She could be at work. She could be with Mark, at his place – or 'Harry's', as I now suspected he was calling himself for Tabby's benefit.

I left my car parked outside the flat and hurried off on foot for the coffee shop. At every crossing I met the 'red man' signal and had to wait. Come on. Come on!

'Tabby's mum – right?' the young male barista greeted me, when I pushed my way inside.

'Yes. I'm sorry – I must have forgotten your name.'

'I'm Oisín. Can I get you something, or were you looking for Tabby?'

'I was hoping to find her.'

'She isn't in right now, but let me ask the boss if she's working today.'

I stood and waited, my heart pounding, as Oisín disappeared behind a beaded curtain.

When he returned, it was with Liv, the coffee shop's beautiful Ethiopian proprietor.

'Caroline – hi. It's lovely to see you. Tabby's got a later start today, but can we buy you a coffee, since it's Christmas? Our cinnamon twist latte gets rave reviews.'

'Thanks, Liv, but I'll have to pass – I'm very keen to find Tabby, and she's not at the flat.'

'Well, if you can punch in a couple of hours round the shops, I can tell you exactly where she'll be – she starts her shift here at twelve.'

I looked at my watch – that was just over two hours' time. 'Where else do you think she might be? Her new boyfriend's?'

'Ah, Harry,' Liv replied, grinning. 'She hasn't brought him to meet us yet, but we're hoping soon.'

'So you don't know what he looks like?'

'I do,' Oisín said. 'Tall guy. Black hair. I saw them walking along the shore together.'

I turned my attention to him. 'When was this?'

'Monday, I think. Yeah – Monday. We were heading to the skate-park.'

I swallowed. 'I don't suppose you noticed – did he have a limp?'

'He *did* have a limp!' Liv gave a playful wince.

'A dark man with a limp – positively Byronesque. Very sexy.'

'Does either of you know where he lives, by any chance?'

'Sorry, no,' Liv said.

Oisín shrugged.

I raked my fingers through my hair and tried to think. 'If Tabby should turn up early, would you please ask her to ring me? It's important.'

'Sure,' Liv said. 'Caroline, is everything all right? You seem anxious.'

'Everything's fine.'

Everything was not fine. Everything was very, very wrong.

27

I left the coffee shop and walked about a bit in a daze. The speakers on the lamp-posts were blasting out Elvis singing 'Silver Bells', as if everyone was feeling festive and great.

What to do? What to do?

I scurried off up a side street, where it was quieter, and tried Tabby's phone again. It rang for a moment, then – at last! – she picked up.

'Tabby! Thank goodness. I need to see you.'

Except it wasn't Tabby's voice that answered.

'Caroline.'

'Mark?'

I wanted to flay him, wanted to strangle him, wanted to beat him with my fists, but I had to keep my cool.

'Mark, Sylvia came to see me. I know now why you're so angry. She told me about your struggle to have a family, about the miscarriages and the IVF. She's worried about you. I'm worried about you, too.'

'Are you?'

'Please put Tabby on. She's the innocent party in this, Mark. She doesn't deserve what you have in mind.'

'And what do I have in mind? Anyway, I can't put her on right now – she's in the shower.'

In the shower – so she had stayed over. It had happened. I was too late.

I still had to get her away from him, though – Mark was ill. He must be.

'Meet me by the shore,' Mark said. 'There's a coffee shack beside the jetty – walk away from that, as if you were heading towards the lighthouse. I'll find you.'

'Now?'

'Right now. What are we waiting for?'

'What will you tell Tabby?'

'I'll leave her a note. She was going home to feed her cat, anyway.'

I found a taxi and asked the driver to take me to the coffee shack.

'Try the flapjacks,' he told me. 'I don't even like flapjacks, but these are a different class.'

I checked my watch again – it was after half past ten and I hadn't eaten anything since breakfast. Although I didn't feel remotely hungry, I knew I'd better have something – this was no time to risk having a hypo.

Sitting on a picnic bench, I watched the water gently lapping against the shingle beach. Back when Mark had still been known to all as 'Wee Maxie', we had spent many happy holidays at the seaside, jumping over waves, shrieking when a big one took us by surprise, pushing each other in, eventually swimming. Josie and Big Maxie lay on their towels, looking beautiful – Mum went bare-faced for sunbathing, but she still looked great, and the big hair and smoky eyes would be reinstated before we went to a hotel in the evening for chicken-in-a-basket.

They sometimes went in the water. Maxie was a good swimmer; Mum could only doggy-paddle. It didn't matter when the car went into the river, because they couldn't get the doors open.

It had been August, the second week of their fortnight off, and Mum and Dad had booked a small hotel – just the two of them. This was the first time we hadn't gone away as a family, but Wee Maxie had started his apprenticeship and couldn't get the time off, and Mum and Dad didn't want to leave him at home all by himself, so I'd stayed, too. In any case, Wee Maxie and I were older, by then – family holidays weren't something we were particularly bothered about.

When Mum and Dad's friends, Scottie and Jan Coulter, regulars at our house, heard where they were going, they hired a little stone cottage a couple of miles away – their children were a bit younger, so they were coming along.

It rained for most of the week, which was why the river was so high. Some days Maxie and Josie met up with the Coulters, others they did their own thing. Same in the evenings. On the first sunny day, the Coulters proposed a barbecue and a bit of a party at the cottage, since they had the kids to think about. Mum and Dad went over, plus another couple the Coulters had met on the beach, and the drink flowed.

It was only a short drive back to the hotel, on little country roads, after midnight on a hot summer night. Maxie wouldn't have thought twice about chancing it. But it was so humid that a thick fog had come down. The roads weren't familiar and they couldn't see the bridge.

I finished my flapjack, scrunched up the paper wrapper and put it into the bin. With my eyes on the lighthouse, I began to walk.

28

I saw Mark coming towards me, from the other direction. Even from a distance, I had no doubt it was him.

Before Mum and Dad's death, the worst thing that had happened in our family was Wee Maxie's accident on Granny and Granddad's farm. Ever since we were little, we had loved to play there, and we had always particularly enjoyed being involved when it was time to bring in the hay. Dad would drive us all over on a warm evening after work, and Mum would help Granny in the kitchen while the rest of us went down to the fields on the trailer.

Dad and Uncle Johnny threw the bales about as if they weighed nothing – Wee Maxie and I struggled to carry one between us. Dad and Johnny passed them up to Granddad, who stacked them carefully on the trailer. I remembered the dusty summer smell of the warm hay and the fibrous binder twine. Once, when we lifted a bale, a frog jumped out of the stack and Wee Maxie and I followed it about the field. We wanted to bring it home, but Dad said that would be unkind.

When my brother grew as tall as Dad, and nearly as strong, he became useful to Granddad, too, at hay time. He was teasing me, telling me girls were weaklings, when he leapt into the stack that hid the pitchfork. It was horrific. There was blood, and Wee Maxie was screaming. There were no mobile phones then, so Dad stayed with him while I ran all the way over the stubbly fields to the farmhouse to ring for an ambulance. Before it arrived, Dad had carried Wee Maxie back. He was quiet, by then, and the ambulance crew said he was in shock. Granddad wouldn't come in from the yard.

Mum went in the ambulance with him, and Dad followed in the car, with me. Wee Maxie had surgery that night and when we visited the next day he was out of it on painkillers. He came home on crutches, and had to start a long course of physio. His therapist was tough, and told him he would have a limp for the rest of his life, but if he did his exercises, it would help keep it to a minimum. Wee Maxie had done them faithfully, yet the limp didn't seem to lessen much – but perhaps it would have been even worse if he hadn't.

'So now you know. I have a daughter,' I said, when he was close enough to hear me. 'She's a good person. She wouldn't hurt a fly.'

'Tabby's very different from you, Caroline. Perhaps she takes after her father. Probably for the best.'

'Now that you have done the very, very worst thing you could ever do to me, will you go away and leave us alone?'

If he did, if Mark was satisfied with having slept with his own niece in order to eviscerate me and just disappeared back to Greece and his hospitality empire, Tabby would never know the dark psychodrama in which she had been involved. She might wonder why 'Harry' had stopped courting her, and why he had suddenly vanished; she might try to trace him and find out she had been seeing a ghost, or a liar, but she would get over that – I would get her over that.

'Let me think about it.'

'Think about it now.'

'Come and sit down.'

'Why?'

'Because I want to talk to you.'

He patted the place beside him on the wall.

An hour earlier, my blood pumping, I could have savaged Mark, bitten him to the bone, ripped his flesh. Now, though, I grasped the need to rise above such violent animal fantasies of tearing at him with my teeth and claws. We were down to damage limitation, if that were possible. I had to manage him, defuse the ticking bomb, remove the threat. Keep calm, Caroline, hold your fire and think.

'Tell me something, Caroline, did you ever really love me?'

With all my mind, with all my blood, with all my heart and with every other organ. 'You know I did.'

'Then why did you kill our baby?'

I closed my eyes, swallowed. 'We couldn't have had a child, Mark. How could we have raised it? And what if it had been malformed, with all kinds of health problems? What we did was incest – it's not a nice word, but it's what it was. There's a law against it, and for good reasons.'

'It wasn't your choice to make. You didn't ask me what I thought.'

'Because you weren't thinking straight, and one of us had to.'

'I still hear that song in my head. It drives me mad.'

I heard it, too. I'd been hearing it a lot, recently. 'Don't'. Elvis and the Jordanaires. It had always been Mum and Dad's 'make-up' song, after they'd had a row. They would slow-dance to it in the living room, Mum's hands linked behind Dad's neck, her head against his chest, and his arms loosely around her waist. This, this was what love between a man and a woman looked like, I thought.

And so, after their funeral, when the other mourners had gone home and we had finally persuaded all the grandparents that we needed some time in the house by ourselves, Wee Maxie and I put on that record in our empty home, to remember them.

I could still hear the sound as the stylus dropped softly onto the black vinyl, the gentle whip of the record turning and the crackle and hiss that came from old discs.

Wee Maxie looked at me, I gazed back, and we stepped into each other's arms, just like Mum and Dad, and slowly danced.

By the time he led me upstairs, he was Wee Maxie no more, but Mark, the name he was christened with, a grown man in his own right, and I was no weakling little sister, but a whole woman.

'I didn't have a termination,' I said. 'I lost the baby before I got that far.'

Mark shook his head sadly. 'I don't believe you.'

'It's true. In the toilets at Great Victoria Street bus station. Alone. I thought I was going to die. I had to hide in there until it was dark so no one would see me walking about with blood on my jeans, and then sit on a plastic carrier bag on the bus all the way home.'

I ached at the memory. Since his return, Mark had forced me to think about things I believed I had put behind me. Now, it seemed that all my previous selves had merely been locked inside me like the layers of a Russian doll.

Mark looked at me. I gazed steadily back – if I looked him in the eye, he would know I wasn't lying.

'I couldn't tell you because you'd already gone. You abandoned me, Mark. You left me to cope with everything on my own.'

'Because you broke me! I told you before! I couldn't bear to look at you.'

'Oh, I know. You cursed me and you damned me. You told me to die. You vowed you'd get me back one day. And now "one day" has come, and you have.'

Surely that was enough.

'Were you sad? When you lost the baby, were you even sad?'

'How can you ask me that? It was ours. It came from our love. Its heartbeat had drummed inside me. Yes – I was sad.'

'But if you hadn't lost it, you'd have got rid of it anyway.'

'Not "got rid of it", let him go. And I don't know for sure, but yes, probably.'

'So the baby was a boy.'

'I believe so.'

'He would be grown up, by now. With a job, a partner, maybe children of his own.'

'Or maybe he would have been born with some terrible ailment and would have suffered and we would have lost him in infancy. You shouldn't have left me on my own. At the time, I thought I deserved it. I thought I had twisted love and it had twisted me in return. But I was wrong, Mark – we were just kids, we were grieving and we fell into something that simply could not be.'

'I had to go. I couldn't stand being around you. Do you think it's possible to love someone and hate them at the same time?'

I didn't know. Maybe. Perhaps with certain kinds of love – if there were different kinds of love. Were there?

'You were the love of my life, Caroline. I worshipped you. I never got over you. People think I have everything, but I have nothing. You're the one who got it all – you said it yourself: you got a second chance; you got your daughter.'

And you defiled her.

Neither of us said anything for a while – we just sat there and watched the waves gently kissing the shore.

When I looked back at Mark, his eyes were vacant.

'Did you have a drink before you came here?' I asked.

He turned towards me, but his face was devoid of expression.

'Mark? Are you all right?'

He sighed, but didn't answer. His demeanour lacked any sort of animation. Was he on something?

A thought suddenly struck me. I shook him. 'Mark?'

He stared back at me, glassy-eyed.

'Mark? Can you hear me?'

I stuck my hand into his deep coat pockets. He didn't say a word. I found nothing, but didn't stop there. I reached for his inner pocket and put my hand on it – a barrel-shaped pouch, about the size of a pencil case. I unzipped it and found precisely what I'd expected. Mark was diabetic.

29

I set Mark's diabetes kit on my lap. Inside the pouch was an injection pen like mine, pre-loaded with insulin, a glucometer and a packet of dextrose tablets. Everything I needed to sort out the hypoglycaemic episode he was undoubtedly having, or to kill him on the spot and for it to look like a self-inflicted accident.

Judging by the apparatus, Mark had been diagnosed years ago and, like me, preferred his trusty old kit, not wanting to move to an insulin pump or get blood-sugar readings on his phone. I already knew diabetes could run in families – we had been warned when I was pregnant with Tabby that it was something to watch out for, especially since I had been diagnosed at such a young age.

If I walked away and just left Mark alone on this remote stretch of the shore, his blood sugar would continue to drop and he might just die. But there was also the chance that a passer-by would come across him, call an ambulance and he would recover. However, if I dialled up a dose of insulin on his pen, and injected that into his upper arm or his thigh – enough to push his blood sugar down still further – it would hasten his demise and there would be little for anyone to be suspicious about. Yes, there would be a puncture wound, but what was another little puncture in the pincushion that was an injecting diabetic's body? It wouldn't flag anything peculiar. Diabetics had hypos. If their sugar levels went so low that they couldn't look after themselves, they sometimes needed intervention to rescue them. Surely it wasn't unheard of for a hypoglycaemic diabetic, unnoticed by other people, to go fatally low.

It was only a small act that was required, just as I was a small woman, with a small family, working on a small newspaper, living a small life and, up until three weeks ago, very content with my little lot. My problems would disappear.

I looked at the contents of Mark's diabetic pouch. There was the dextrose, which would perk him up in minutes, or the insulin, which would shut him down for ever.

I had to choose.

Epilogue

Noah and Lucas have just zoomed Tabby and me so we could see them in their new pyjamas.

'I hope you're going to leave out a mince pie for Santa,' Tabby said, and Noah took the iPad and showed her the plate, the glass of sherry and the carrot, lined up on the hearth.

Tabby is a little pensive – it's the first time she's ever broken off a relationship, so it's new territory for her.

She didn't sleep with Mark – the man she knew as 'Harry'. She had intended to, but then her period came early and she asked him if they could wait. Somewhere that evening, she had decided that, attractive though he was, and attentive though he seemed, this wasn't what she wanted. He was so much older, and must have baggage of some sort. Tabby wanted to meet someone special, of course she did, but she had always assumed they would scrimp and save together to buy their first place, and roll up their sleeves in partnership to sand and paint and paper and furnish. They would 'go up the hill together and go down the hill together', as Doris would put it. Tabby wanted a family, but 'Harry' was already in his mid-fifties – how was he going to play football or run behind a bicycle when any kids were six or eight or ten? She had ended things that morning, before I met him on the shingle beach. She hadn't been in the shower at Harry's, when I'd rung. She must just have been on the loo.

'I know he's not much older than you, Mum, and I'm not saying you're old, but you wouldn't date a twenty-five-year-old,' she had observed.

'How did he take it?'

'He wished me every happiness.'

'Good.'

In the end, I had stuffed Mark full of dextrose tablets and sat with him while his blood sugar climbed back up. When it came to it, I simply didn't have it in me to kill the only other person in this world who had lived in the little house with Maxie and Josie, who remembered what I remembered, revered them like the king and queen, even while we watched them dance and drink and take care of our home and put away the shopping and cook dinner. I didn't want to be the only one left who recalled Mum in her kimono dressing-gown and Dad sitting in his armchair, striking a match on the sole of his shoe, and Granny and Granddad and the farmhouse, and Nanny and Papa with their good furniture draped in antimacassars. As well as which, if his dead body turned up by the shore, wouldn't it come out who he was? How we were related? Wouldn't Tabby discover too much, if not quite everything?

Mark had fallen into unconsciousness and slumped beside me, before the sugar had had a chance to work. I couldn't know for sure that he would wake up again – that I'd caught the hypo quickly enough. In repose, his face looked as it had done when we were kids. It was still beautiful, despite everything. He had asked me whether it was possible to love someone and hate them at the same time and I knew in that moment that it was.

Eventually, he had opened his eyes, come round, realised what had happened and that I had helped him. 'That was your opportunity,' he said.

Once Mark was fully alert, we had talked again, and this time he had wept. 'I have hated you for so long,' he said, through sobs. 'I thought I didn't know how to stop, and I didn't try to stop, didn't want to stop. And now it turns out you weren't who I thought you were for all those years.'

He cried, but the furious eyes had softened.

'All I wanted to do was punish you. I fantasised about taking away everything you cared about. But now you're here and you're not the monster ... you're not the bitch ... you're just ... you're just ... and you're Tabby's mum, and Tabby's a great kid.'

I had flinched at that, and Mark saw. 'I never touched her. I swear.'

He was telling the truth. 'Say "swear"', was what Maxie and Josie always said when absolute honesty was called for. No one in our family ever abused the word. It was infallible. So I knew then that he had not been intimate with Tabby, after all. He had spared me that. I was the kitten who had been held down drowning in the bucket, now suddenly released, bursting matted and pink through the surface of the water, finding air. Tabby was unharmed, more or less. I was unharmed, more or less. Mark was a mess. He had hurt people; but he had stopped short of the very worst he could have done. The timing device ceased ticking; the bomb was inert.

'You must have kissed her – that's bad enough. Why "Harry", anyway? And why say your mother was a shrink? What was that all about?'

Mark shrugged. 'I wanted her to trust me. Harry's a trustworthy name. Being answerable to a smart mother figure felt like it made me reliable.'

'And the cat allergy?'

'I didn't want to deal with the housemates. They might not have liked me.'

'And you pretended to Suzanne you were some hotshot features editor – she's going to be disappointed.'

We were silent for a moment.

'Are you going to report me to the police?'

'For what?'

'Everything. Stalking you. The little creep I punched at the hotel. The suave guy by the canal.'

'I should. It's the behaviour of a vile thug. But how can I? Tabby would be bound to find out.'

'I think I'm having a breakdown.'

'I think you're probably right.'

'I don't know what to do.'

Our roles had reversed. Mark was the one who was lost now, and I was still standing.

'Go home.'

'To Greece?'

'If that's where you belong. Do you belong with Sylvia?'

He dried his eyes with the back of his hand. 'I don't know if I belong anywhere.'

'Do you *love* Sylvia?'

'I don't think so.'

'She loves you.'

'That's not enough.'

I thought of Eric Haffey. 'I know.'

We had walked back along the shore. I got Mark a cappuccino from the shack and stirred three sugars into it. 'I don't want to spend the rest of my life looking over my shoulder, Mark,' I said. 'I need to know that this is over and, if it really isn't over for you, that you'll get help so it can be. I could threaten you with what will happen if you don't, but I'm just about sick of threats and warnings and promises of retribution. Just tell me you'll find someone to speak to.'

Mark looked out to sea. 'I've thrown away my entire adult life despising you, pitying myself, and for what? I was wrong about everything.'

'Not everything.'

'I should just take my own life.'

'Don't, though.'

Mark sobbed again. 'I don't know what to do.'

After what he had put me through, after the maelstrom of recent weeks, should I have seen his distress as just deserts?

'Slap it up him,' Madeleine might have said. 'Good enough for him. Serves him right.'

But it wasn't that easy. Because deep, deep down, some part of me understood. What we'd had all those years ago ... it had been electric, ecstatic. It might have defined me, too, had I not had Tabby to redraw my outline and fill me in anew, and Ray, and his mum and dad, and then Noah and Lucas had come, too.

Such lucky encounters had shaped me into becoming kind, patient, nurturing, sympathetic – even if my moral compass pointed somewhat awry, especially in matters of attraction – and I couldn't unmake myself from being those things.

So, because of both the past and the present, in spite of everything he had done, I felt a familiar urge to comfort Mark. Of course this was the one thing I could not do.

Instead, I phoned a psychiatrist I knew. He had helped Amy Madden after Katrina's accident. Amy had stayed at an expensive private clinic of which he was a director – nothing like the grim NHS wards, but with fresh flowers in the rooms, daily therapy, a swimming pool and woodland walks – and he and I had become involved for a while. It had ended amicably, and I had no hesitation in calling him, particularly since Mark undoubtedly had the means to pay.

I rang Sylvia and she said she would come. Perhaps that was wrong, knowing that Mark didn't love her, but I couldn't fix everything and I wasn't inclined to try.

When Mark and I parted in the grand, panelled hallway of the clinic, there was no embrace. We were like two Midases who must stand six feet apart, our arms outstretched yet not daring to touch, because when we did, all would be gold, but all would be death.

'This has to be the final goodbye, Mark. Now that Tabby's seen you, I can't exactly have you in my life.'

'I know.'

He looked at me, and his eyes were searching. 'It was a real love affair, though, Caroline, you and me – wasn't it?'

'It was. But it had to end.'

'Mum? You look like you're miles away. I said, "What are we going to watch?"'

'Sorry, Tabby. Daydreaming.'

'Want to hear the options?'

It was nice to have options. Next year, I was going to do things. I was going to ghost Ralph's memoirs, write more for the *Weekend Tribune*, make better friends with Blooming Marvellous June Black because she was fun, and drink much less. I would also try to mentor Suzanne somewhat.

It was a better outlook than Jodie and Ray had suddenly found themselves facing. Days after Jodie had bought the empty unit next door to her gift shop, in order to expand into baby equipment, the highly desirable chain of Le Grenier Clair announced they were moving into a substantial part of the nearby premises left empty by the departure of Debenhams. Le Grenier Clair, one of the most sought-after retailers for any high street, specialised in the kinds of highish-end gifts and homewares Jodie sold on her shelves, only they had the space and the financial backing to go bigger and better. Within a day, Bumps to Babies revealed they were taking over the rest of the former Debenhams' downstairs, bringing the best-value brand-name nursery goods in the country into our town centre.

Jodie was apoplectic. She spent a whole day on the phone, demanding the council, the Chamber of Trade, the planners, *someone* step in and keep out the newcomers. How were small independent traders, the beating heart of the town, supposed to compete with such chains and all their buying power? Jodie's shop had been serving the community for ten years – didn't that count for anything?

Much to her chagrin, everyone but Jodie seemed to be thrilled about the two new shops.

'Tell them you don't want to buy the new unit after all,' Ray suggested. But it was too late – the paperwork had been signed. Pop and Nana had done an equity-release deal on their bungalow to fund the purchase.

'That's it. I'm ruined,' Jodie complained. 'Honestly, you try to bring a bit of class to this crappy town and when something new and shiny comes along everyone drops you like a hot shit.'

I doubted Jodie would be ruined. She would probably lose money, though – possibly a great deal.

But then, to add to the trauma, Fran, Ray's top photographer, left him to set up his own picture agency, and took two of Ray's staff with him, plus a list of all Ray's contacts and regular customers. With a clear knowledge of Ray's pricing policy, he immediately swooped in to undercut Ray by 20 per cent and wiped out 80 per cent of Ray's January diary.

'I'll fight back, obviously,' he told me, with a shrug. 'But it'll kill me for a while. What with Jodie's shop, the timing's pretty bad.'

'But you'll recover,' I said.

'Up to a point, maybe. But the pie's only so big, and now Fran wants a slice of it. I was never a businessman, Caroline – you know that. I just took pictures. Do I really want to spend my fifties giving myself high blood pressure? I'd be quite happy working for someone else, letting them worry about profit margins and VAT and paying everybody's national insurance and pension contributions.' He laughed. 'Maybe I should ask Fran for a job.'

'Sometimes I don't know if you're joking.'

'Sometimes I don't know either.'

'Mum? Have you just bumped your head one too many times, or are you going low? Shall I pour you a Coke?'

'No, no. I'm not low, just thinking.'

'That's allowed. But a bit annoying. What were you thinking about?'

'Just that I love you, Tabby.'

'And I love you, even though you're too pretty and it gets you into trouble. Shall we put off the TV and have a chat?'

'Sure.'

Tabby zaps the television and I reach across Lennie for my mug of hot spiced apple juice – the stuff I'd bought at the craft fair. 'I was thinking – how would you feel if we just stayed for lunch and pressies at Dad and Jodie's tomorrow, and then came home?' she asks. 'They're not exactly fun to be around, right now, and I also think it's time you took a step back from them. Sad to say, but they both use people, in their own way, and you don't need that.'

Tabby, Tabby, you're growing very wise.

'It would suit me well,' I reply. 'But what about the boys? It would mean leaving them in that atmosphere on Christmas Day.'

'We could kidnap them,' Tabby says. 'Bring them here.'

'It would be an opportunity to try out their new sleeping bags!' I suggest. But, no, we agree that it would be unreasonable to think of taking Noah and Lucas away from their parents on Christmas Day.

'Tabby, we both love the boys very much, and sometimes we wish they had a better deal at home, but we have to accept that your dad and Jodie are their parents, and while they might not be perfect, they're OK. You and I are only in a supporting role. We can do our very best for them, and love them to pieces, but that's all.'

'I know,' Tabby says, with a sigh. 'I do know that. But let's push to have them here with us on Boxing Day. Lucas can suck his thumb and Noah can wear your nightie and everyone can relax.'

'You know about Noah?'

'Mum, I've always known about Noah. *Carols from Trinity*?' she asks, going to the CD player.

It's a digital recording, of course, so no little kiss of the stylus landing on vinyl, no crackle and hiss.

'Good idea,' I say. '*Carols from Trinity* would be lovely.'

I suddenly remember the Christmas of my new bike, out on the tarmac behind our house, and Dad asking Wee Maxie to take a turn holding the back of my saddle so he could have a break.

'Promise you won't let go!' I cried.

'I'll never let go,' Wee Maxie answered.

I shiver.

Acknowledgements

I am going to use the words encouragement, support and enthusiasm rather a lot, because I am lucky enough to have received buckets of all three.

Thanks go to my agent, Faith O'Grady, at Lisa Richards, and to my publisher, Ciara Considine, at Hachette Books Ireland, for everything they do, but above all for their initial gratifyingly positive responses to the manuscript.

I am very grateful to Emma Dunne for challenging me to make this story the best it could be, and to Hazel Orme – one classy copyeditor – as well as the eagle-eyed Aonghus Meaney.

Thanks are due, too, to all the Hachette team, especially Elaine Egan, Ruth Shern, Joanna Smyth and Stephen Riordan for their hard work, support and kindness.

I would also like to thank Dr Nikki Thompson and Dr Charles Saunders for their expert guidance – any errors in depicting medical matters and fishing are entirely my own. Thanks also to Nikki for being an insightful, enthusiastic and supportive early reader.

Warmest wishes go to my dear friends in the playwork world, the legendary Pauline Martin and Mairéad Prunty, who cherish every child in their care and create a home from home – they would never in a million years employ a 'Roberta'.

To Ruth O'Reilly, Joanie Arthurs, Julia Porter and Anthony John Clarke, I extend heartfelt gratitude for their enthusiasm and supportive friendship.

Thanks, too, to the Halliday, Thompson and Crozier clans and connections who have generously got behind my writing endeavours.

Lucy Crichton continues to provide the most practical encouragement, by word and deed, on a weekly and sometimes daily basis – thank you so much. I am also grateful for the support of Andrew Shaw and Alice McIntyre.

Helen Yendall and Patsy Collins have taken time from their own busy writing careers to give me a leg-up. This is much appreciated.

Thank you Mum and Dad, for your enduring encouragement and for being generally amazing – an anchor and a firework. What a combination.

Thanks Keir, Clem and Nye for all kinds of stuff and for being interested enough to get involved. Thank you Lara and Matt, just because.

Thank you, Niall – always.

And thank you very, very, very much to anyone who picks up this book and gives me a chance to entertain them. I hope you will feel it was worth your while.

'Taut and spine-tingling, *I Know I Saw Her* journeys
through the apparent normality of suburban lives to expose
the hidden terrors behind closed doors – a riveting read'
LAURA ELLIOT

Parnell Park is an ordinary suburban street. Alice from number 25 has a quiet life but she craves more. So she watches the street's inhabitants – taking a special interest in Kevin and Kim, the beautiful, charming couple from across the road – wondering what goes on behind closed doors.

One day, on a visit to London, Alice sees Kim on a passing train. But when she later mentions this to Kevin, he tells her she has made a mistake, insisting that his wife is on holiday in the West of Ireland.

But Alice knows what she saw. So who is lying? Kevin, or his wife?

Alice feels compelled to investigate, and her concern for Kim quickly intensifies. And as she enters a high-stakes game with shadowy rules and hidden dangers, Alice is soon to find out that the thing you crave can be the most dangerous thing of all.